Jeffrey Penn May has published many short stories, poems and articles, and he has won several short fiction awards, including one from *Writer's Digest*. His work has appeared in the US, UK and Canada. Jeff was a consultant for a St Louis theatre company, and he wrote and performed a short story for Washington University radio. As a technical data engineer, he helped write manuals for fighter jets. As an educator, he published feature articles and appeared in radio and television spotlights.

Jeff rafted the Mississippi, searched for artifacts in Mexico, and climbed mountains from Alaska to Colombia. His adventures provided expertise and inspiration for the diverse settings in *Where the River Splits*, from Manitoba to Missouri, Wyoming and California, and Jalisco in Mexico. Jeff currently teaches writing and fly-fishing in and around St Louis, Missouri.

Contact Jeff through his website www.askwritefish.com

The right of Jeffrey Penn May to be identified as the Author of this Work has been asserted by him in accordance with the Copyright, Designs and Patents Act 1998.

Copyright © Jeffrey Penn May 2008

All characters in this publication are fictitious and resemblance to real persons, living or dead, is purely coincidental.

All rights reserved. No part of this publication may be reproduced, stored in a retrieval system, or transmitted, in any form or by any means without the prior written permission of the publisher, nor be otherwise circulated in any form of binding or cover other than that in which it is published and without a similar condition being imposed on the subsequent purchaser. Any person who does so may be liable to criminal prosecution and civil claims for damages.

ISBN 978-1-905988-71-6

*Cover by Sue Cordon*
Published by Libros International

www.librosinternational.com

Printed and bound in Great Britain by
CPI Antony Rowe, Chippenham and Eastbourne

# Where The River Splits

Jeffrey Penn May

Libros
INTERNATIONAL

# PRAISE FOR *WHERE THE RIVER SPLITS*

"In my 15 years as a Trade Book Publishers Rep., I've seen an awful lot of first novels. Jeff Penn May has succeeded with his by combining a unique style with crafty plotting. The result is a thriller that has all the right stuff: suspense, intrigue and a high page-turning quotient. An accomplished debut." **David Einig, Director of Sales, Publishing**

"As an outdoor enthusiast, I loved the wilderness scenes, but even more impressive was the psychological tension between the two main characters. This was a fun, fast-paced, page-turning read! I highly recommend this book." **John Zavgren, PhD. Mathematics, Network Architecture, Network Security, Open Source Software Developer.**

"This is a page-turning story of evolution, of a man and woman who drift apart, discover life, drift back to the acceptance of both the good and evil in one another and the resolution of love. A wonderful read." **Dorry Catherine Pease, Published Author, President of Writers' Society of Jefferson County, Member Missouri Writers Guild***

*"Where the River Splits* is one of those novels I look for, but rarely find. You don't just read it; you inhabit it - the characters, the locale, the marriage that is both complex and fragile. May's writing is fluid with generous details, and it carries you effortlessly to the climax." **Robin Theiss, Author, Poet, and President of St. Louis Writers Guild**

"May's book is RIVETING! I started reading it in my office at the end of a very long day and stayed up all night to finish it. I simply could <u>not</u> put it down. This is a well-crafted book - just like a river - with surprises around every bend – and you can't predict what will be next! For me, reading May's book brought up memories of countless wilderness trips, past lovers and struggles to find the 'meaning of it all.' Read it!" **Lin Shook Schalek, Choreographer and Artistic Director of Perceptual Motion, Inc., Avid canoeist and lover of nature.**

"*Where the River Splits* is the perfect read for a quiet vacation on the beach or a winter weekend curled up next to a roaring fire. As an experienced broadcast producer, I think this book would make an excellent movie script! I thoroughly enjoyed it, and anxiously anticipate May's next adventure." **Dan Dillon, KMOV/Channel 4 St. Louis Broadcast Producer, Author of** *So Where Did You Go To High School?* *

"The river is both the opening setting and a fitting metaphor in Jeffrey Penn

May's wonderful novel, 'Where the River Splits'. As a river meanders and changes course in surprising and unpredictable ways, so, too, does this novel's story line. Through alternating points of view, the reader follows David and Susan as they face grief, surprise, betrayal and tough choices, culminating in a satisfying ending that will leave you wanting to go back and reread all over again." **Denise Pattiz Bogard, Author, Founder and Coordinator St. Louis Writers Workshop**

"Real people, real relationships, and real suspense—all delivered in smart and beautiful language. May writes with wisdom, humor and heart." **Julia Gordon-Bramer, Poet, Writer, Founder and Editor of Nighttimes.com.**

"A captivating debut, May takes marital posturing to a new level in this highly believable tale of deception and intrigue that carries the reader every step of the way through the foothills and mountains of the American West to the highlands in central Mexico." **Elizabeth Ketcher, Founder and Director, StudioSTL**

"I dare say most wonder at some point in their lives, 'What if I had taken the other path? What if I just walked away and left it all behind? What it would it be like to go to that unknown place and be that unknown?' This book takes you through it all and lets you taste each morsel, the bitter and the sweet… Whether you are an outdoors lover or avoider—this is the adventure for you! You will put the book down sweaty and tired, sure you survived/thrived in person! And you'll never have to wonder again…." **Andi Boyd, Outdoor Experiential Educator, St. Louis, MO**

"WHERE THE RIVER SPLITS is an account of the unexpected vagaries, dangers and promise of adventure, whether in the wilderness, in marriage or in career. These most major of our decisions are taken with optimistic expectations, but no sure knowledge as to what really will unfold, when, where or why. Mr. May addresses the struggle confronting someone who has come face to face with the unexpected, the traumatic and the disillusioning, and who such a person will discover himself to be. Events in the wilderness are compellingly and faithfully rendered and will excite the back-country enthusiast and casual day-hiker alike. The question of what might have been had a different path been followed will surely appeal to a wide audience. The book drew me in and challenged me to think." – **P L Wakefield, MD, Rafter, Backpacker and Retired Mountaineer**

**\*Full Reviews**

**Review-Where the River Splits by Jeff Penn May**
**Dorry Catherine Pease, Published Author, President of Writers' Society of Jefferson County, Member Missouri Writers Guild**
Be prepared for a wild ride into the unimaginable life of two people who love and love and love, but are not sure how to live as one. You will not be able to put it down…I couldn't.

Start with a great adventure, two real to life people, Susan and David, marriage problems and a world not quite in sync. Put this together with a camping trip that goes wrong from the start, a forest fire and a river that has no compassion and you have a story that draws you in, page by page. Follow David as he struggles to find Susan lost in the river, cry with him as remembers the good times and bad, the loss of a love he hopes to recover. Follow Susan as she awakens in a hospital and begins to understand what the true meaning of relationship is as she toils to reconcile her acceptance of David's death with the subtle threat of her rescuer knowing only that life must go on.

This is a page-turning story of evolution, of a man and woman who drift apart, discover life, drift back to the acceptance of both the good and evil in one another and the resolution of love.

A wonderful read.


**Dan Dillon, KMOV/Channel 4 St. Louis Broadcast Producer, Author of** *So Where Did You Go To High School?*
Jeffrey Penn May's *Where The River Splits* is a thrilling, intelligent adventure that chronicles two years in the life of a young couple torn apart by a freak accident. To help save their crumbling marriage, David and Susan Brooks plan a Canadian wilderness vacation. Their canoe capsizes, and the raging waters pull the two in different directions. Each survives, suspecting the other has perished in the river.

As the two characters establish their new lives alone and apart, May takes the reader on an engrossing, twisting saga through the United States, Mexico City and Aztec ruins near Puerta Vallarta.

*Where the River Splits* is the perfect read for a quiet vacation on the beach or a winter weekend curled up next to a roaring fire. As an experienced broadcast producer, I think this book would make an excellent movie script! I thoroughly enjoyed it, and anxiously anticipate May's next adventure.

# Acknowledgements

When my brother jabbed a short stick at a rattler and its fangs parted the hair on his forearm, I was thankful it didn't bite him. But I was even more thankful that the snake (minus its rattle) didn't slither around and sink its fangs into me. So is gratitude doled out by degrees? I would like to thank almost everyone I've ever known, maybe list them in some sort of comforting order, but that's not possible, is it?

Therefore, I'm attempting to acknowledge only those who have read my fiction and, directly or indirectly, said something that I remember. For example, "Yeah, good stuff, but what the hell are you going to do with it?" Excellent point. Writers know the problem. Either publish or quit, but quitting is impossible, even when real jobs and relationships are crumbling around you.

So, thanks to my wife Kim for this novel's precipitating idea, for her love and tolerance, for providing middle-class normalcy, especially our children, Sam and Sarah (who are of course the best looking and most intelligent children in the world).

Thanks to my editor, Candace Stroot for her enthusiasm, encouragement and professionalism.

I tried to list the rest of you in "random order" because, among other things, storytelling involves trying to organize chaos. Thank you for your input and for suffering my presence.

Doctors P Lynn Wakefield, Kenneth Yorgan, and John R Zavgren. Lin Shook and Dr Clarie Wooster. Julie Shargel. Hunter Crabtree. Mary Beth Wilczac. Sex therapist Dr Bob Meyners. Lisa Caplan. Stoney Breyer. Barry Gold. Andi Boyd. Eric Hahn and Julie Hahn. Eric Chaet, writer, poet, American original. Author/professor Howard Schwartz. In memory of Dr Luis Clay-Mendez, professor and friend; we searched the highlands. David Carkeet, professor and author of some favorite books. Jim May and Walter May. David

Einig, Joey Einig, and Beth Ketcher. Robin Theiss, Julia Gordon-Bramer, and Kathy Behrens.

And of course those of you not on this list, but are still with me in a clear stream with a strong current, in a '69 VW rattling into a redwood forest, in a long line waiting for a cold shower in the Northern Andes, or merely still in trouble. Maybe we shook hands, said goodbye and, as you passed, I smelled sweat, smoke, and our last beer. Or you smelled vaguely like daffodils, reminded me of my backyard and childhood possibilities, and your long hair brushed across my face in the wind. Wherever you are now, I remember… and I thank you.

# Author's Note

Have you ever bought a book based on the blurbs and found yourself skimming? Perhaps that's when we most crave our favorite authors. But we read faster than our authors can write so inevitably we take chances on unknowns. Sometimes we are pleasantly surprised. Other times, we find ourselves wondering why some books are published at all, and we concoct theories. Maybe it's technology, word processors like tomato slicers. Or a publishing conspiracy, repetitive scenes designed to increase page count and by extension retail price. Or the slick binding that makes it difficult to distinguish the small publisher from the self-publisher. If we are feeling generous, we might say that the writing style was not to our taste, or the plot twists didn't interest us, or the main character was a jerk.

While I can't guarantee you will like *Where the River Splits*, I can assure you that it was not hastily written. No conspiracy was involved, nor was it self-published. I did use a computer though and, while this is my first published novel, I am not a first-time novelist. I used to sweat over manual typewriters, and I still write drafts longhand. Perhaps because of my experience, I work hard to omit unnecessary scenes so you won't have to skim.

I hope you enjoy *Where the River Splits*. If not, maybe you will take pleasure emailing me a scathing review. I can be contacted through my website www.askwritefish.com

*Jeff May*

PS: Jeffrey Penn May is my birth name. Penn, as may seem obvious, is a family name. However, I've never introduced myself by saying, "Hey, hello, I'm Jeffrey Penn May." That it appears on the cover of this book indicates a lifelong struggle between Jeff May and Jeffrey Penn May.

For Kim, Sam, and Sarah

# Chapter One

Arriving at a resort cabin with Wilderness Outfitters carved over the doorway, David Brooks finally relaxed enough to appreciate the cool Canadian air and anticipate the canoe adventure awaiting him and his wife, Susan. They endured hours of airport lines and security checks, and they managed to be polite to each other through it all. Except, David thought, for their usual disagreement about what was important; in this case, she wanted to visit the Manitoba Museum of Man and Nature, and he wanted, as always, to escape into the wilderness. In that respect, the security delays worked in his favor. He had made reservations for a canoe and a ride upriver. They simply did not have time to stop for side trips.

As a tanned young outfitter listed the obligatory warnings and conditions of rental, David only half-listened. Instead, he wondered what being in a canoe for a week would do for them. He'd never been to Canada, but he heard the rivers were so clean you could lift your paddle and let the water drip into your mouth. Standing next to the outfitter's truck with their canoe strapped on top, he told Susan about the water, but she doubted its reliability, citing studies that indicated otherwise. He stared at her, and said, "Right. Thanks for pointing that out."

She climbed into the truck, and the young man, wearing what David thought was a pretentious safari hat, drove them over narrowing, unpaved roads, finally ending on a two-track path at the water's edge. David quickly loaded gear, and stood, waiting impatiently for any other instructions, but the outfitter seemed more interested in flirting with Susan than anything else.

"Okay," David said. "Let's go."

He shoved off, into the clear water, map in hand, Susan in the bow. He heard the outfitter yell something about dry conditions but, David thought, must not be that important if the guy almost forgot about it. He paddled with the current, the air smelling of pine, and the sky bright blue, a few white clouds. As they floated around a bend, thick forest engulfed them. The first few hours, David paddled eagerly, and happily, but eventually he got tired, and he wanted Susan to help.

"You having fun?" he asked, trying to sound sincere, but feeling testy.

"Sure," she responded. "Aren't you?"

"Are you interested in paddling at all?"

"No," she said sarcastically, "I just thought I'd let you do all the work."

For several minutes - felt like hours to David - she sat, not helping, and he paddled harder. Finally, she said, "Are we in a hurry?"

"No . . . no hurry."

"You hungry?"

David hadn't thought about it, but it was past lunchtime. He scanned the shore, nothing but thick woods, and he realized that most places were swarming with blackflies. He couldn't stop just anywhere. After another half-hour, they rounded a bend, and a gray rock came into view, flat and appealing in the sunlight. He paddled up to it, misjudging the current and rammed it, almost tipping over. The current turned them around bumping flush with the rock, and David jumped out, pulling the front of the canoe out of the water.

They sat eating peanuts, raisins, apples, then lay on the warm rock with the sun on their faces. With his wife lying so close, David was hopeful that they would overcome the differences that had seeped into their marriage. They fought often. And when they didn't, their words were obviously strained, pressure always lurking beneath their careful conversations. He listened to the wind in the pines and thought about other wilderness trips where Susan had difficulty keeping his frenetic pace. She lagged behind, often looking at flowers, while he pushed on, then had to wait for her to catch up.

"This is much better," he said, a breeze whistling through the tall pine. "You don't have to worry about keeping up."

Susan shielded her eyes from the sun. "What's that mean?"

"Nothing," he said, thinking that it would take more than a few hours on the river for them to work through their difficulties. "Let's go," he said, and started putting the food away.

David climbed in the stern and Susan shoved off. Once on the water, he felt better. Lunch had helped, and the smell of pine and the cool breeze made him feel alive as it always had. He looked ahead to a short set of rapids. Susan paddled as they zipped past boulders, swayed into side currents, and straightened into a calm pool.

"That was fun," David said, laughing, challenged by the white water, but also wondering if he had overestimated his canoeing experience.

They found an opening in the forest and even though the sun was well above the horizon, David steered them to shore. "This might be the best spot for miles," he reasoned.

"You would know," she said.

David looked at her, unsure if she was being sarcastic again. "*How* would I know? I've never been here before, have you?"

"What I meant was, you have the map. That's all."

"Right," he said, remembering a time when their conversation showed nothing but admiration for one another, when camping meant making love in the open air and falling asleep in each other's arms. Now they were ready to argue about maps; he loved maps and their possibilities, but Susan showed only moderate interest.

As the sky turned dark blue, they sat silently near the coals of their fire, and David wanted his wife back in his arms, like it used to be.

"Next time, we could go to Mexico," he said, trying to find common ground. He'd been there years ago, but she hadn't, and she talked about it during the planning of this trip. He added, "I've always wanted to climb one of those volcanoes down there."

Without looking at him, she said, "Not Popocatepetl. It's had several eruptions recently." She paused. "It would have to be Ixtaccihuatl."

David was impressed with her ability to not only remember the names of the volcanoes, but to pronounce them correctly. Didn't surprise him, though. Susan knew a lot about history. At first her constant need to study the past intrigued him, but now it seemed she used her expertise more like a weapon. Whenever he talked about exploring a new wilderness, she wanted to bog it down with historical baggage. History was about dead people, he thought. He stared into the fire and said, "We should see lots of stars tonight."

Susan sipped her tea and said, "Stars were always important for navigation."

David wanted to lie on the cool earth and gaze up at the universe with her holding onto him. It used to be so easy – deep pleasure in her smooth, soft skin, her craving lips and the sheer revelry in their lovemaking. Maybe a little too easy. From the very beginning he felt she was withholding something and whatever it was created a wedge between them, widening with each day. Not that he told her everything, especially about his land in Wyoming, nothing more than a few acres of arid foothills with a shanty perched on a slope. But it was a safe place in his heart, at the base of the Wind River mountains, gray jagged snow-covered peaks. Even though it lay a thousand miles west of their home in St Louis, just knowing it was there helped him cope with his job, and later, his deteriorating marriage. He had tried to tell her on several occasions, and he'd come close. But she kept drifting away and he held back, never feeling comfortable enough. Maybe on this river, he thought, with much needed luck, he could share Wyoming with her, and what it meant to him.

"I'm tired," she said.

He was too, but reluctant to crawl into the tent next to her where he would lie awake trying to figure out what to do, while she slept. "What is it?" he asked.

"What?"

"Why are you being this way?"

"Me? It's *you* who leaves *me* behind."

They'd been over this before, but he hoped for a new resolution. "I know," he said.

"Know what?"

"That we have our differences."

"That's not everything," she responded.

David knew what she was getting at; she'd complained of it before, that he came home from work irritable, sullen, and she had to put up with his bad mood. Having her bring it up now only made him tense, and threatened his enjoyment of this gorgeous river. As before, David took the offensive and asked about *her* job, and listened to her typical response.

"There's nothing wrong with being a secretary in the history department."

He looked up at the stars  and responded, "I never said there was." But, why didn't she finish her degree?

"Then why do you always bring it up?"

Because, he thought, she would have to pay the bills, at least for a while. He was told to use up his vacation time, and when he asked why, his boss just stared gloomily and walked away. And now David had to face up to the inevitable. Logically, he understood how he'd come to this point. After five years of verifying new attack systems on warplanes that dropped "smart" bombs and "surgical-strike" rockets, he was transferred to the commercial division. Then the terrorists attacked, and people lost their jobs. But he still felt like a failure, and he hated to fail, probably more than most people.

Stars filled the northern sky. Susan sat a foot away, and it felt like miles. He would have to shout, and she would shout back, and they would get into a horrible argument. Maybe in a few days, it would be easier. Perhaps if he resolved it in his own head, he could talk to Susan. Was their marriage doomed from the start? Were there clues? He sat staring at the coals glowing red, a small molten world where he tried to decipher their past.

*** 

Passenger jets screamed overhead as they drove past houses in disrepair - paint peeling, windows cracked, lawns full of weeds - then the houses disappeared altogether. The subdivision was being demolished so the airport could expand. Instead of homes, vacant lots lined the fractured streets, bushes overgrown and trees blocking old sidewalks. What an improvement, he thought. Get rid of the suburban sprawl and return it to the wilderness. In this case, however, the trees would be bulldozed and paved over with a concrete runway, the air full of jet fuel.

David turned onto what once was a cul-de-sac but now resembled a private drive, only three houses remaining on the court. Susan's childhood home looked like the others, bushes growing onto the driveway. When David tried to use the doorknocker, a screw fell out, leaving it hanging lopsidedly. He shoved the screw back into the rotting wood and rapped the door with his knuckles while Susan remained distant, looking at the other houses, sparrows fluttering from the trees. What's with her, David thought, her tension filling the air around him.

Susan's mother met them with an onslaught of talk in stark contrast to her daughter's careful silence.

"Hello, David," Mrs Moore said, peering over her glasses and smiling, as if she'd known him a long time. "Come in. Sue's been keeping you a secret. I'm so glad to finally meet you." She offered him something to drink, and led him into the small kitchen that smelled of roast chicken. Out the kitchen window, he could see nothing but trees and bushes. Susan's mother handed him a beer. He thanked her, noticing that she had big blue eyes and a beautiful smile like her daughter, the crow's feet wrinkles only making her more attractive.

During dinner, Susan's mother asked David about his work, listening intently and sympathetically, stopping to inject her own views and observations, then steering the attention to her daughter. "You know, you're the first one she's brought home in a long time. Or maybe the first one I've liked." David blushed, and tried to hide it by drinking more beer. He liked her as well.

As the evening passed and the beer gave way to wine, then brandy, Mrs Moore became even more wonderful, the meal settling over him like a warm blanket. He swirled the dark roast-colored brandy in its glass, took a sip, and stared at Susan, her curving neck, big eyes, and moist lips. While his conversation flowed smoothly, he had a nagging question begging to be answered, and no fluency for asking it.

"Where's *Mr* Moore?" he finally asked.

Susan bowed her head over her plate.

David drank the rest of his brandy. "Sorry," he said, "I—"

"My daughter should have told you."

"Why?" Susan said. "What difference would it make?"

But her mother waved her hand in the air and tried to explain, tossing the facts onto the table as if they were antacids, unpleasant but necessary to avoid ruining the meal. Susan was still a young girl at the time. Her dad was a history professor, a "repressed archeologist," Mrs Moore said, who loved fieldwork, so much so that, when he couldn't get grant money, he'd use his vacation time, occasionally leaving them alone for months. One summer, he met a friend and colleague from Mexico City, and they explored the Yucatan Peninsula looking for evidence of Aztec influence beyond its empire. His friend, Menendez, returned as promised to his family while Susan's dad stayed on "obsessively" and "let" amoebas perforate his intestines. "Just like him, didn't pay attention to his fever, I'm sure." He couldn't walk, couldn't move, stuck on a dirty cot, delirious, apparently speaking in English even though he was fluent in Spanish. "We don't even know what he said before he died. *Probably* told us he loved us, but who would know? Could just as easily been a lecture on pre-Columbian civilization." The doctor arrived too late. Officially, the cause of death was dehydration, but the coroner also wrote "Montezuma's Revenge" on the certificate.

"But life must go on. He would have wanted it that way." Mrs Moore picked up plates from the table and set them on the counter. "Sometimes," she said, "I think that's why Susan hasn't gotten married yet. You know, she loved her dad more than anything, and he was gone during a very important stage of her development."

"Oh, come on, Mom, I know that psychology crap. I'm fine. I just haven't met anyone. . ." She glanced at David.

"Sure, honey, but no one shrugs off something like that." Mrs Moore rolled her glass around in her hands. "You were just a girl."

"But you told me he was part of everything, that he would always be with me. I believed that."

"Right, but you're twenty-eight and you haven't —"

"Gotten married? I know, you don't have to harp on it." Susan turned to David. "She thinks that I'm afraid *all* the men in my life will leave me."

David shrugged, sipped his brandy, and looked at her hoping she could read his eyes, thinking, *I won't*, poised with his drink ready to say he would never leave.

But Susan turned to her mother and said, "Besides, look what you did? How did you deal with it?"

Mrs Moore spoke to David. "She thinks that spending two weeks alone on a South Sea island was a little odd. I call it healthy. And I also tried to climb an 18,000-foot pass in Nepal. Would've made it if not for that blizzard. But I didn't do *that* one alone. I'm not crazy."

David poured them all more brandy, and listened carefully.

Mrs Moore continued, "It's great to see Susan getting out into the woods, experiencing life as she should. You're good for my daughter."

David felt excited by the possibility that Susan could be like her mother, adventurous, climbing mountains, and breathing in views that only a select few would ever see, and together they could scale grand peaks. He could envision a long, satisfying relationship.

A few days later, they hiked deep into woods and camped. Susan pointed out Orion the Hunter in the starkly clear night, and he suggested the hunter looked lonely, and needed a partner. When she turned to him, her gaze falling upon him like leaves in a breeze, she captured his heart. In the warmth of the moment, he proposed, but felt like it was a mutual revelation, the commitment feeling comfortable, the right thing to do.

The wedding took on a life of its own, with Susan's mother swirling around them arranging everything - a small ceremony and the reception at her house. Several drinks into the party, David stood outside looking at all the open space, the empty lots, and thought it strange to be celebrating his wedding in a doomed house. He went back inside and bumped into his old climbing friend, Jack Savgren, in St Louis for a conference on nonlinear equations. Savgren quickly launched into a discourse on probability theory, his wire-rimmed glasses and scraggly beard emphasizing the chaotic nature of his theories. David didn't understand much of it, but he had always marveled at how Savgren coped with the death of his first child, a son who died eleven hours after being born.

"If there are an infinite number of possibilities," Savgren said, "then it is easy to imagine alternate realities."

David nodded, sipped his drink, and searched for Susan. "I'm sure," he said, then started to leave.

Savgren grabbed his arm and stared at him through the distorted lenses of his wire-rim glasses. "Don't worry," he said. "If it doesn't work out for you, you can always leap into another universe."

David looked at him, unsure if his friend was joking, implying divorce at a wedding. But he decided Savgren was drunk, like he was, and was just pondering probabilities. David broke free, bumping into people, feeling like a random thought. He looked for Susan but she had disappeared into the crowd, the sound of low flying aircraft suddenly overwhelming the celebration.

They moved into a refurbished house in the city. Susan liked it because of its historical charm, built during the boom after the 1904 World's Fair, and she talked about the broken statues and grand pillars buried in various places around St Louis. But he listened half-heartedly, unconcerned about people digging up useless statues from the turn of the century. With the cold winds of winter, the windows rattled loudly, and David worried more than ever about his job. Lying in bed, late, he listened to rain pounding the house, his wife sleeping soundly next to him. He shook her awake, wanting to talk, but going about it in such a circuitous way that she became irritable, and he ended up asking her why she "settled" on being a secretary. Then he asked her if it had anything to do with her father, saying that she was acting childish. She responded with penetrating silence that drove him outside for a walk in the cold night, his breath white, the clouds low and gray, rain changing to swirling snow. He passed a corner bar with music reverberating through the walls, the door opening, the music spilling out onto the glimmering city streets, and two young women stumbled into the night. David looked at them, thinking they were attractive. Must be nice, he thought, to live a purely superficial life, unconcerned about anything but the next drink, easy laughs, and good times.

Walking back, he felt warmed, relieved by the exercise, but when he returned, the front door was locked. Rather than ring the doorbell, and risk another fight, he dug into Susan's flower box, looking for an extra key he had recently hidden. His hand was deep into the box, scooping out dirt, when she opened the door.

"What are you doing?" she asked incredulously.

"I hid an extra key," he said. "You locked me out."

"You locked yourself out," she said, then added, "Thanks for *telling* me about the key."

"I thought I had," he responded. "It's a good idea for both of us."

"Or maybe for a *burglar* to use?"

"No thief," David scoffed, "would bother digging around in a flower box. They would just break a window."

"Of course," she said. "You're always right." Then she slammed the door and it locked automatically, and he shoved his hand back into the dirt.

## Chapter Two

By the end of the second day, David thought the camping trip was a mistake. He had wanted them to be together, but the canoe only made things worse. Unable to get out and hike alone ahead of her, he felt trapped, hopelessly enmeshed with her movements. Every time she shifted, he had to react, keep them from capsizing, or hitting a rock, or scraping bottom. Each moment in the wilderness separated them not only from civilization but from each other.

They set up camp gloomily, not saying any more than absolutely necessary, and had just finished eating when black clouds rolled in to match their mood. Lightning cracked across the dark sky. David ran to the canoe and pulled it up the riverbank while Susan picked up food, clothes, maps and threw them into the tent. When he returned, she was waiting with her wool shirt buttoned up to her neck. He waited for the storm, wanting to feel the torrent, let the downpour soak him. "The wind's cold," she said, turning away and crawling into the tent.

David considered staying outside and waiting for the storm, but slid into the tent next to her. Susan wanted him to zip up the thin, fabric door, keep the rain out, but David left it open, lying on his back with his head resting outside. He wanted to feel the cool, cleansing rain on his face.

The wind blew fiercely, flapping the nylon tent and bending the thick pine forest around them, then came waves of rain spattering their camp. Lightning struck close by, just over the ridge, brilliant jagged flashes followed immediately by deafening thunder. But the downpour never came. He crawled outside and stood, thankful to be free of the tent. Susan gathered dinner plates, carried them to the riverbank, and scrubbed them with sand, almost losing them in the swift current.

The sky cleared, dark evening blue. Their campsite was in a small open area surrounded by the thick parched woods. Through the forest, he noticed a red glow to the North, just beyond a low ridge. Susan set the plates on a rock. "I hope the canoe's okay," she said, looking toward the river.

"Why wouldn't it be?" he responded tersely, then looked at her wide, blue eyes, hair pushed back.

"Must've rained upriver," she said. "The water's come up a little."

"It'll be all right." He had tied it to a tree. "I'll check it in a minute."

The glow on the ridge grew brighter and smoke bled into the night sky like black ink. David imagined trees exploding in white flashes, crackling, red-orange flames devouring the forest. He had seen fire before, from a roadside in California, marveled at the destruction, and felt vaguely worried about the future. Then it had been easy to deny reasons for the rampant wildfires, simple to just drive away and file the memory. But now he couldn't flee so easily. His car was far downriver, and he watched intently.

Susan stood next to him. "Looks like a fire," she said.

He shrugged. "Yeah, looks like it." And he wanted to add that they could be in serious trouble soon, but didn't share his concern. Things were tense enough already between them.

"Are we safe here?"

"Sure we are." But he knew they couldn't escape through the thick woods in the dark, and if both shores were in flames, they would have to run the river at night, a treacherous alternative. The rapids had been manageable so far, but with the river rising, they could be interesting. Small animals scurried in the underbrush. A deer bounded into their campsite, then leapt back into the woods.

"We better pack up," he said, trying to sound in control, but his stomach was in knots and his teeth were clenched.

Susan crossed her arms as if holding onto herself. "It's bad, isn't it?"

"Doesn't hurt to be ready."

They loaded the canoe, leaving the tent for last, hoping they wouldn't have to go. But the fire moved in fast, exhaling ash and smoke, swirling along both sides of the river. Another deer, with its hide burning, the smell stinking, jumped at them, then veered off into darkness. A blast of heat surged from the forest.

Susan pulled down the tent and stuffed it into the canoe, while David barked orders. "You get in first. I'll push off. Listen to me. Hurry up!"

They splashed through the water. She jumped in, the canoe tilting. He pushed off, slid in carefully, and they glided smoothly on the black water. They paddled away from the acrid-smelling blaze, into the cold air on the river. Their campsite receded quickly behind them, consumed by flames lapping along the bank, even the water "burning", reflecting yellow-red. The river curved back near the fire and a tree fell just behind them, spitting steam, the heat choking them. Susan coughed. He tied a bandanna over his mouth and nose. Their clothes, drenched with perspiration, stuck to their skin. Orange embers floated, borne by the wind, and followed them, as the current pulled them through the bend and downriver away from the sooty pall into open, cool air.

Moonlit mist lingered over dead pools, casting a ghostly aura over the river. As they glided swiftly toward huge boulders rising out of the mist, David heard the roaring of white water. He looked to the bow, Susan hunched over, gripping her paddle. As the river lifted them into the luminous white rapids, he shouted, "Left side. Left! Now right." He tried looking ahead but couldn't see. They rammed into a boulder, spun around, and shot backwards into a chute, David paddling furiously, guiding them through stern-first. She screamed, hands clutching the canoe and her paddle pressed uselessly across her legs. Working hard, he turned them around, maneuvering in preparation for the next rapids. He knelt on the seat but could only see his wife's back.

"Goddammit," he yelled over the water crashing into rock. "Don't just sit there." At least make a suggestion, he thought as his mind raced, which way?

"And do *what*?" she yelled.

"I don't care. Paddle!"

The current gripped them and pulled them past a boulder; the canoe turned sideways, the aluminum frame scraping against rock. Susan screamed, "Watch out!" She paddled frantically. They slammed into rock and tilted, the current pounding against the canoe, foam surging to its rim and held there for a moment before dark water poured in. The canoe went under, sucked down by the current, and they were in the river.

Trying to keep his head above water and his feet pointing downstream, he went under, hit something and came up choking and spitting, bobbing. Cold currents dragged him under again and again, as if something were grabbing at his ankles. No, he thought, no, and each time he clawed his way back to the surface, gasping.

Finally, the rapids fanned out into the smooth surface of a large pool and he floated easily in the swirling water. "Susan!" he called but heard nothing in return. Her name echoed in his head, Susan, and he felt sick, his stomach knotting. *I need to find her*, he thought, twisting his head around, looking for her in the slow, swirling current. *Was she on shore*, he thought, *why doesn't she answer*? The water felt smooth, almost caressing, and for a moment, he imagined that he and his wife were playing, swimming together. All he had to do was find her and touch her in the cleansing water, then everything would be okay. But his teeth started chattering, and he was miserably cold, aching to the bone. *Move*, he thought, *must move now*. He swam, not sure which way he was going, knowing only that he had to get out of the river. He swam into black shadows from the forest, then stumbled onto the wooded bank.

David's head throbbed as he touched the bridge of his nose, the skin loose around a jagged gash, the blood sticky. He used his right hand to steady himself against a tree, but when he applied pressure, his wrist buckled, pain shooting to his fingertips. Holding the hand up close to his face, he could see two fingers protruding unnaturally, pale and crooked in the moonlight. "Damn," he muttered, then tried to reassure himself, okay, it's not that bad. *Not bad. Could be worse.* His clothes smelled like wet charcoal. He tasted blood. But the hot wind was gone, and no animals were scurrying for their lives.

"Susan," he yelled and scanned the white water above the pool. Nothing. No sign of the canoe. While pushing through the underbrush, branches scraped his arms, and he was unable to see much but the turbulent white of the rapids. He climbed onto a boulder, then onto another, and leaned precariously over the river, searching the far shore. She must have swum to the other side, he thought, not drowned. No, that couldn't be. She had to be okay. A noise floating above the roar of the rapids could have been his wife screaming for help, couldn't it? He listened intently. Was it her?

David slid off the boulder and banged his shin on a fallen tree, then lurched forward into sharp branches, slicing skin from his palms. He caught his leg between the branches and fell. Lying flat, his face against the rain soaked pine needles, he fought for breath. Easing his foot free, he crawled out from the jumble of dead limbs. With the white water raging and reverberating around him, he stumbled along the shore, falling into the water again, hands sinking into the bottom, the foul stench of rotting trees bubbling to the surface.

Struggling to his feet, he waded into the moonlit pool. Standing knee-deep in the swirling water, he called, "Susan!" A small object rolled to the surface. As he moved in deeper, up to his chest, his heart pounded with his love for Susan and the fear she might be gone, the water pressing against him, cold and constricting. He struggled to breathe and the current, even in this pool, pulled hard, again nearly taking him under. He lunged, falling and going under but catching the object before it was swept into the next set of rapids. Frantically splashing back toward the shore, he stood, knowing what it was by the feel of the laces and the sole - one of Susan's tennis shoes. Looking downriver, he thought, the current almost killed me, what chance did she have? Overwhelmed by the gruesome possibilities, he stumbled back, sitting in the shallow water near the shore. He fought to keep back tears, remembering how he had helped her when they crossed streams, her hand in his. He focused on the opposite shore, listening to the rapids blend into the swishing of tall pines in the wind. The moon cast shadows in the forest and the shadows moved like ghouls. Rocks lined the shore - small, round faces sneering at him. Maybe something was lurking in the dark woods.

David looked down at the moonlit water reflecting white and swirling around his legs, then at the looming boulders pounded by the torrent, and he felt light-headed, like he was floating above the forest, unbound from earthly emotion. Suddenly, he shuddered, teeth chattering, and he tried to gain control. The small shoe fell from his hand and he watched it bob in the turbulent water, the current suddenly taking it swiftly toward the rapids, and the boulders.

"No!" he yelled. "Susan," he called again, but again no response. "Susan."

He imagined his wife underwater, frantically swimming to the surface. Maybe she made it to the other side, but hit her head on something. That's why she didn't respond to his calls. Or maybe, she just couldn't hear him above the noise of the rapids. Lightning flashed overhead, followed by a crack and rumble, then a hard, cold gust, chilling him. He looked to the far shore one last time, the pointed outline of treetops against the dark sky lit by lightning. Was that her? If Susan were alive, he thought, she must be on the other side. He turned into the forest, thrashing his way through the thick woods, determined to find a way across the river.

Warmed by the pumping of his blood, he slogged through the forest in a heavy downpour, the stale smell of rain-soaked ash lingering on his clothes. Had he fled an inferno only to fight his way through this freezing muck? He followed the river, his mind fixed on a vivid image of their map - a footbridge, downriver. *When* he made it to the bridge, there would be a trail also, the trail leading to a town.

David thought about Susan, pulled deep into the cold water and how she hated the cold. He remembered when they first met, the way her body fit next to his and the soothing warmth of their bed, thick blankets, with cool winds blowing over them from the open windows. David scowled, his jaw tight, remembering their arguments. But he loved her. And he felt guilty. He should have worked harder at solving their problems, the way he did on the warplanes when his business degree left him unprepared for complex engineering jargon. He earned promotions and raises by memorizing what he could and nodding in approval at the right moments. Had he worked that hard on his marriage? The job was lost. Was he now losing his wife? Or had he already lost her? Don't feel anything, he thought. That's best. Emotions were a weakness, and now they could be fatal.

The lightning split the sky and heavy rain glistened like jewels falling out of the blackness. He hiked through the forest, following the bank, remembering trips into the mountains before he met Susan, often alone, the sinking feeling at the end, standing at the trail head, a parking lot full of cars, the pleasure of the climb giving way to the dread of having to return.

Now, fighting for survival in the wilderness, he felt confident, strong, sure that Susan would be all right. When he found her, she would be banged up maybe, but otherwise okay. He had to think she would be okay, unable to bear any other conclusion, the image of his wife returning easily, her soft, curving cheeks, her smile. But suddenly gloomy images replaced the good, Susan being hurled through the darkness, mutilated by the sharp rock. He slowed, staggered, and nearly crumpled to the ground. "No," he said. "You're okay, Susan. You must be." He leaned against a tree, his body cooling rapidly, thinking, I must analyze . . . and re-analyze. . . . And move, he thought, and keep moving, because that was the only way to survive.

By morning, nausea and fatigue overwhelmed him, but he did not stop. He couldn't. He had to press on. The rain eased to a drizzle as he thrashed through the thick woods, blackflies landing on his arms and leaving red welts, blood, as if they were chewing into his flesh. Once, in Maine, while hunting with his father, he had killed a moose that was fleeing the marsh during blackfly season. His father had jokingly thanked God for the flies that drove the moose into the sights of David's rifle; David could see it fall, and the spurting blood, while his father marveled at the shot and praised him for the beautiful kill. Then later, they ate moose, washing it down with beer, and making jokes about women, his mother complaining when they tracked dirt and specks of blood onto the carpet. He let his thoughts linger on the moose for quite some time until he became aware that he was thinking about the moose and not Susan. Her absence from his thoughts unnerved him. Must focus, can't waver. Need to keep believing she is alive.

The sun broke through the clouds and was shining in his eyes when he struggled over a rise and came upon the bridge, and the trail out. Unimpeded by underbrush, he hiked over the footbridge and crossed the river. He knelt on the opposite bank, cupped his hands and drank from the river, remembering his conversation with Susan. *Yes,* he thought, *I am right, you can drink the water*. But he also now wished he were standing next to her, alive, in a museum. Museum, he thought sarcastically, of man and nature?

The town was ten miles further. If he backtracked along the river, searching for his wife, it would take him at least a day, maybe two, struggling through the dense underbrush. Then another day or so just to make it to the town.

With this realization, his legs felt heavy as lead, and he staggered into the forest, slumping to the ground and settling into a bed of pine needles. Hungry and aching, he passed into a delirious half-sleep. In a dream, he saw Susan rolling in the current, her body emerging, glistening water dripping from the apparition, then he saw himself drowning, water filling his lungs. He woke in a panic, unable to breathe, his battered nose clogged with mucus and dried blood. Holding one finger at a time over each nostril, he blew them clear. He rubbed his face and head, careful to avoid his wounds, trying to block any thought about the pain continually throbbing to the surface. He sat, thinking about her.

"Maybe she's dead," he muttered. After all, he had barely survived; she might not have. She loved the outdoors but often struggled through it, at least at his pace. He should have shared the map, and he might have, he reasoned, if their arguments hadn't gotten in the way. He stared at the sunlight filtering through the dense forest, exhausted at the mere thought of going back to look for Susan. She's gone, he thought, then rubbed his face. No, he thought, he had to survive, emotions now . . . will only . . . "No," he cried, howling in the wilderness, his body shuddering as he fought to keep back the tears, feeling like a child lost in the woods, alone.

That strange floating feeling returned, like he was above the forest looking down at himself. It disturbed him, thinking that he was dying as well. No, he thought, he would survive. He had to. Recovering, he thought about what happened, how things could have been different with just a small change here or there, wanting to go back and relive it, do it right. They should have taken the rapids before camping, but he had decided to stop for  just one more effort, he thought, to reconnect with her. In hindsight, they should have gone on, and ended the trip as early as possible, then . . . divorce? What happened? He thought about when they first met, before they were married, before their relationship died like lightning bugs left in a jar to suffocate. Had she *ever* loved him? But he couldn't go back and do it over and, in the end, they capsized. He could barely see the trail through the brush. He needed to push on, use the daylight. Get to the trail, he thought, and go fast. But he was too tired and decided to take a short nap, regain some strength, easier to sleep in the warmth of daylight. Just for a few minutes.

David was lying on his back when he woke, opening his eyes, but not moving, birds chirping and fluttering from branch to branch, sunlight casting long shadows. He was unwilling to move and face the pain. Nose must be broken, he thought, and pushed at it carefully. His whole body hurt. While preparing himself for the agony of getting up, he heard something moving in the forest behind him. Slowly turning his head, he peered out from the brush.

On the other side of the footbridge, a hiker emerged from the forest, dragging one leg stiffly along. David tried to get up, but his legs throbbed and his lower body felt numb. *Am I paralyzed?* He couldn't move. He pounded on his legs, then looked at the person who now fell onto the path, long wet hair slapping against her face. She leaned against the bridge post, then wearily looked up and down the path. David tasted the blood on his chapped lips, and exhaled, trying to clear his throat, feeling like he'd swallowed pine needles. Move, he thought, grabbing his leg, then looking up in time to see the hiker struggle to her knees and peer into the woods. Susan? He watched her turn away and stagger down the path, away from the town, deeper into the forest. He opened his dry, parched mouth - *that's the wrong way* - but no sound came out, and Susan vanished. *No*, he thought, *that was not her. I'm hallucinating.* But then he thought, she must've recovered gear from the canoe. While he had slept, she must've kept on,

33

probably delirious, out of her mind. *If* that was her. How could it be? His heart was beating fast. Get up. Do something.

What's wrong with my legs? He punched one leg, feeling it tingle, then worked on the other, suddenly feeling an excruciating pain in his back. He twisted around, reached behind him and felt a sharp rock in the pine needles. *I'll be okay, able to walk, just wait, the nerves will come back.* He pushed and massaged his legs until the blood pumped into his legs like hydraulic fluid lowering a jet's landing gear.

Rolling onto his knees, he struggled to his feet, and almost blacked out, taking two wobbly steps. He leaned against a tree, forced another step, legs heavy as lead, and started hiking, following the hiker deeper into the wilderness. Was it Susan? He hadn't really gotten that good a look at her. Did it matter, he thought. Whoever it was, she was in trouble. But so was he. Had to be her, he thought.

As he warmed, his pace quickened. Where was she? How could she be that far ahead of him? Had she stumbled off the path somewhere? Had he passed her by? He turned around and hiked the other direction, but then stopped. Was he going the wrong way now? He sat and leaned against a tree, his heavy legs sticking out into the path. He stared at his crooked fingers. He needed to think. Maybe he should head for the town, get help. But Susan could be dead by the time he returned. But if he kept searching for her, he could also die. What was the point of that? But wouldn't leaving her now be murder? The woods were peaceful now, the light from the descending sun filtering through the trees and glistening on damp ground. Get up, he told himself. Just the thought of failing to save her made him sick. He would rather die than fail.

The path narrowed, slightly downhill, the direction that offered the least resistance, his legs thudding on the path as he kept a slow, steady pace. He hiked into a small clearing, long grass stirring gently in cool wind, dark blue wild flowers, and a cabin. David tried to yell, but it came out as a hoarse whisper. A faint yellow light glowed in the window, a curl of smoke from the stovepipe barely visible against the darkening sky. Shadows crept across the front porch, the sun a red ball pierced by the tall pines, the air cooling rapidly. Had she come this way, to this cabin? If she had not deviated from the trail, then she must be inside. He yelled, his voice stronger but still hoarse. No answer. Blackflies swirled around his face, a few landing to suck more blood, red welts rising.

David crept onto the porch, the planks creaking. When he tapped on the front door, it opened. Inside, a black potbelly stove burned near a plank bed where he found his wife lying motionless, on her back, arm jutting out stiffly, knotted hair covering her face. He collapsed in relief, sitting on the dirty cabin floor, leaning against her, exhaling, touching her. He pushed her arm onto the bunk. She felt cold. He leaned close, felt her pulse, and listened to her faint breathing. Yes, she was alive.

A cold gust swept through the open door, swirled around the cabin, and rattled the vent on the stove. David stirred the dwindling fire and it crackled reassuringly. Carefully, he lifted hair from her face, now softly visible in the firelight. Lingering over her, David touched her cheek, the smoky smell of the cabin inviting, but also unnerving, like the forest fire. He stood, feeling wobbly, and looked for more wood. The cabin was small, one room. He found a table, with a bottle of tequila, almost empty, and next to it a box of bullets, and a few empty shells, the brass shells shiny in the diminishing light. He looked around for a gun, but didn't see one. Looks like a public use cabin, he thought, rustic, he'd seen plenty of them. They were cheap, and hunters often rented them. But the tequila bothered him. Not that he didn't drink, but he recalled when he was a teenager, his father warning him against alcohol and hunting. Of course he didn't listen and his friend almost shot him, buckshot whizzing past his head. They laughed about it then, but David never forgot it.

The flames from the potbelly stove went out, and the cabin

felt cold. David looked at his wife, then opened the door and stepped outside, looking for firewood. There wasn't any on the porch, so he circled the cabin, finding only twigs. He headed into the forest, but the ground nearby was depleted of good firewood. He had to go much further than he wanted to, eventually finding a fallen tree, dead branches jutting through thick brush. He grabbed a branch, his injured fingers swollen and unable to grasp anything, but he tried, and pulled hard. A branch snapped off in his hands, stinging. David suddenly realized how exhausted he was, taking deep breaths. He needed more wood and was ready to try again when he heard something, at first unclear, but quickly becoming discernible - twigs snapping, the clanking of a metal cup against a backpack. He stood still, listening, gripping the branch like a club, and thinking about the tequila and the bullets. Any normal person would help them, he thought. "Susan," he whispered, and started to run back toward the cabin, thrashing through the brush, then stopped. Wait, he thought. Don't make noise. He stepped carefully, crouched down just before the clearing, and listened again.

A looming, shadowy figure of a man approached the cabin and stopped, the resulting silence abrupt. The man dropped a pack, equipment clanking, and cautiously stepped onto the porch, then inside, emerging a few moments later with a lantern, and peering out into the descending night. David could see him clearly - leather boots, army fatigues, red flannel shirt, thick beard, and long tangled hair. The man hoisted his pack, turned to have another look around, then went back inside.

From the brush, David crawled to the side window and peeked in. The man immediately grabbed the tequila and drank it like water, straight from the bottle, then pulled it away from his mouth, staring at his bunk. He knelt carefully over Susan, gently pushing her shoulder. She moaned, but did not wake. The man touched a small puddle on the floor, blood dripping from Susan's leg; he unbuckled a sheath from his ankle and pulled out a knife, wide blade glistening in the firelight, and thick handle wrapped with black tape. He set the knife down, then stood quickly and headed for the door.

David ducked beneath the window and retreated into the underbrush. Hide, he thought, buy some time, come up with a plan. The man stepped outside, gripping a rifle, then receded into the shadows of the porch. David froze, thinking, the bastard must be paranoid, half-animal, six senses. He waited, listing his options - yell out, beg for help. Run away? *I'm an idiot*, he thought, why not just go to the door and ask for my wife? But he felt sure that the tequila-guzzling, long-haired man in fatigues was dangerous. David held his branch like a club and started to circle the cabin, thinking he would attack from the other side. Save Susan. But after only two cautious steps, the man emerged again and shouldered the rifle.

David ran thinking the bastard was going to shoot, the bullet would hit him in the back, tear through his heart. But he heard nothing. Only his own thrashing as he ran far into the woods, suddenly tripping, sprawling into the brush, hitting the ground hard and blacking out.

As he regained consciousness, he tried to recall what had happened. His head pounded from the back of his neck through to his already-cut face. Stars were glittering across the big sky. He tried to stand but felt too wobbly. Crawling through the underbrush, he found his club, and used it to push himself up onto his feet. He lurched, then staggered recklessly toward the dark cabin. He stumbled onto the porch, pushed the door open and lunged inside ready to fight. Like he should have done before, he thought. Wind rattled the windows, shadows moved with the wind, and wood planks groaned. Standing with chest heaving, trying to catch his breath, the emptiness of the cabin slowly settled on him like the end of a three-day drunk. His arms shook, the cold gripping him. He opened the stove door and held his hands over the warming coals, then noticed a torn piece of brown paper pushed onto a nail, a note with heavy-handed, uneven print. "Had to go.

Woman hurt. You go without me this time."

David stepped back outside. "Susan?" he called. Nothing but strange yelping in the distance. Maybe coyotes. Then wind. He had failed miserably. He had miscalculated the danger running the river, failed to stop her from going in the wrong direction on the path, and worst yet, failed to save her at the cabin, misjudging the situation, and letting a strange man carry her to safety.

While sitting on the porch, he stared into the dark woods. Now what should he do? Drag his stiff, aching body back inside? Sleep by the fire, and wait? For what? Some hunter to rescue *him*? He'd rather the hunter shoot him. That would be a just fate, wouldn't it?

The moon rose brightly over trees, and David watched the black shadows slice across the clearing. The silhouette of one tall tree jutting up into the moonlit sky like a warplane taking off, straight up. He recalled his unwanted transfer to commercial airlines, and thought his own marriage seemed to mirror the ensuing economic deterioration.

A breeze stirred the trees and the shadows moved. Was that someone? He stood and walked into the clearing. "Who's there?" he called. No answer. He looked back at the cold, confining cabin, then at the moonlit path, and he started hiking. As long as he kept moving, he didn't feel so bad.

Susan would be okay, he thought, wishing he could go back, before they were married, and . . . then he recalled Savgren's odd comment at the wedding. He stopped, standing in the middle of the path, staring at the sky, the moon falling to the west, and the stars brightening. Doesn't work out, you can always . . . What? Leap into another universe? Not possible, he thought. At least not literally. But what about an alternate reality? Each movement, each choice he made now, would determine his reality, the future possibilities unfolding before him. No, he thought, shaking his head, rubbing his face, feeling outside his own body.

Had the man *seen* him? Had Susan? If either had, he'd be

with them now, wouldn't he? Didn't matter. He could choose to emerge from the forest, and return to his old life. Then what? Let his wife, a woman who clearly lacked ambition, who would rather study the irreversible past than explore future possibilities, let her take the lead? Cling to her for financial support while he waited in unemployment lines? Even if he found a job, wouldn't they fall into the same trap, with him working hard and coming home to a wife who apparently didn't love him? Escape, he thought, flee his miserable life and go to Wyoming, where he had felt at peace before. That possibility made him feel light-headed, unburdened, floating like before, but without any fear. Free. If he just disappeared, they would search the river for *his* body, not Susan's. Eventually, they would conclude that he had drowned. Or they might think he had died trying to save Susan, that he was some sort of hero instead of a pathetic failure.

"No," he said, then looked around at the dark forest, as if someone would hear him. "Hello," he yelled, hearing a slight echo. *Or was that in my head? Am I talking to myself, or my alternate self?* Theoretically, there were infinite possibilities, he reasoned. Just like Savgren had said. Couldn't he just *choose* one of those alternatives? Who would care, really? His wife. Yes, maybe, at first, but then she would realize that she was better off without him. No more arguments. Family? Maybe. But, living in a different city, they had rarely communicated. They would get over it. Why not choose a new life? He shivered, and his whole body ached with the cold. Had to move, he thought.

By the time he'd made it back to the bridge, he was suffering from exposure, fatigue, his body no longer generating enough heat. He needed food. If he stopped to sleep, or to rest, he would risk hypothermia. He scoffed at the paradoxical idea of freezing fast, his body temperature shifting so suddenly, the cold coming in on him so fast that it freezes his core, stops his heart in mid-beat. Speed created heat, not cold. With the town only a few miles further, David ran, feeling more like an escaped convict than a free man.

## Chapter Three

Susan dreamed that she was lying on her back, underwater, staring up at a distorted, bearded face leering over her. She heard fire crackling, and tasted bittersweet pine. She opened her eyes, waking to the odor of disinfectant and the clatter of silverware on plates. The room was white, sterile. Her vision was blurry at first, the bearded man in her dream fading away, replaced by a thin-lipped, tight-faced nurse with a hangover.

The bright light irritated Susan's eyes and a tear dropped from her cheek. Her tightly bandaged leg itched unmercifully and rested on a stack of pillows. "David?" she asked.

"Go back to sleep," the nurse commanded, then tossed dishes onto a cart and pushed it rattling out the door.

A green curtain divided the small room, and she heard the squeak of bedsprings from the other side. "David," she called, then grabbed her bandaged leg and pushed it to the edge of her bed. She stood and knifing pain jolted her spine. Lunging, she grabbed the curtain, metal rod collapsing and clanging to the floor, then she heard a cry. Clutching the edge of the other patient's bed, she stood, staring past a mound of blankets, into the terrified face of a young woman.

"Where's David?" Susan demanded.

The nurse ran into the room with two attendants, and they worked quickly, lifting Susan back into her bed, pulling the covers cocoon tight, then someone pushed a needle into her arm and she felt the dull pain. Soon she relaxed so much that she didn't care about the hubbub around her and the objections from the woman's husband.

Waking groggily, Susan looked up at a tiny window high on

the wall, sun beaming in, blue sky. She remembered flying into Winnipeg, their brief stay in the city, the great open plains of wild grassland bending with the North winds. Then the forest. She had wanted to spend more time in the city, go to museums, and learn about the Indian cultures.

The doctor came back and asked how she felt. But Susan's lips were numb. She could only mumble, and the doctor explained that the numbness was normal, telling her that a man brought her to the hospital that morning. "Found you in his cabin last night. Treated your wounds, then rigged a backpack. Carried you twelve miles, in the dark." Susan remembered the rocking motion, then she thought about her father, carrying her piggyback, after a long day of playing. "They found your canoe wreckage where, presumably, you left it. I'm sorry, they haven't found your husband yet. But you made it okay. And your leg will be fine, no infection." Susan nodded. She closed her eyes hard, trying to make it all go away, but tears seeped out and she pressed her face into the pillow. The doctor touched her shoulder, held it there, then turned away, giving the nurse instructions for more sedatives if needed.

Susan rolled over in the sagging bed and fought to keep her eyes open, but she succumbed to the drugged sleep, her body cringing at lightning striking all too realistically, and she gasped for breath as the torrent poured from the sky. She screamed for David, hearing nothing but the roar of white water.

"Wake up," she heard. "It's okay." She felt her arms being squeezed, her mother holding her tight like a little girl, and she sobbed. The nurse came in with a needle, but Mom waved her away.

Susan eventually stopped crying. She opened her mouth, but couldn't talk, her mind spinning in the rapids, pounding her, spinning deeper, deeper until she knew she would drown, the current like an animal grabbing at her and pulling her under, then her struggle to shore, choking and vomiting and praying for David, never finding him.

She sat up straight, pushing against the metal headboard. "I need to get out of here."

"I know," her mother responded. "It's okay, I'll get you out."

Susan tried to roll over, slide out of the bed, but the pain gripped her. She shut her eyes tight, only to see fire surrounding her. Pressing her face against the pillow, she struggled to bury the nightmares. But she saw herself digging through pine needles, scraping up mud over her leg. She opened her eyes. "Mom, I . . ." She wanted to tell about the twisted canoe, dragging it onto shore, building a shelter. "Remember how Dad used to build forts with me?"

"Yes," her mother responded. "You dug up our yard to make a moat."

Susan nodded. "And ramparts . . . Escarpments."

Mrs Moore grabbed a tissue and wiped tears from under her own eyes, then she reached into her purse and pulled out a notebook, and an ink pen. She stared at the blank notebook, and said, "I'm sorry . . ."

"What is it, Mom?"

"When your father died, your Uncle Jim helped me take care of finances. You wouldn't believe the mess." She touched her daughter's face and brushed back her long brown hair. "I didn't know a thing. Didn't want to. Couldn't even find the checkbook."

Susan remembered her uncle helping in the only way he knew how: going through files, making sure they were in order.

"I'm just trying to help," Mrs Moore said. "You know that, don't you?"

"What's wrong?"

"I reported the accident to your insurance company."

"Okay." Susan waited for more.

Mrs Moore took off her glasses. "They're sending someone."

"Who is?" Susan asked.

"David's life insurance . . ."

"Life insurance? David?" She remembered him scoffing at the idea, calling it death insurance.

"About 300,000." Mrs Moore put her glasses back on and held her pen ready. "At first I thought maybe it was an investment, but all you get is death protection."

Susan stared at the white walls. She thought she heard someone say her name, but then suspected it might be a hallucination - David screaming at her while she crawled out of the cold water. "Mom? Is he alive?"

"I'm sorry, I don't think so. They've searched the area thoroughly-"

"But it *is* possible?" Susan insisted, resisting feelings she knew all too well, the room filling with emptiness as she faded into the wall and stared at people, unable to join them.

"Anything is possible."

"Does the insurance company say he's alive?" Susan could hear David's voice, one of their many "discussions". She hated the way he made her angry.

"Yes, of course, dear. But that's the way finances work - nobody cares how you feel."

"It's just really *hard* . . ." she cried.

The doctor arrived, asking, "Everything all right?"

Susan still felt drugged, and only half-listened to her mother insist sedatives weren't needed, asking when her daughter could be released from the hospital. Then Susan fell into another restless sleep, waking to the sound of voices. At first she thought them part of her dream, but realized they were coming from outside her room. She tried to listen while watching the walls change from white to gray, the light from the small window diminishing, shadows from the lattice looking like bars on a jail cell.

The door opened, and she heard the nurse insisting, "I told you, she needs to sleep."

Then she heard an unfamiliar male voice. "She's probably awake right now." With the nurse telling him to stop, a man moved quickly to Susan's bedside. "Is there anything I can do for you?" he asked. "Something to drink? Eat?"

Susan looked at his closely cropped hair, yellow tie, his brown eyes staring at her. "Who are you?" she asked.

"Excuse me, I didn't introduce myself. Bad habit. Mike Jurgan, of Jurgan Insurance."

Susan pulled the thin sheet up and folded her arms across her chest. "I've never heard of you," she said, "or your company."

Jurgan pulled up a chair and sat, leaning forward. "We're a small, two-state operation, based in St Louis."

Susan thought that it all sounded like a sales pitch, and the hospital an odd place for an insurance salesman.

"We sell affordable term-life to people like your husband," Jurgan said, "and homeowners' insurance."

The room felt small and Susan wished he would go away. "So why are you here?"

"For *our* company," he responded, "this is a big claim."

Susan looked at him. "I still don't understand."

"Mrs Brooks," Jurgan said impatiently, "I know this must be difficult. But if you could please answer a few questions, we can settle the claim quickly."

She glanced toward the door, then at the agent waiting for her to respond. "Okay," she said.

"Actually, there is one very important question . . . " He paused, straightening his tie, brushing lint from his shirt, then asked, "Did you actually *see* your husband's body?"

Susan stared blankly. Now, thanks to him, she did see her husband's body, tumbling in the current, hitting jagged rocks, white, floating in the moonlight - a carcass, like the bloated deer she had seen once floating in a pond. Her father took her there to fish, and he tried explaining to her that it was just a dead animal and the bloating was natural, but Susan didn't listen. She just stared.

"Mrs Brooks?"

"Get out."

"I apologize, I should've given you more time, talked to

your friend, what's his name? Mr Blucuski? Kester? I just thought —"

"Get out!" she shouted. "Get out!" She looked for something to throw at him. The desk lamp? But the insurance agent backed away, and she could hear him cussing under his breath as he left with the attendants. Jerk, she thought, he only cared about his money.

The nurse turned off the lights, and a gray pall lit the room, Susan wanting to see the sunset, but figuring the room must be facing east. She tried to read a magazine her mother had left. Kester, she thought, the bearded man in her dream? The man who saved her? When she was a child, her father often saved her from imaginary burning castles, and later, the burning temples of Tenochtitlan. She tried to imagine Kester Blucuski. The name did not conjure up knights or conquistadors. No, she thought, the name had a more basic, savage quality - maybe he was indigenous - the "noble savage".

As the last light faded from the window, Susan turned on the table lamp, and the room smelled faintly different, like an old coat left outside. The door eased opened and the smell filled the room. A man stood by the door, not speaking, standing in the diffuse lamplight. "Hello," he said in a deep, almost soothing voice.

"Kester?" she asked, sure it had to be him. He wore a thick red mackinaw over a sweater, olive-drab fatigues, and he inched forward, kneading his knit hat through his hairy fingers. He sat next to her and smiled, but then his thick eyebrows furrowed.

"You were hurt pretty bad," he said. "Lucky you made it to my cabin." He squeezed his hat into a ball and stuffed it into his pocket.

"You carried me out?" Susan asked.

"Yes," he responded slowly. "You needed a doctor . . . "

"Thank you." She relaxed, his voice calming her.

"It wasn't anything." His big hands touched her covers.

She let her mind drift - thoughts about home and sleeping in her own bed, her cat curling up next to her. "I'm tired," she said.

Kester leaned close, his pupils black, glossy. "Where you from?" he asked.

Susan pulled the covers close to her neck. "St Louis . . ." But she stopped, wishing she'd kept her mouth shut, not wanting to become too familiar with this stranger who did not seem all that noble.

"No kiddin'?" Kester smiled, but Susan thought it looked more like a grimace. "I'm from St Louis. My buddy rented a cabin up here for a couple weeks." His eyes narrowed. "You feel bad about your husband?"

Susan glared. How was she supposed to feel? Good? And what right did he have asking about David? It only made her feel worse.

Kester placed his heavy, dirty hand on her arm. "You should spend a few days with me at the cabin. Help you get over things. Do some huntin'. Do you like to hunt?"

"Thank you," she said, "for taking care of me; you helped save my life. I'm grateful." Be polite, she thought, and he will get the hint, feeling torn between gratitude and aversion.

"If that's a no," he responded, frowning, "just say so."

"How can I repay you?" she asked.

"Come back with me," he said. "That's more than your husband can say, isn't it?"

Susan stared at him, dark circles under his shifting eyes. "What do you mean?"

"Nothin'. Except that *he* didn't save you, did he? I did."

"Please leave," she said, thinking she'd better remain polite, that Kester was a little off-center. And David *would have* saved her if he could've. "Thanks for what you've done, but please—"

"Sure, whatever you want." He stood, one side of his mouth turning up. "See you later," he said.

Susan gripped the covers for a long time after Kester left,

47

and she stared into the dim-lit room unable to stop thinking about her husband. Was he still alive? Somewhere in the woods? Her mind vacillated wildly, praying that David was alive one moment, then plunging into a morbid desire to see his corpse, to verify that their marriage had ended with his death. She suspected he was going to leave her anyway. But not like this. This was unbearable. Eventually, she gave way to fatigue and slept again.

In a never-ending nightmare, Susan searched the dark woods looking for her husband, her life jacket ripped, hanging uselessly from her waist, sobbing and searching the moonlit pool below the rapids. David, she cried, while stumbling along the riverbank, blood spewing from a gash above her knee. Then she found her father standing alone in the forest, reassuring her in the nightmare, her father calmly telling her that she would soon be a woman, and how proud he was of her, then the voice drowned in the roar of white water.

She woke at noon, sweating, more determined than ever to get out of the hospital. She struggled to get dressed. After an hour, she was limping back and forth, using a crutch, ready to beat the doctor with it. Finally, her mother arrived, checking off items on the list.

Susan was anxious to get outside where she could think clearly. Where, she hoped, the accident would fade away, a bad dream, and David would emerge from the woods. Maybe a little beaten and bruised, but alive. He couldn't have died, she thought, not David. He was like the rocks that he loved to climb. Solid, unbeatable, not one to succumb easily. Too solid? Hard to read? At one point, she believed that if she learned how to climb, it might help her understand her husband. But, she thought, their relationship had been even more complex than climbing mountains.

"Let's go," Susan said.

"Okay." Mrs Moore checked off an item. "We fly out right after the meeting with our lawyer and Mr Jurgan."

## Chapter Four

Near the trailhead, David sought high ground, which was difficult to find in this land of gently rolling hills and pine forest. He always felt better on mountaintops, able to see things in perspective, the troubles of the world far below and insignificant. David stood on the trail, in a rocky glade, and for a moment thought he understood himself and his marriage, the main reason it had failed. He worked hard, going to the edge and beyond, while she went in the other direction, never willing to push herself, settling for a secretarial career that didn't even come close to exploring her potential.

David hiked past a granite outcropping, the huge rock jutting up from the forest floor, and he stood on a bluff overlooking a lake with morning sunlight glistening from the blue surface. A motor boat skipped across the blue lake. Cabins lined the shore, and through an opening in the trees, he could see the smooth green surface of a golf course. He tried to recall the name of the resort community on the map. Where exactly was he? But the towns, lodges, outfitters blurred together in his mind, all with indigenous names: Brokenhead, Seven Sisters Falls, Wekusko.

Gray clouds billowed above the far end of the lake. David stuffed his hand into his pocket and found a US twenty-dollar bill. He had meant to put the money with the rest of their cash, securely attached to the canoe, but had forgotten. He'd been distracted by his own anxiousness to get on the water while Susan had casually organized her space in the bow. He had wanted her to move faster, more efficiently. Now he wondered if she were safe, maybe in a hospital. Had the stranger carried her on this same path? But, he thought, as the trail neared civilization, it split into several different directions, offering many possibilities.

David nodded and smiled at tourists who stared at him in his ragged clothes. He picked dried blood from his face as he stood in a store and looked at overpriced shirts. For a moment, he considered stealing a shirt, but the shopkeeper was watching him.

"Been camping?" the shopkeeper asked.

David set a roll of adhesive tape and a shirt on the counter. Camping, he thought. Yes, that was it. He was just a tourist on a camping trip, nothing more. "Sorry," he responded, "I don't have any Canadian money."

The shopkeeper shrugged. "Happens all the time."

David thanked him, taking the Canadian change, then walked a short way before finding a lodge with a restaurant where he cleaned up as best he could, washing away the dirt and blood. He changed his shirt and bandaged his face, making him feel a little better, hungry. He seated himself at a table away from a couple busily attending to their two small children, and an older couple, glancing at him. David had found a flat stick, and now he pressed it against his finger. Using his teeth, he pulled on the adhesive tape, the ripping sound loud in the restaurant, then taped his fingers together around the stick. When the waitress arrived, she set a glass of water in front of him. He ordered bacon and eggs, then gulped the water. As he set the empty glass down, the older couple stared at him and whispered.

David ate slowly, trying to act normal but, as the food warmed him, the abnormality of his situation hit him, and he felt isolated. There are always choices, he thought, even in this new reality that he was forging. No longer was he a hard-working husband with an unloving wife. But who was he now? Who would he become?

The food was expensive, and he spent most of his money paying the bill, leaving no tip, hurrying before the waitress found out what a cheapskate he was. Outside, the clouds had turned black and were looming overhead as he walked along a narrow road leading to the highway.

The rain came down hard and he hitchhiked with his back to the wind as trucks roared by, spraying water. For now, he thought, his thumb was the only control he had over his life. Finally, one of the semis rolled onto the shoulder, squeaking, hissing and groaning to a stop. He ran, and climbed into the truck cab where warm air blasted out of large vents.

"Kinda wet out there, huh?" the driver said, glancing at him.

"Yeah," David responded, leaning against the window, staring at his own distorted face in the big, rectangular side mirror - the warped reflection of tape crossing over the bridge of his nose and blue-black bruises under his eyes. "Thanks for stopping."

The driver grunted, then shifted, the huge tractor-trailer lurching and slowly growling into motion. David looked over his shoulder at the gray spot of highway where he'd stood. Rain and mist swirled in the vortex of the departing truck. His chest tightened, and he inhaled deeply, then coughed.

"Ya gonna be okay, buddy?" the driver asked.

David nodded his head, and stared blankly at the cracked vinyl dashboard. Sure, he thought, he was going to be just fine, as soon as he figured out what he was going to do. What was left of his past life? Could he go back to their historic home? When he thought of it, he felt like a failure. His parents had managed to stay married for thirty years, but David's marriage fell apart right after it started. Could he go back, rewind time and be with Susan before they were married? What would he change?

"You get in a fight or somethin'?"

David looked at him. "A few miles back," he said, "in a bar."

"Yeah, which one?"

"I dunno, back there somewhere . . . it wasn't me, I tried to break it up."

"Sometimes it's better ta let things be." The driver shifted again, voice drifting in the warm air blasting out from the truck's heater. "Where ya headed?"

David looked out the rain-splattered windshield at the gray evening. "Where are we now?"

"On our way to the border, then the Cities."

"Minneapolis - St Paul?"

The driver muttered, "Yeah, that's right."

David settled back in the warmth of the truck cab, leaned his head on the unyielding, rumbling seat, and closed his eyes. He slipped into a half sleep, and remembered that he had once thought about being a truck driver. Make lots of money just sitting on your rear end. Drink coffee and eat bad food. He even researched a few driving schools, but then he landed the job in aerospace. What sort of life would he have had as a truck driver? Could he choose that path now? Maybe, he thought, he had been trying to meet his father's expectations all along, working for the aerospace company. He was always expected to do well, fit the mold. But he didn't fit. His vacations were always into the wilderness. Often alone. Sometimes with Savgren. His climbing friend's numbers provided some solace. Numbers represented pure thought and logic. He could almost hear his friend's words, "If it doesn't work out . . ."

The rain let up and a fiercely red sunset cut the black clouds from the horizon as the truck squeaked to a stop next to a diesel fuel pump. The driver walked away stiffly, rubbing his lower back. David waved goodbye, and soon hitched a ride on another truck, this one barreling into the night at breakneck speed, the new driver white-knuckling the steering wheel, and talking about deadlines, his nonstop talk interrupted only by his downshifting and swerving around slow-moving cars. They drove south then east, nearing Chicago with its huge buildings surrounded by clogged curving highways and a glowing orange shroud reflecting city lights.

David was grateful to get out at a rest stop while the truck roared off toward the big city. He stared at junk food in a vending machine, but all he had was Canadian change. He tried to use one of the coins, but it fell clanking into the coin return. He slumped between a wall and a soda machine. A little girl stood in front of him and stared. "Mommy, why is that man so dirty?"

"He's a bum, sugar. He doesn't earn a living like your daddy." She dragged the little girl outside where the headlights flashed across the building as cars pulled onto the highway.

David's mind echoed the mother's answer. A bum? *No, that's not quite right, lady, I'm a businessman, in aerospace. Been one for several years. Good job, lots of money*. But that wasn't right either. He had no job and he no longer existed. He wasn't a bum, but the description would fit him as well as anything, at least until he gained an identity. In reality, he thought, people changed their lives all the time. Many of his colleagues were "let go" and they merely shrugged and moved on. Different jobs, homes, divorce, countries. Why not do it all at once? Why not jump entirely into a different life? He curled against the warm, humming soda machine.

Sirens out on the highway woke him, and red numbers from a digital wall clock flashed four in the morning. He stood and stretched, his stiff body reluctant to move. Outside, the air felt cold, but the sun would be up soon.

While trying to hitchhike on the exit ramp, David braced himself against the rush of wind as cars and trucks accelerated past him, the smell of exhaust lingering. Down on the highway, city-bound traffic roared by, people rushing to work. He probably wouldn't have stopped either. He waited hours, standing, sitting, lying in the tall grass along the ramp and watching the clouds while his thoughts drifted. What was it about Susan that caused so much friction? Was it because he did whatever he wanted while she reflected on the past? His earlier moment of clarity faded. Sure, he worked hard and she settled for a job as a secretary, but why?

As the sun beat down, the stink of hot tar choking, he began waving his arms wildly at motorists as they sped past him. A highway patrol car roared past, then pulled into the grassy medium and made a U-turn. David ran up the hill, across the exit ramp, and hid in the tall grass while the patrol car slowed, pulled onto the shoulder, then sped away. Probably, he thought, some law against highway vagrancy. But, if so, he decided to play the part and ignore it. He started hitchhiking again.

Around one in the afternoon, an old pickup truck full of hay chugged past, the hay flying out, then pulled onto the shoulder. David ran to the driver's side where an old farmer offered him a ride if he didn't mind sitting in the back. "That's okay," David said, and climbed in, coughing as straw stuck to his skin. Anything to get off that ramp. After a few hours of rattling and bouncing, eating straw and dust, eyes watery, David leapt out of the pickup as the farmer stopped on a side road bordered by six-foot high cornfields.

David immediately climbed down the embankment to the highway, but again had no luck, the sun settling red into the flat horizon. He gave up and retreated to the cornfields. While lying on his back, staring past the large, tasseled ears of corn, he watched stars fill the night sky. Another day, he thought, tomorrow maybe, and he would be home, or what once was home, his alternate self emerging haphazardly from the aerospace businessman.

# Chapter Five

Susan frowned at the prospect of meeting with the lawyer and the insurance agent. But logically, her mother was right - she had to deal with the business details, no matter how bad it made her feel.

As they pulled into a gravel parking lot, Susan thought the location for the meeting curious - a tavern on a secondary road, surrounded by forest, the air smelling like cooked meat, with puffs of smoke swirling into the blue sky. Why not just meet in the city? Winnipeg had plenty of clean libraries, lobbies, office space.

Inside, the tavern was cluttered with empty beer bottles and animal heads - moose, deer, buffalo protruding from the walls, fake eyes. A few locals dressed in jeans and mackinaws nodded at them as they seated themselves at a round wood table with hearts and obscenities carved into it.

Her mother sipped tea and glanced repeatedly at the entrance while reassuring Susan that the lawyer would arrive soon. When he did finally show up, Susan shook his hand, his grip firm, eye contact steady, a distinguished-looking man with nearly all white hair and silver wire-rim glasses. In his business suit, he stood out in contrast to the irregularly dressed locals, and he immediately went to work, explaining the legalities of the claim. Susan only half-listened, deferring to her mother who knew how to handle the situation.

When Mike Jurgan arrived and shook hands with the lawyer, Susan looked away and stared eye-to-eye with the buffalo head. She wondered what the eyes were made of, then tried to identify the beer bottles lining the walls. Anything, she thought, but listen to what was happening around her. She didn't want to think about the accident, all so fresh in her mind, her nerves on edge, feeling like the slightest reference to her husband - dead - mutilated by rocks - drowned - would reduce her to tears.

"Hope you're feeling better, Mrs Brooks," Jurgan said.

"Yes," she responded. "Thank you."

Jurgan clicked open his briefcase. "First," he said, "I want to say I'm sorry for what happened before, at the hospital." He pulled out a stack of papers and a legal notepad. "I didn't want to make you uncomfortable."

Susan looked at the buffalo head, and thought, maybe the eyes were glass.

Jurgan smiled. "I'm just doing my job, that's all."

"Some job," she responded.

Jurgan shuffled through his papers. "Are we ready to start?" he asked, waited, then read, "Efforts to recover the body of Mr David Brooks proved unsuccessful. A complete search found only inanimate objects."

Susan stared at the menu - burgers, buffalo stew, beer. She shut it and laid it on the table. She shifted in her chair and counted the number of animal heads. Inanimate objects. One, she counted. Search for the body. Two. She didn't want to cry. Maybe the eyes were plastic, she thought.

The lawyer adjusted his glasses and referred to his own stack of papers. "Given a search of the area, it seems reasonable to assume that Mr Brooks drowned—"

"Yes, that's right," Jurgan interrupted, "but there is no indication that a body will be recovered." He set his papers down and looked across the table. "Without a body, his death *must* remain assumptive."

The white-haired lawyer took off his glasses. "There is more than enough evidence to suggest Mr Brooks is dead." Susan flinched, and looked at her mother who was paying close attention to the conversation.

"Yes," Jurgan responded, "but the law reads . . . the date of

56

death is determined by . . . the absence of the deceased." He quickly turned over a paper. "By law, death is assumed at the end of seven years." Jurgan's eyes flashed up as if he'd stumbled upon the wrong bit of truth. "There you have it."

The lawyer smiled. "Yes, it's obvious that you'll have to pay eventually."

Jurgan leaned back in his seat, looked at his watch and suggested, "What if he's alive?"

Susan took a drink of ice water, spilling it. Her stomach twisted. If she ate anything, she'd be sick. She had survived and, if David had also, they would be together. Probably fighting, she thought sarcastically. Then she tried to remember the first time she'd met her husband, unable to recall a specific moment. He sneaked into her life and they were married. She wanted to be married; she knew that much. But she never thought they would become so distant so fast.

Susan tried fixing her eyes on a mirror behind the long wooden bar and saw Kester Blucuski coming toward her, his black beard and dark eyes. He had the look of an animal, loping, lacking a connection to the rest of humanity. She tensed, gripped the table as if bracing herself for an attack.

Jurgan stood and shook Kester's hand. The lawyer introduced himself, then asked, "Are you a friend of Mr Jurgan's?"

"No," Kester said. He stared at Susan, and she thought, why are you here? Then it hit her. Jurgan must have arranged to meet at this tavern. The waitress set a beer in front of Kester.

"So, Mr Blucuski," Jurgan said, "maybe you could tell everybody exactly what happened when you saved Mrs Brooks here."

"Maybe."

Susan tried to remember what happened - her arms wrapped around Blucuski's neck and rubbing against his beard while he carried her to safety. Now, out of the hospital, Susan viewed him with a slightly clearer head, and she noticed that his social interactions were awkward, staccato attempts to communicate that always seemed misdirected. She always felt he wanted sex, the way he looked at her, the inflection in his voice. But, she thought, he seemed like he wouldn't know the difference between lovemaking and rape.

Jurgan looked at Kester, then asked, "What about those sounds you heard?"

"No big deal." Kester took a drink, the beer suds dripping from his beard. "I thought there was something in the woods."

"Was it some *thing* or some *body*?"

Kester shrugged. "Maybe just an animal."

Jurgan frowned. "A man *is* an animal, isn't that correct?"

Susan heard laughter from a nearby table. She remembered a deer with smoke rising from its back leaping out of the woods, the fire closing in. Now she looked at the head on the wall, a buck with huge antlers. Her hands were sweaty, cold. Fire's gone, she told herself, but felt panicked anyway.

Kester's eyes glazed over and he grunted. "Yeah, pal, that's right, a man is an animal, you got that right."

"Oh, come off it," Susan yelled. The discussion seemed senseless. What difference did it make what Kester thought he heard?

"That's not what he said before," Jurgan protested. "It could have been a person."

Susan remembered the dark woods full of dangerous animals. "If you think David's alive, then where is he?"

Jurgan shifted in his seat, frowning. "There's no body . . . I thought *you* might tell us where he is."

The lawyer laughed. "What you're implying is ridiculous. You're accusing Mrs Brooks of being a thief. That's libel. Make it easy on everybody and pay up."

"Maybe we should take it to court." Jurgan sat back, his eyes shifting from one person to the next.

Susan's stomach cramped. Her leg stiffened and she felt like running, the tavern suddenly too hot, all the dead animals staring at her. She didn't want to stand in front of a judge and bloodsucking lawyers. And what if they were right? What if

David was alive? If he was, then why wasn't he with her now? Maybe he was still looking for her, or maybe he was lost in the woods. But David never got lost, she thought, he always knew where he was going. No, the only rational explanation ended with his death, and each time she had to face that conclusion, it made her heart sink and long suppressed feelings about her father's death suddenly reappeared and overwhelmed her.

Susan glared at Jurgan. "What do you want? Money? Or do you just like seeing people suffer?" He pursed his lips ready to object, but she stopped him, saying, "There won't be any trial. If it takes the law seven years to figure it out, that's fine. By then, maybe I'll be able to handle all this." Maybe, she thought, her mother had been right all along, maybe her fear of losing men she loved had somehow caused the canoe to capsize - all her fault. But that explanation seemed inadequate, if not ridiculous. It was an accident. Nothing more.

"But, Susan," Mrs Moore protested, "it's your money. You shouldn't have to wait one day."

"I don't need a bunch of legal hassles right now, Mom."

Kester laughed, leaned across the table and grabbed Susan's arm. "Maybe your husband didn't want you, but I do."

Susan felt his warm breath, the smell of beer, and his smooth voice as he leaned close. "Let go," she said, as her gut twisted, jaw clenched tight.

Kester slowly released his grip. He stood, downed his beer, and pushed over a chair as he left.

When the waitress arrived to take their order, Susan waved her away, then stood, refusing to listen to the developing squabble between Jurgan and the lawyer. She limped through the tavern and went outside where the cool evening had settled in around streetlights. She imagined her husband emerging from the dark forest, grinning, and saying something like, "Susan, where have you been? I've been looking all over for you," as if they'd been separated in a shopping mall. She could almost hear his voice. Then, suddenly, she did hear something rustling in the underbrush, and her heart leapt in anticipation.

Kester appeared from the woods, zipping up his pants, laughing. "When you have to go. ." he called, holding out his hands and shrugging, then opening the door to a rusted-out truck. "Maybe I'll see you back in St Louis," he said and, climbing into his truck, yelled, "I don't give up easy."

# Chapter Six

David reached the outskirts of St Louis at nightfall, feeling hungry, tired, more like a tramp with each passing moment. From the highway, he walked south along the main avenue, past people milling around the YMCA, the grocery store with cars pulling in and out of its small parking lot, and the starkly clean, well-lit old folks' home. He stared vacantly through the clear glass window, old people sitting on properly arranged sofas and sipping coffee, eating cookies. At least they didn't go hungry, David thought. He remembered how his wife waved at the old folks and how they always returned the gesture and smiled. He had never bothered with them and now in a way he envied them, their food, warmth, and apparent contentment.

The familiar sour-sweet smell of burning hops wafted up from the brewery, and the thick, late-August air feeling good compared to the cold, northern rain. Maybe, he thought, he could just obliterate the past few days, reconnect with the daily routine. For a second, he felt like he could just as well be returning from the grocery store with a carton of milk.

David turned up his street, the amber lamps obscured by trees. As he walked past the old houses, some re-bricked, others crumbling, someone turned on a porch light. He stopped. Neighbors might recognize him. What then? He would have to answer awkward questions about his vacation and his wife. When did they get back? Thought you would be gone longer? Everything okay? He hurried to his house. Shadows of the big oak tree played across the white stone. If she were home, he thought, would he confront her? Demand an explanation for their marriage? He'd given his word - until death do us part. But the wilderness had provided death. Accept it, he thought, complete the leap into a new reality, gain an alternate future. Make it a clean jump. No job. No wife. No failed marriage. What lay ahead depended on the calculated steps he took now. Get what he needed from the house, money, buy some food. Go to Wyoming, where he had felt content before. Whatever it took to get there. Wyoming and peace of mind.

He scanned the neighbors' houses, making sure no one was looking out their windows. Nearing the front steps, he could see the flower box and, hopefully, the buried key. Suddenly, he was overwhelmed with images of his wife opening the door, stepping onto their porch, waving to him. He looked up and down the street. Neither of their cars was parked on the street where they normally would be. Had Susan recovered from the accident and come home? When they went on vacation, they always parked the cars at her mother's.

David slipped into the shadowy, narrow walkway between houses, along the privacy fence. He reached through the gap between the fence and its door, easily lifting the latch. In the small enclosed yard, he crouched below the kitchen window and peered in. As he had hoped, the one small light over the sink was on, just as they'd left it. The kitchen looked the same, even a water bottle he'd forgotten on the counter. He went to the bedroom window where another light was on, clothes scattered all over the bed. Was she there? Then his insides knotted as he remembered the church down the street and the parking problem. If services were being held when she arrived, she could've parked on the next block. He waited for what seemed a long time, waiting for Susan to walk naked from the bathroom, her small breasts, nipples erect, her wet hair dangling . . . but she did not come into the bedroom. He did not become a voyeur, peeping at his own wife. Maybe she had been there and left, or someone had come to get her some clothes, and she was still in Canada. In a hospital? The thought of Susan, still hurt, without him, made him feel guilty, again a failure, but he repressed it. Different life, he thought.

He waited, but saw no movement inside. He ran back around to the front, up the steps onto the porch. The large oak swayed in gusts of wind, and the lights shifted between black shadow and streetlight. He fished through the flower box, pulling up a handful of the rich dirt and letting it slide back into the box. Come on, come on, he whispered to himself. Hands shaking, careful not to spill the dirt, he lifted another handful, sifted through it and found the key. He shoved it into the lock. From the shadows, something jumped out at him, and his heart pounded. Susan's cat purred and rubbed against his leg. He remembered evenings when he slept on the couch while the cat curled next to his wife.

As he turned the key, the lock clicked. He stood still a moment, then pushed the door open. The cat scampered inside. David carefully buried the key back in the flower box. He eased through the entryway, locking the door behind him. He crept across the squeaking hardwood floors, checking each room thoroughly.

In the bedroom, he stood over his wife's clothes: underwear on the floor, a skirt bunched up on the bed, nylons draped over the back of a chair. The mess was uncharacteristic; she always kept clothes neatly folded in drawers. He opened his dresser and pulled out clean underwear, a shirt, and socks, pushing them into a canvas duffel bag. Something rattled around in his bottom dresser drawer - an empty prescription bottle, Volmax, the label indicating one refill. He hadn't needed the allergy medication in years, and then only once or twice, but he stuffed it into his pocket anyway. Shuffling through his closet, he lifted out a jacket, trying to take only clothes that might be useful in the outdoors, cautiously avoiding anything that she might notice.

In his study, he turned on the light and found it exactly as he'd left it. He turned on the computer and examined an entry of the last check he'd written - number 934 for groceries,

63

dated 8/11, a few days before they had departed. Now, just after the last entry, he typed: "8/12/935/trip expense/4000." Then he made the check out to himself for the 4000 dollars, also dating it 8/12. He pressed the enter key and heard a loud cha-ching, and quickly turned off the speakers. The check appeared perfectly along with all the other 8/12 transactions, leaving a workable balance of $439.35. David sat back, stared at the screen, and considered his plan. Would Susan question the 4000 dollars? She knew very little about the costs of trips and asked few questions. He frowned when he thought about the bank posting the correct date on their monthly statement, maybe even stamping it on the back of the canceled check. What were the chances she would even look at it? While she was clearly an intelligent woman, she hated keeping financial records. She was happy to let him track their money.

Next, he opened his file drawer and pulled out the folder containing mortgage papers. He flipped through copies of the note on their house, the closing statement, inspections, then crammed the file back in place; he dug through a miscellaneous file and finally came to a small brown envelope. In it, he found what he was looking for: the deed to his Wyoming property. He stuffed the check and the brown envelope into his coat pocket, then reached far back in his desk drawer and pulled out a fifty-dollar bill. He sat back and took a deep breath, then got up and went to the bathroom. While there, he thought about taking a shower, letting the warm water soak his head, steal time from his past life. But he heard a car door slam shut, and his heart fell. He ran to the front room and looked out the window. Nothing. On city streets, car doors slammed all the time

The cat followed him, meowing incessantly, until he picked it up by the nape and set it back outside. Then he retraced his steps, painstakingly checking each place he'd been, turning off lights, making sure the house appeared undisturbed. Scanning the kitchen, he thought, why not take everything? Become a burglar. For a moment the idea was intriguing, but of course impractical. No way he wanted to be running from the police with arms full of stolen goods. Never mind that he had stolen them from himself.

In the dining room, a small lamp lit photos on the wall: David and Susan together on a trail in Colorado, the inn at Mount Rainier, photos of their wedding day - her dress and his suit and tie. Another photo of Susan alone in a mountain pasture with a blue wildflower stuck in the buttonhole of her wool shirt. He stared blankly at that, turned off the lamp, then heard the click of the front door lock. He looked down the hall, toward the back door, the kitchen and the enclosed porch, searching for an escape. Impossible to get out without being seen.

## Chapter Seven

Susan's mother was unusually quiet on the flight from Winnipeg to St Louis, adjusting her seat, reading, trying on headphones. Susan finally asked, "You think I should've forced a trial?"

"I don't know . . . makes no difference to me."

"Since when? You *always* have an opinion." Susan had in fact counted on her mother's advice. Especially now, when she felt so lost, so unsure about her future.

"That's not what I meant, dear. You are very important to me, but you knew what you wanted without me telling you . . . the way you dealt with Mr Blucuski . . . and Jurgan."

But, Susan thought, it was often easier to let someone else make the decisions. And she wouldn't mind it so much now. She stared out the plane's window at the tops of gray clouds while her mother sipped wine and talked all about her next vacation.

"You shouldn't be alone in your house," her mother said. "Too many memories. I know. Took me quite a while to go home after your father died."

Susan remembered their little "vacation" at her cousin's, when she was a young girl, not fully comprehending that her father wouldn't be coming back. When they did finally go home, she searched room after room. She waited up late at night listening to car doors and tires on pavement, expecting that Dad would walk through the door at any moment, pick her up in her arms, and tell her again that he would always come back to her, that he would love her forever.

"Maybe," her mother said, "I should cancel my trip."

But Susan knew that Mom had paid for the trip far in advance, and would lose money if the plans changed. "No, I'll be okay."

Landing in St Louis late at night, Susan stepped out of the airport terminal, the hot, humid air suffocating. While squinting against the swirl of lights and waiting for lost luggage, she fought to keep from crying, her leg aching, finally settling into a taxi that reeked of stale cigarettes. She spent the night with her mother, waking often to the sound of jets roaring overhead.

In the morning, Susan drove to her house, following a familiar pattern - the exit ramp, the street parking, the oak, as if nothing had happened. The house looked the same. Brick two-story, white stone front. Had she expected anything different? Inside, she found the mail where the neighbor had piled it on the dining room table, mostly junk and bills. Susan stuffed it all into a grocery bag and carried the bag out to the car, then returned for clothes.

While standing on the front porch, ready to leave, she called for the cat, remembering how it liked to curl into the neighbor's arms, strong for a man in his fifties. But Karl wasn't home either. She called and whistled, then searched the yard, the alley, then back inside. She worried about her cat, but knew that he often went away for a day or two, always to return, hungry and looking scruffy. She wrote a thank you note with a phone number and slipped it through Karl's mail slot. She considered staying, but knew she couldn't escape the memories, so she drove away, following Mom's advice.

Several houses on her mother's street had windows boarded up and orange numbers spray painted across driveways. Inside, she found her mother scurrying around the bedroom packing last-minute items. "Why don't you come along?" Mom said. "You could use a vacation."

"I just took one." Susan picked up a photograph from the nightstand, an old wood frame, and a picture of her father.

Suddenly, she felt woozy, spinning, the memories embracing her, pulling her under, swirling, like the cold current in Canada. She tried to focus on what her mother was saying.

"I know . . . but why not a *fun* one? From Switzerland, you can go almost anywhere. Like Spain."

Susan looked at her mother. "You're not planning on running with the bulls or something, are you?"

"Of course not . . . but sounds interesting."

Susan held the picture, her father slim, smiling, handsome to Susan. He wore a khaki shirt and had both hands in his pockets, and he bore a vague resemblance to David, except that Dad wore wire-rim glasses and always had a five o'clock shadow. As a little girl, she remembered scraping her hand along her father's face and giggling. She remembered how he would explain things to her, the significance of past events. She set the photo down. Tears dropped from her cheeks. Her whole body hurt. "I feel so alone," she muttered, light-headed again, overwhelmed by a feeling of loss that seemed to pull her deeper than the river in the wilderness.

"Did you say something?" Mrs Moore pushed a suitcase closed and turned to face her daughter.

Susan wiped her cheeks. "No," she said, "I'm fine."

She picked up the suitcase and carried it into the kitchen. On the table, Susan noticed a newspaper, the county journal, a free paper that Mom usually picked off the driveway and immediately tossed into the recycle bin. It was spread open on the table. Then she saw the article, "Local Woman Battles Canadian Wilderness". Two photographs were arranged side-by-side, David's blurry work photo, and Susan, an old college picture, her smile suggesting she'd been drunk. "Forced from camp by a forest fire, Susan Brooks, of South St Louis, battled the elements and won. After an extensive search, David Brooks's body was not recovered from the river." The article described their ordeal with the fire and white water, Susan's struggle through the woods, her courage in making it to Kester's cabin. The story read like a TV "re-enactment", not what really happened.

"How do you like it?" Mom said. "I called a friend. He said it was a good local interest story."

"Suppose I didn't want my picture in the paper?" The article seemed to over-inflate her importance and she felt a little embarrassed by it.

"Come on. It won't hurt anything. You're heroic. Maybe you'll get a better job."

Susan recognized the tone, the implication that she wasn't living up to her potential. She remembered having similar discussions with her husband. "There's nothing wrong with being a secretary."

"Of course not."

At least, Susan thought, her mother wouldn't keep at it the way David had, turning it into a big issue, something that had to be settled.

Susan offered to drive her mother to the airport, but arrangements had already been made. Mrs Moore and her traveling companion were going to arrive at the airport two hours early, plenty of time before the flight, and have lunch together.

Her mother peered out the window and spoke quickly. "David's parents called from Pittsburgh. They're proud people. Talked about how David liked to take chances..." A plane flew so low Susan could almost see passengers in the windows, and the crushing roar of the jet engines obliterated all other sound. She had not spent much time with David's parents and wanted to know more about them. With the jet noise still ringing in her ears, Susan tried hard to listen to her mother saying, "They want to arrange a . . . service."

Susan blinked. "A funeral?"

"Sure, that would be appropriate, but don't worry. Since there's no rush, I've convinced them to wait a couple weeks."

No rush, Susan thought morbidly, because there was nothing to bury.

"I liked him, honey; I don't know if I ever told you that, but

I thought he might be good for you. I really wanted it to work out."

"You make it sound like we got a divorce. He drowned. I couldn't help that." She felt defensive about her marriage. But why? Arguments were a part of living together, weren't they?

"I know. It's not your fault, Sue."

"Then why do I feel like it is?"

"It's just part of grieving. You'll get over it."

After hugging her mother, forcing a smile, and watching her drive away with her friend, Susan returned to the empty house, voices from her childhood echoing in her ears. With the encroaching evening, the jet noise got louder and more frequent, and the house creaked in the dark, a mere shell of a previous life. She looked at the newspaper article and remembered crawling through the muck, those first painful steps and each succeeding step through the wilderness.

Just part of grieving? Maybe, she thought. But she felt that more than simple grief was involved. Their marriage had deteriorated to the point where they could only talk about superficial things, and even then their words were strained. She wanted to know why, and didn't feel like she could learn anything by avoiding the home she'd shared with her husband. Under the roar of the low-flying jets, she chose one lost past over another, and left her childhood home.

With the brewery smell hanging heavy in the night air, Susan drove by the taxis at the edge of the park, then turned up her street. She parked the car crookedly in a small space, one block from her house. The cat leapt out onto the sidewalk, startling her, then rubbed against her legs and mewed. She picked him up and hugged him, but the cat yowled, and leapt from her hands. The cat scratched at the front door. Susan shook her house key loose and shoved it into the lock.

She stepped inside, the cat leaping onto the couch, back arched. Susan turned on the overhead light, then heard a thumping sound like someone was on the basement stairs. She hesitated, heart racing, then turned and ran back onto the porch and into Karl's big hands. She almost screamed but caught herself. "There's someone here," she gasped.

# Chapter Eight

David ran down the stairs into the basement, unlatched the door and pushed it open, then stopped. While staring at the crumbling concrete steps rising to the backyard, he thought he couldn't just leave and reveal that he *knew* about the key, evidence that he was still alive. The house should look burglarized. So he pulled shelves away from the window, knocking paint cans clattering across the floor; he yanked on the thick wire mesh popping free from the window frame. Outside, he kicked the window into shattering pieces and ran out the back gate into the alley. Someone shouted for him to stop and a car screeched to avoid hitting him. He cut through a yard and out the other side, then walked casually. The shout echoed in his mind, the familiarity of the voice suddenly hitting him - the neighbor. Must've thought Susan was home or he'd come to feed the cat. Maybe, David thought, if he had just hidden, waited a few minutes, Karl would have left, and he could've sneaked out without being seen.

But after walking awhile, he remembered the disagreement he'd had with Susan. By returning the key to the box, in a way he'd gotten the last word. Susan would have to admit that no burglar would bother digging around in a flower box, that they would, as he had suggested, just break a window.

A police car sped along the avenue, siren blaring, and turned up their street. David ran into the park where old trees loomed high and blocked light from stars and the surrounding streets. He slowed to a walk, eyes adjusting to the darkness, and suddenly an old man with rags dangling from his arms lurched out of a ditch and begged him for money. "Spare change?" the beggar asked. "For food?"

But all David had was the fifty-dollar bill he had just stolen from his own house. "No," he said. "Sorry."

Then a police car rolled into the park, spotlight flashing into the trees. David ran again, this time hiding in one of the park's nineteenth-century gazebos, the spotlight flashing over him. He waited, and considered sleeping in the gazebo, but thought the police might return, or more beggars.

David ran out of the park and hailed a taxi. Before the trip to Canada, he often jogged by the parked taxis, the drivers either sleeping or drinking coffee, seldom going anywhere. Now, he climbed into a cab where food containers and newspapers littered the floor. The driver started the meter and asked him where he wanted to go. Wyoming, David thought, but first he needed to cash his check, and he needed to eat something. He gave the driver the name of a small diner not far from the bank.

David closed his eyes but couldn't rest. He picked up a crumpled newspaper, one of the county journals. He folded it open, the yellow cab light forcing him to squint, but his own face clearly stared at him from the page, Susan next to him. He read the article. Everybody believed he was dead. But the article focused almost entirely on Susan and her bravery, no credit to him, no hint that he had died trying to save her. At least, he thought sarcastically, they hadn't criticized him for failing to get them through the rapids.

David paid the driver and climbed out, carrying the newspaper, stuffing it into a trash can before opening the door to the diner. He found a seat at the counter, near the wall. He ordered, then watched the crowd, no newspapers. Not that they would identify him from the picture. He was worn and dirty. Besides, who would try to recognize a dead person? Even so, it made him feel uncomfortable. He devoured his burger, then wiped up ketchup with the lettuce garnish and ate it, cleaning the plate. He drank coffee, but felt his nerves wind tight with each refill. The diner was no longer crowded, but as he glanced down to the other end of the counter, he saw a man reading a newspaper. That made him nervous. David left a meager tip and, while walking past the man, noticed the Post-Dispatch, not the free paper with his picture. He walked stiffly out into the night. He had time to kill before the bank opened in the morning. He walked down the street to catch the eleven o'clock movie. He'd seen it already with Susan about two months ago. It was just the sort of romantic comedy that she liked. He could sleep through it.

But the theater's air-conditioner blasted cold. The seat was hard, the volume was turned up too loud, and he still felt uptight from the coffee. When the movie ended around one, he hurried away from the crowd, his eyes darting from one face to another in the marquis lights.

A 60-degree "cold front" had moved in, what the local weather forecasters always referred to as a "blast of cold Canadian air". To David, it usually brought relief from late August heat and humidity. But now, having just come from the cold theater, the air made him shiver, and he felt empty and anxious for sunrise. He walked past the bank, hands in his pockets, feeling the crumpled bills and change, what was left of his fifty. Not nearly enough for a motel room, even if there was one nearby. He kept walking, the movement providing warmth again. He stopped at a small city park, and lay down on a bench concealed by trees. He rolled over, tossing and turning, dozing off, finally waking as a gray patch of light appeared.

Feeling beaten, cold, he walked back toward the bank, thinking about Wyoming. He would be all right, he thought. Just had to get away from St Louis, obliterate his life there, and move on, where he could start anew. He could find peace and contentment at the base of the mountains in Wyoming. He was sure of that.

At a convenience store, he bought a necktie and new bandages, plastic razor, and soap, then went to a fast food restaurant across the street from the bank. After locking the door to the bathroom, he splashed water on his face, trying to revive himself. He stared in the mirror, the black bruises under his eyes gradually fading to brown and yellow streaks. When he pulled the bandage from the bridge of his nose, he saw a thin gash running diagonally between his eyes, healing around the edges. After washing and shaving, he checked his hand. The tape around his fingers was dirty and ragged. He unwound the tape, exposing his crooked fingers, white and stiff. Using clean tape, he wrapped them again. He washed his hair in the sink, rinsed it, and was combing it when he saw the doorknob twist, and someone pushed against the door, calling.

"Anybody in there?"

"Just a minute," he responded.

David pressed Band-Aids onto his nose, pulled out the necktie and pushed everything else back into the gym bag. The tie, he thought, was an instant source of credibility. If he were going to cash a $4000 check, he wanted to look credible. But tying it around his neck with his damaged fingers was difficult; the voice behind the door boomed.

"Are you all right?"

David fumbled, eventually tying an acceptable knot, pushing it tightly to his throat, then he opened the door. A teenager nodded at him, their eyes met and, for a horrifying moment, David sensed that he'd been recognized. He exited quickly and rushed outside, his mind racing, trying to place the face. Where had he seen it? Probably someone's son, or perhaps the brother of a friend, or the friend of a friend. Damn, he thought, could be anyone. Or no one. His lack of sleep, he concluded, made *everybody* look familiar. For a moment he considered leaving town without the money.

David walked across the street, a car slowing to let him pass. Inside, he sought out a teller who looked young and inexperienced, reasoning that he could deceive her. Probably a mistake, he thought, as he slid the check to her. He smiled, but felt too damn uptight and exhausted to say good morning. She would probably ask someone about the check, and they would take the opportunity to teach her all about clearing it. He'd have to wait for an eternity, then surely someone would recognize him, or that he'd put the wrong date on it. Then what? If he hadn't lost his ATM card in Canada, he could've avoided humans. But ATM machines, he thought, had a withdrawal limit. He needed lots of money, and this was the only way to get it. He glanced up at the monitoring camera pointed at him, recording him alive, a thought that made him cringe and feel like running. But that would only alert them. No reason to panic, he thought, no reason for them to replay the video, especially if everything looked normal.

The teller studied the endorsement, stared at the amount, then looked for someone to ask how she should process the check.

"I'm buying a car," David explained, trying to smile again. "Used car. Owner wants cash."

The teller entered his account number into the computer, then waited while it beeped erratically before showing the balance on the screen, enough money in account. But she looked around again, and David's mind raced for something to say. A woman appeared from behind a partition, and the teller waved at her, but the woman rushed through a door, and shut it.

A line had formed behind David. The teller looked at him and shrugged but still did not start processing the check. He smiled and shrugged also while she tapped the check up and down. She looked one more time for help, then put the check into the computer to print out the transaction on the back, but she pressed the wrong sequence of buttons. David leaned over the counter to look at the computer with its irritating message WRONG ACCESS.

"What's the problem?" David asked, trying to sound calm, but feeling wound tight.

"Oh, this computer . ."

"They can be difficult." He felt sweat dripping down the

inside of his shirtsleeve. Come on, he thought, give me the money.

She looked around. The woman had yet to return.

The line behind David grew longer. "I don't mean to be pushy," he said, "but the guy might sell his car to someone else."

She stared at him. "It's frozen up."

"Can't you use a stamp?" he asked tersely, then tried to make light of it. "After all, we didn't always have computers."

The teller again looked over her shoulder, then opened a drawer and shuffled around in it, finding a rubber stamp, pushing it hard onto the back of the check. Then she scribbled down the date and account number, pulled out a stack of 100-dollar bills, looked at him and asked, "Are hundreds okay?"

"I'd prefer smaller bills," he said.

"I'll have to go get change."

"No," David said, stopping her, "that's okay. Hundreds are fine."

She counted, laying one bill at a time on the counter. David grabbed the money. "Thanks," he said, and hurried out, trying not to run. He started walking toward the highway where, as a teenager, he and his high school friends used to hitchhike to the State Park. Too many memories, he thought.

At the highway, he felt like a fool. What if someone he knew stopped, stuck their head out the window and yelled, "Hey, Dave, you in a wreck or something?" He couldn't let that happen. He needed to get far out of town quickly. He walked to the Laundromat on the corner and called a taxi.

Settling into the backseat, David relaxed. Except that the driver, with wide-set eyes and black receding hair, looked like someone that used to be in his evening college class. David sat forward and talked about the weather, the baseball team, the brewery, until he was sure that the taxi driver was no one he knew.

The taxi passed streets that led to friends' houses, any one of which would have, if he were still alive, gladly let him spend the night. But he told the driver to head west, at least fifty miles before bothering him. David leaned his head back against the ripped vinyl seat cushions, and slumped into a deep sleep.

## Chapter Nine

Susan watched the neighbor run inside, and down the basement stairs, while she stood in the front room. She expected more of a mess - furniture knocked over, dirt on the floor, at least a picture hanging crooked or broken. But everything was in order. She heard the screech of tires, ran to the back porch and looked out the window, a car stopped with headlights shining down the alley. From her angle, Susan could see between houses, a narrow view of the main avenue, a shadow, somebody disappearing around the corner.

Karl came back up the basement stairs. "Old woman almost ran over some guy," he said. "Shook her up… thought she hit him." Susan remembered the key and ran out to the front porch, shoving her hands into the flower box, digging. Then she felt it on the bottom of the box. She pulled it out of the dirt just as two police cars rounded the corner, lights flashing, siren blaring, cops getting out. One held a gun and headed toward the back yard, the other commanded them to get on the sidewalk, and ran to the front door. Only a few minutes passed before both officers came back out the front, the younger one saying that it was okay, then driving with his spotlight flashing into the park.

Susan rolled the key in her palm, potting soil crumbling away. She watched Karl explain to the remaining officer that he'd seen lights go on and off, shadows, then a little while later Susan pulled up and went inside. That's when Karl called the police.

The officer walked to his car, the lights still flashing, and he came back with a clipboard. A breeze rustled the leaves of the oak. Karl asked Susan if she wanted him to stay. "Sure," she said, thankful for the help.

Susan led the officer from room to room. Everything looked the way she'd left it, except the basement where the shelves had been pushed over, power tools lying on the floor covered with red paint already starting to thicken. The window's wire mesh lay in the corner, splattered red. Broken glass jutted from the paint like knives.

The officer stood by the mesh. "They must've come in here and then just unlocked the door, there." Susan looked at the mess, then at the officer. "These sort of burglaries," he explained. "Usually teenagers . . . gangs."

"What about fingerprints?"

"We can do that if you want. Maybe find your prints. Or maybe your husband's."

Susan looked down at the policeman's polished shoes. "You don't think you'll be able to catch them?"

"To be frank, Mrs Brooks, no. Consider yourself lucky that you weren't hurt." The police officer held his clipboard ready. "If you'll just come up with a guess," he said, "make it whatever you want."

"A guess?"

"The estimated loss. Whatever your insurance will pay."

Susan watched Karl picking up the power saw, trying to wipe it off with a rag, the red paint smearing on the blade and into the trigger. "The window," she said, "a new power saw, and a drill. They're ruined. And paint." But, she thought, what difference did paint make? Could she change the color of her life? Karl set the saw down and shut the basement door, then found a board, and a hammer, and started pounding in nails, covering the broken window.

On the sidewalk, the officer handed Susan the report number, then drove away, turning off the flashing red lights.

Karl came out the front door and stood next to her. "I don't know," he said. "I been in the city all my life and been robbed too, and this one just doesn't seem like it was teenagers."

"Why not?"

"Usually they go right for the good stuff . . . "

"They didn't have time?"

"Maybe," he said, and wiped paint from his hands.

Susan thanked him for everything. As he left, she heard him mumbling, "Maybe . . ." She looked at the church on the corner, the busy avenue, and the park. If not a gang of teenagers, she thought, then who? Was there any chance at all that it could have been David? But she recalled feeling the same way when her father went away, always looking for evidence that Dad still lived. Often finding it. Proof in the most common things, missing toolbox, found later, clothes disappearing, thrown out by her mother. Unlikely, Susan thought, that her husband would break into his own house. She held the front door key in her palm, remembering their argument about it. The key to their failing marriage, she thought, then shoved it into her pocket, went inside, and locked the door behind her.

# Chapter Ten

David's lips were chapped and his teeth covered with dust as the hot wind swept across the Red Desert. He hiked along the cracked concrete shoulder of Interstate 80, staring ahead at the horizon, low desert mountains, the road shimmering, and his mind drifted longingly back to Gannettt Peak - Savgren roped up behind him, matching his push to the summit step for step, black clouds rolling over the Divide, lightning flashing overhead. In the rarified air, he had felt alive, nothing but pure adrenaline, the hollering and laughing while glissading down a glacier.

An RV roared past and nearly blew him into a ditch. From the back window, a teenage girl gave him the finger. David had paid one hundred dollars cab fare, and more money for a cramped bus ride, only to be dumped at the exhaust-filled station in downtown Kansas City. He had no choice but to hitchhike. He needed to save money, and liked the open highway. He'd already come this far. Wallowing in the past would get him nowhere. Everything would be fine when he got to his Wyoming property.

As he stared across the desert at the sagebrush and cactus, he recalled buying the property. After climbing Gannett, Savgren had to fly back for a conference, leaving David to get drunk and celebrate by himself. At the Ram's Horn Bar, he met Evert Carson, and they talked well into the evening about God, oil, space, real estate. Evert just happened to have info on a "real interesting chunk of land" and David, drunk, climbed into Evert's truck. They drove up a narrow, rutted route into the hills, beer foaming onto their hands, spilling and flowing like rivers across the floorboard. Then David heard loud thumping and Evert stopped. They got out - shredded tread hanging from a flat tire. They changed it but the spare emitted a loud hissing sound. Evert quickly squirted it full of fix-a-flat, oozing out of the tire and foaming like the beer. That's when Evert grinned and said, "You don't wanna turn around, do you?" And David looked out at the vast land, the sky full of stars, and agreed to buy the property "sight unseen". Then he nodded off to sleep while they bounced back down the road. But when he woke they were on pavement in the wrong lane headed for an oncoming car. David grabbed the wheel and pulled, Evert waking up and yelling, "Oh shit!" They swerved onto the shoulder, tires and rock flying, the bad tire stretching and flopping. Evert steered back onto the pavement, and drove slowly, eyes wide. "I owe you one," he said.

The next day, nursing a hangover, David rode with Evert back up into the hills, turning onto the unpaved road, then slamming on the brakes. "Look!" he shouted. "A freak!" David squinted, trying to figure out what a freak was, then spotted an antelope with one of its horns twisting down across the snout, the other standing upright from the animal's head. When they finally reached the property, David got out and stood, looking at the shanty tilting downhill toward the creek. "Real interesting," he told Evert. Now, alone and hitching with tumbleweeds skipping onto the highway, he smiled at his reaction. As Evert had been quick to point out, David was paying for the land. The shack was an "extra". Right now, he thought, it was home, and he stuck out his thumb.

A pickup truck pulled onto the shoulder. The man inside wore an old baseball cap with "Wyoming" across the front, and a cooler in the passenger seat. "Better get in. You look beat."

David climbed in and set the cooler between them.

"Wanna beer?" the driver asked.

The beer felt good on David's chapped lips as the driver headed north on Highway 287. David looked at a map lying on the dashboard, and tried to figure out where they were going. Looked like they had just driven into the Great Divide Basin when they pulled onto a gravel road, stopped, and the driver jumped out to pee.

David climbed out of the truck, hoping that he would feel the joy at being in the middle of nowhere with no hassles, none of the high pressure pace of the city. But he just felt stiff and tired. On the road too long, he thought, disappointed that the surrounding country had yet to lift his spirits. He stood on his side of the truck, relieving himself in the dust, and looked out at the vast expanse of low ground, the Great Divide Basin where everything evaporated. No rivers flowed from this land, he thought. Maybe the basin would evaporate his past, and when he came out of it, into his land near the Wind River mountains, maybe then he would regain his spirit. That's it, he thought desperately, still feeling the pull of his past, and grasping for a future that was so far proving to be elusive.

David looked up at the sun. A dust devil swirled over the sagebrush. Beyond that, red dirt and sparse sagebrush - sandstone outcrops, no other vehicle in sight. He called over to the driver. "Guess our piss goes nowhere, right?" No response. David felt disconnected from his surroundings and wasn't sure the driver understood, so he clarified. "It evaporates."

"What does?"

"Our urine."

The driver climbed back into truck, and asked, "Where did you say you wanted to go?"

"Some land, near Dubois."

While listening to the steady hum of the truck, David drifted in and out of sleep, and dreamt of the freak antelope with its twisted horns. He woke, stared at the paved road ahead and touched his head, running his fingers down along the tape between his eyes. Then he looked up at the sharp blue sky. No clouds. He closed his eyes and saw *fire in the Canadian forest, the river pulling Susan under.* No, he thought, that was in the past. He was leaving that behind. Some other David was the lowlife who tried to "save" his wife and failed. That was over, and now this journey west would bring him peace. But as he drifted off to sleep, the fire returned, *blazing on both sides of the river, forcing them to run the rapids at night.*

David jerked, opened his eyes. Dubois. He recognized the real estate office, the wooden sidewalks, and down the street, the Ram's Horn Bar.

"Gotta go," the driver said. "Supposed to be in Jackson tonight."

David thanked him, then walked up to the real estate office, but it was vacant, so he went to the Ram's Horn and sat with the mid-afternoon crowd, occasionally pulling out the deed to his property and looking it over. Finally, he asked the bartender where he might find Evert Carson. "Liar's Creek. Try up there."

David hitched a ride in a rickety old flatbed with rust-eaten doors. The owner in a cowboy hat, front teeth missing, spit on the floorboards while driving on the curving road full of ruts and gullies. The Wind River mountains stretched along the western horizon, gray and black, white-capped against a darkening blue sky, and the smell of sagebrush filled the cool air. A jackrabbit leapt out wildly along the road before darting back into the brush. The truck hit a deep rut and the wheels slammed against the fenders and stopped. David got out, thanked him, and watched as the truck rolled back down the road.

In the dusk, chilling breeze coming off the mountains, David breathed deeply trying to rouse past feelings, the joy and exhilaration, the simple peace of being in the high country. But now, standing on the edge of the vast wilderness, he felt nothing. He tried to remember the good times. His escapes always rejuvenated him before. No reason to believe they wouldn't do the same now. After he fully crossed over into his new life, he would be okay. That was it. But where was the passage? He'd hoped that just getting out of the Great Divide

Basin would help. What did he expect? A sunbeam from the heavens to lift his soul, make him feel alive again? Was that asking too much from his beloved mountains?

A narrow path lead him into the shadows where the shanty's stove pipe rattled in the wind, spewing white and gray smoke. Up along the ridge, a herd of mule deer ran. A golden eagle soared over a jagged rock outcropping. He saw a sudden flash, and heard the roaring blast of a shotgun, then jumped belly to the ground, dust blowing in his eyes. Sage in his face, the smell sharp, bitter. Then he saw someone standing near the shanty, facing the opposite direction, shooting at something, then a cackling, devilish laugh.

"Evert?" David yelled. "That you?"

"Sure, but who the hell are you?"

"David Brooks."

"Dave?"

"Yeah, it's me."

"Well, come on in."

David stood, dusted off, and stepped inside. Evert's eyes were red, bloodshot, his mouth full of tobacco, and he spat on the floor, then leaned close. "You don't look so good."

David drank a shot of whiskey. "You look pretty crappy yourself."

"Guess I do." Evert stroked his stubble face.

"You always drink alone?"

"Why do you care?" He drank. "Business ain't too good and my wife left. Funny, huh."

"Yeah," David said, "hilarious." But he didn't laugh, nor even in the least bit feel mirthful. In fact, talking to Evert forced him into a world that did not meet his lofty expectations. A world of domestic troubles and hassles like the one he'd left.

"Wife and I got into it last week. Not too sure what happened. All I know is, we got into a fight about somethin' and I got so mad at her I almost smacked her."

David looked into his whiskey, caramel-colored liquid

glinting in the dim light. "You don't mind, I'd prefer my wife didn't know I was here."

"You havin' the same sorta trouble?"

David unzipped his jacket and dust floated around him. "Actually, there's more to it." He felt himself settling into his seat like the dust.

"Always is."

"But there really is in this case." He looked at Evert. He felt disconnected again, as if the alternate reality was the wrong one, and a thin, invisible barrier encapsulated him, kept him from finding the tranquility and peace that he sought. Maybe he needed to talk about what happened, or maybe he just needed to rest, then climb to higher ground. At the very least, he needed Evert's help in crossing to the new reality, gaining a new life. Evert would be the bridge, no matter how rickety. David looked at him, remembering their near-fatal accident, and thought, the cowboy owed him one anyway. "She thinks I drowned in Canada."

Evert stared. "Now that's funny."

"You're the only person who knows I'm alive."

Evert closed one eye, tilted his head and said, "I ain't Jesus." David looked at him. "If you're gonna be dead, I damn well ain't gonna make you alive again."

# Chapter Eleven

Sitting at her husband's desk, Susan opened a drawer, and the sudden overwhelming need for money engulfed her - David had numbered the files, one-receipts, two-taxes, three-banking, all jumbling together in her mind as she pushed the folders back. Pulling out the insurance file, she found the policy, with Jurgan Insurance Company in large black scroll on the cover. She skimmed through it, but it was full of incomprehensible terms like "residence premises" and "negotiable instruments". She looked for a phone number, but couldn't find one. Probably intended that way, she thought, then flipped through David's phone directory, pausing, recalling the names of his friends, people who had moved out of town since their wedding. She found the insurance company's phone number, dialed, let the phone ring three times and was ready to hang up when she heard the singsong voice of the secretary.

Susan quickly listed information about the break-in.

"Thank you," the secretary said. "We'll send someone out."

Susan hung up, leaned back and looked at the wall, a photograph of her husband standing on the edge of a bluff, smiling, the rolling Ozark hills in the background. She took the photo off the wall, and set it face down, then took a drink of coffee before opening the mail. Mostly bills, she thought, cockroaches crawling in to torment her, past-due notices threatening her with lawyers, liens, bad credit ratings. First, she threw out all the junk, the false assertions that she was a valued customer, the exhortations for her dead husband to respond. Then she made phone calls, shedding unnecessary expenses, cable TV and cell phone, her old cell likely nothing more than fragments like pebbles washing onto the riverbank. She arranged the bills, those that could wait and those that needed to be paid, carefully entering each check into the computer. She stared at the screen, trying to fight off the lethargy she felt when dealing with household finances. She hated it. Always had. Probably associated it with her uncle helping Mom and that time in her life.

Susan meticulously entered ATM withdrawals and deposits, then started to reconcile the account, comparing the bank statement to the list on the computer screen. Check number 935 was not on the statement. Trip expenses, 4000, dated August twelfth. While the amount seemed high, it was typical of David who liked having money "on hand," or "just in case". Logically, she thought, a check cashed on the twelfth should appear on this statement. More hassle. Was she supposed to call the bank, try to straighten it out? Maybe they lost the check. And she should keep her mouth shut. She could use the money. With that thought, however, she felt dishonest, and phoned the bank, discovering that the 4000-dollar check was posted on August 22nd. That explained why it did not appear on the bank statement. She hung up the phone, then stared at it, touching the receiver again. Why didn't the bank cash it until the 22nd? But what difference did it make? The money was gone. Who cared when? Obviously, they had misplaced the check. Too bad they didn't lose it altogether, she thought.

Susan stood up, walked away from the desk, and wandered around the house before standing in front of the refrigerator, staring at leftover pizza, a jug of rancid orange juice, and a Tupperware container with mold blackening the lid. She threw it all in the trash, tied off the bag and dragged it through the back gate to the alley. Someone in a gray jacket buried his head into the dumpster. Street scavengers often wheeled broken grocery carts up and down the alleys, foraging through the trash, finding food scraps, aluminum cans, occasionally a valuable item like a bent bicycle or winter coat. Susan waited for the tramp to finish. But the jacket looked expensive, and the shoes were new white running shoes. "Excuse me," she said.

Mike Jurgan's head emerged from the dumpster. He wore designer jeans, and a blue knit shirt, and he pushed bent, wire-rim glasses back into place. "You called about a break-in?" he responded. His left eye was swollen, black and blue.

"That explains your interest in garbage?" she asked.

"Burglars throw stuff in here." He picked up a binder that he'd set on the ground. "Especially if they're in a hurry."

As she heaved her garbage into the dumpster, slime splattered on his new shoes. "Too late," she said. "It's been emptied."

Jurgan wiped his shoe on weeds. "You called the office . . . Since I had been personally involved . ." He fingered his glasses.

Susan looked him over. She knew there was more to it. His appearance here had nothing to do with personal interest. She remembered him in Canada, talking about how big a 300,000 settlement was to their small, two-state company. She stared at his eye. "What happened?" she asked.

"A guy hit me." Jurgan shrugged. "I was sleeping with his girlfriend. He was an idiot."

Susan looked at him and wondered who the idiot was.

"May I look at the damage?" he asked.

She led him to the basement. Everything was as she left it - broken window, shelves knocked over, red paint now dried thick on the tools.

"The mesh is okay," Jurgan declared, "glass should be easy to replace. Did you get an estimate?"

Susan frowned. "No, I haven't. That's what you're supposed to be doing."

"Okay," Jurgan said, opening a folder and writing, then he said, "Now let's go upstairs."

She kept staring at his black, bloodshot eyes distorted behind the thick lenses.

Jurgan explained, "I lost a contact lens when I got hit. It's difficult to focus with one eye." He squinted.

"You can read the police report. You don't need to go upstairs."

He held up his binder and said, "Paperwork."

Susan didn't want him snooping in her life. She felt bad enough trying to deal with her loss. But she had a sense that he wouldn't be easy to ditch. Maybe, she thought, if she just gave him what he wanted, he'd go away.

Susan turned away and climbed the stairs, Jurgan following her. In the front room, he walked around, pausing at the window, apparently admiring the view, then went into the living room and looked at the photographs hung on the wall. "You made a nice couple," he finally said. "Mr Brooks looks like he was healthy. Was he a runner or something?"

"He stayed in shape," she said, and tried to remember what they had in common. What went wrong?

"His eyes as good as yours?"

"Yes . . ." Susan remembered the early days of their relationship, how good David smelled after a workout and shower, and she felt like crying. She went to the kitchen. If she were going to cry, she thought, she wanted to do it alone. But Jurgan wouldn't leave. He pulled a form from the binder, wrote her name and address, checked off a few boxes, then filled in the amount. "Please sign here." After she finished her signature - Susan Brooks - Jurgan started to get up but stopped. "I know you must feel pretty bad—"

"I *feel* like he's still alive. Mostly because of you." Susan rubbed her eyes. "But he's not. Is he?" She stared at the wall, a bulletin board on which she and her husband used to post notes. "I have things to do." She turned and walked to the front door, then waited, watching Jurgan take his time, inspecting the house as if he were buying it.

He lingered on the front porch. "I am sorry," he said.

"Forget it." And she wanted to add, just leave, now. *Please.*

Before getting into his car, Jurgan looked up at her and waved. How ironic, Susan thought, telling him to forget her husband's death when she was the one who had to forget. Back inside, she stood next to the fireplace, the mantle cluttered with her dead husband's belongings: a Colombian machete given to him by a previous girlfriend, a small round bottle of mescal with the worm on the bottom, the skull of a coyote found on a trail in Wyoming. Each memento had its link to her husband, who lived in her thoughts. Even his clothes, hung almost exactly as he left them, suggested to her that he was alive. She carefully slid one hanger to the side, his business suit, then another with his overcoat, trying to visualize their last day together in this house, packing for the trip. For a moment, she allowed herself to dream about David holding her, as if he'd die without her, lying with her in their warm bed. But such passion was short-lived. And the dream shattered into the reality of an empty house. She yanked things from the hangers, throwing them onto the bed, angry at her husband for being dead, the bastard. She held a tie she'd bought him for Christmas, professional pinstriped pattern, and threw it on the mess, then sat on the edge of the bed and cried.

Susan carefully folded his clothes and stacked them into boxes. His blue jacket was missing. She had packed their clothes for their Canadian adventure, and she did not recall packing his blue jacket. Perhaps the burglar had made his way into their bedroom and taken it. If so, maybe she should report it to Jurgan, and get more money. But why would a thief be so selective when ransacking a home? Ridiculous. David must have stuffed it in at the last minute, and there was no reason for him to tell her something so trivial. He never told her much of anything, trivial or otherwise. He always wanted to move, to hike faster. Was that his way to avoid talking? And she followed him into the wilderness, hoping for those moments when he opened up, when he seemed at peace with himself and ready to talk about their life together, their future. Why, she questioned, did she marry him in the first place? Was it because he seemed so solid, so unflinching and strong, unlikely to leave her? When did their marriage fall apart? There seemed to be no single event to define it, only a steady decline from the beginning, and they couldn't reverse it. Should she have done more to confront him, force an explanation from him? Did he even have one? Susan packed everything into boxes - clothes, mementos, papers - and pushed it all into a dark corner of the basement.

# Chapter Twelve

David rolled over on the hard bunk and looked out the window at sunlight reflecting from high peaks, wisps of snow in the wind. He smelled smoke. In the kitchen, Evert huddled near the wood stove, both hands around a cup of coffee. Without looking up, Evert said, "Hope you don't mind me stayin' on awhile."

"Not at all," David responded, pouring himself coffee. He rubbed his stiff, slightly crooked fingers. They'll be okay, he thought. Maybe a hairline fracture in one, but it was healing. Hopefully, it would eventually return to normal. "I'm going for a hike," he said. "Want to come along?"

"Nope. Gotta go to town, get supplies."

"Maybe I should go with you," David said.

Evert looked at him. "Ain't you supposed to be dead?"

He shrugged, and watched Evert drive down the narrow two-track road, then he started hiking, crossing the creek, over the hill on the other side, and he was alone in the foothills of the Wind River mountains. He hiked further, passing boulders, along a ridge into woods where an eagle circled above him. The cool morning air had burnt off, sunlight now searing into his eyes. Sitting on a rock, he scanned his surroundings - sage, wild flowers, mountains, the eagle soaring.

David closed his eyes. For days, he sought this moment, praying that it would make everything all right, that he would feel the contentment, the sheer joy of the mountains. But now he sat, tired, worn down. His surroundings somehow detached from the person he'd become. Where was the Epiphany?

His mouth dry, sweat on his forehead, he laughed about what an idiot he was. No water. With the cool morning, he decided not to bring water, thinking it would be a short hike. He knew better. In the distance, over on the next ridge, he saw a deer staring back at him.

Shielding his eyes against the blinding sun, he looked at the pale blue, cloudless sky. Nothing. The air still as death. No wind. The deer stood motionless. Had it moved? The resplendent wild flowers meant nothing. He had to get back, but his body ached and he didn't want to move.

A cloud drifted over the mountains, and the deer was gone. David stood like an old man, believing that if he could get moving, he would feel better. He headed toward where the deer had been, recklessly seeking that elusive feeling that he knew existed somewhere in these mountains. He'd felt it before. Those moments when he felt the surge of adrenaline wash away all of life's pressures, leaving nothing but his clean, clear, exposed soul. But now he stumbled and struggled just to make it to the next ridge where he fell, rolling in the dust, sagebrush scraping him. He felt disoriented, and sat, looking around. He was in a depression. Like the Great Divide Basin, he thought. He searched for his tracks, and thought he saw them but concluded that they were from deer or antelope. He climbed up the ridge, and stood. The only things he could be sure of were the mountains behind him and the foothills rolling on forever around him. If he hiked down the wrong gully, he could be lost for days.

As the sun set behind the mountains, casting long shadows, David knew he had gone in the wrong direction. But he also knew that when he found Liar's Creek, he could follow it. The air cooled rapidly in the shadows, and he hiked fast, kicking up dust, thirst wrapping itself around his throat like a noose. He came over a rise, the creek snaking through the foothills, and he almost fell while rushing to feel the cooling waters. Lying on his stomach, he looked at hoof prints in the gravel and sand and worried the water was full of cow manure. He stuck his head into the creek and let the water run over his lips, but didn't drink.

He leaned back, wiped water from his face, and stood, then followed the creek, weaving in and out of the brush and aspen. He heard a rattle, stopped, and looked down, a coiled snake with its forked tongue sliding out and back in, ready to strike. David froze and started to ease away, but fell, the snake lunging, missing his leg as he scrambled away kicking dirt, getting up and running, feeling like his shoes were full of lead, but making it back onto the higher ground. His heart pounded and his nerves felt frayed. Not the sort of adrenaline rush he had hoped for.

He hiked along the ridge but was drawn back to the rushing water sounding like voices. Shadows from the aspen like animals scurrying at his feet. He tripped on a rock, splashed knee-deep into the creek. Twisted scrub branches hissed in the wind. Frantically, he stumbled out of the water, falling, sagebrush scratching and gouging. He rolled over onto his back and stared up at the vast expanse of stars filling the sky, Orion rising from the eastern horizon.

# Chapter Thirteen

Every day, Susan felt overwhelmed by even the most simple of chores. Returning to work felt impossible. But she forced herself to start working for a few hours at a time. She thought it strange the way her co-workers gathered around her and admired her "courage". Nothing that happened in the wilderness had anything to do with courage, she thought. No, it was the daily, lonely struggle to earn a living, go on and act as if everything was "normal". That was courageous.

Susan measured her life in days and hours, and didn't think about the funeral until it was upon her, the event overtaking her like a sudden squall. She changed outfits several times, her black dress too stylish, red too bright, finally settling on a gray skirt and white blouse.

The church service itself went okay, she thought, providing her with structure, the security of knowing what to do, having people usher her to her seat, say things about her husband. All she had to do was listen. The eulogies were mercifully short, the priest spoke about the afterlife; a business associate talked about him as a hard worker who deserved better. Susan wondered about that comment. Deserved better than what? Drowning? Cracking his head open on a rock and bleeding to death? Then there was the mathematician, Jack Savgren. She remembered him from their wedding: David's old climbing pal. Savgren's eulogy recalled David's confidence in the wilderness, then saying that mountain climbing was statistically safer than driving on the highway.

As they filed out, she worried about the "gathering" at her mother's house. What would she say to David's parents? How was she supposed to show her grief? She had been offered several rides, but declined them all. She didn't see any sense in having to shuffle around cars and, while lonely, she felt safer driving herself, pretending she was going somewhere else, some other occasion where she'd be less likely to cry.

Turning onto her old street, she saw that almost all the houses had disappeared, leaving her mother's house like a stray country estate surrounded by forest and lawn. Susan remembered the trees that remained. They used to shade the large back yards of her childhood friends.

Mrs Moore had decorated the front of the house with red geraniums. Inside, flower arrangements adorned desks, tables, and hung from the walls at odd places. When Susan looked closely, she could see that the flowers hid peeling paint and cracks caused by the low-flying aircraft.

"You look terrible," her mother said, face tanned from the Alps, and handed Susan a vegetable platter. "It's because you're going out, right, having a good time."

"Yeah, that's it." She set the platter on a table in the dining room.

"Have you met someone?"

Susan didn't want to "go out" with anyone. "Mom, it's only been a month."

"Seems longer." Mrs Moore handed her a glass of wine.

Susan greeted people as they arrived - David's parents, his father saying, "I know we didn't get a chance to spend much time together . . . but my son picked you. You're the best of the bunch."

"We loved *all* our children," his mother said, as if a mother's love distributed equally could prevent death. Susan looked at her husband's older brother and younger sister, both of whom she'd met only once. David, as far as she knew, was not close to his family. "Did he talk much about us?" his mother asked.

Susan lied. "We were going to visit you . . . on our next vacation."

David's mother nodded, and wiped under her eye, then

looked at Susan. "Did he say anything about us . . . at the end?"

Susan tried to recall. She thought he might have said something like "Goddammit." But she replied, "I don't remember. I'm sorry. It happened so fast."

His mother frowned. "You seem so calm."

Susan explained that she had been crying for weeks and had no tears left. Then she watched the room full of people sipping cocktails and telling amusing stories about David, then drifting to the gossip of the day, anything to fill the void. Susan stood tight-lipped. She finished her wine, and was headed for more when she turned and bumped into Jurgan. While startled, she wasn't surprised. *You jackass,* she thought, showing up at a funeral to protect his money?

"Why are you here?" she asked.

"I was invited."

"By whom?"

Jurgan smiled. "Your mother, of course." He handed her the check for the break-in. She looked at him, and knew the normal response should be a thank you. But she felt sure there was more to this than good service. She started to leave. But he stopped her. "Wait, there is one more thing."

"What?"

"I'm supposed to go through a checklist with you. It might take awhile. Maybe we could do it over dinner or something."

She squinted. "I don't understand."

"Your mother said you were ready to make the claim."

Susan searched the crowd, the diffuse light, the noise of everyone talking, and she was ready to deny everything when Mom stepped up next to her and said, "I said she *might* be ready to make a claim."

"Even if you want your money in seven years," Jurgan said, "I need to process the papers."

She looked at him, the thought of any more paperwork making her stomach knot up, and she walked away, into the kitchen for more wine. She filled her glass, then carried it,

99

spilling on her hand, avoiding her mother and Jurgan. She stood in an obscure corner and watched. Looks like a party, she thought. David would have been amused by it. He was never one to acknowledge the past. Everyone had to pursue the moment. Then she noticed Savgren standing alone, peering over his thick, professorial glasses and drinking a beer. She made her way over to him, and after the customary exchanges of sympathy and acceptance, Susan asked, "His death was a fluke, wasn't it?"

"Flukes happen all the time."

Susan sipped her wine. "How often?"

"You don't really want to know."

"Yes, I do." But she had trouble following his lecture about probability theory, and she eventually had to interrupt. "So you haven't heard from him lately?"

Savgren laughed, then stopped. "Sorry. But the chance of me communicating with the dead is nil."

"I know . . . but . . . sometimes I feel like he's still alive." Susan felt strange saying it out loud. She had been so busy defending herself from the idea, because of Jurgan mainly, that she hadn't been allowed to express her own doubts.

Savgren looked over the top of his glasses. "Are you okay?" he asked.

Of course, she thought, but suddenly wasn't so sure. "Do you think he was happy?"

"I don't know . . . he seemed fine. He liked to move fast, especially near a summit."

Susan looked across the room at Jurgan talking to her mother. "But where's his body?" she said absently.

Savgren stared into space, then rubbed his beard. "If he were alive, he'd probably be in Wyoming. But the guy's dead, and if not, he might as well be. I mean, he's lost everything - home, wife, family, job." Then Savgren smiled. "But of course, statistically, anything is possible."

As the evening wore on, Susan wished everyone would leave. She leaned next to her mother who was laughing along with one of David's work associates. "You think anyone would notice," Susan asked, "if I went home?"

Mrs Moore looked at her, and said without hesitation, "You can do whatever you like. But wait. I have something for you." She went to her purse. "I know it isn't much." She handed her a check for seven hundred dollars.

"I can't take this." Susan shook her head, feeling worthless, like a charity case. Had she been a burden on her mother all these years? It must've been hard for Mom, supporting her daughter financially, emotionally, and dealing with her own feelings at the same time.

"You'll need whatever you can get. Enroll in classes. Finish your degree."

"No, I . . . "

"Take it. I need to slow down on my travel anyway."

Susan escaped into the night, jets circling overhead, waiting to land, the drive home lonely as she slumped against the steering wheel wanting only to sleep. But she couldn't help thinking about actually following her mother's advice: finishing her degree.

Opening the front door to her house, Susan pushed mail across the floor, a letter from David's work on top of the pile. She carried it all upstairs and sat on the couch, opening the letter first. It contained a stock disbursement for several thousand dollars, the sudden rush of money buoying her spirits. Then she read the letter explaining that David, and by extension, his wife, would not receive the full package of benefits granted the others, such as retraining expenses, because his demise occurred before his official last day of employment. What? Susan's mood fell from its lofty ebullience to guilt. David had lost his job? Did that explain their fight on the first day of the canoe trip? Hardly, she thought, they'd been arguing long before that. Then she became angry. Why didn't the bastard just tell her? How could she trust someone who never shared his thoughts? Their failing marriage was *his* fault, wasn't it? She tossed the stock disbursement aside and, still thinking about what a jerk he was, she looked at the rest of the mail, belated notes of sympathy from distant friends. Most of the cards had come from David's work associates, impersonal, standard condolences with nothing more than signatures inside. One dreary card with pastel flower arrangement on  the front had the usual canned sympathy. But at the bottom, below the floral, she read a one-line, typewritten message – "In your heart, he lives".  She looked at the envelope. No name. No return address. She read the card again. Who would send such a thing, and what were they trying to imply?  That David was alive?  Implying also that she *knew* he was alive? Savgren had helped convince her that David was, as seemed obvious, dead. So why did a simple card arouse such suspicion in her?  Just as easily, she could have read it differently - her husband would always be alive in her heart and with her forever. But why then did she jump to the other conclusion?  Frustrated, she ripped the card into pieces and stuffed it into the trash.

## Chapter Fourteen

Staggering down the slope to his shanty, David Brooks thanked God that he'd made it, shutting the door and listening to the empty shack rattle in the wind. He gulped too much water too fast, and the room started spinning like he guzzled bad booze. His knees buckled and he sat with his head down. Evert pushed open the door, carrying full bags, and said, "Get off your butt an' help."

David grunted, then said, "Sure." No problem, he thought, he would drag his battered body out of his chair and help unload groceries. No matter where, or who, he was, he had to do his share of the work.

Later that night, the rattlesnake slithered into his dreams, lunging at him, fangs stabbing into his arm, venom coursing through his blood, and he fell into the creek. Fighting against the rushing water, he stood and, in his dream, a serpent rose from the water, eyes red, the tail coiling around and rising, turning into a second, identical head, both mouths smiling, sharp teeth dripping blood. The tailless serpent-monster wrapped around his neck suffocating him, both heads ready to devour him. He gasped and woke from his dream, yanking the blankets away from his face.

David watched the darkness turn gray and waited for Evert to wake up, handing him a cup of coffee and sitting across the small table, watching him slurp it down.

Evert looked up from his coffee. "What ya lookin' at?"

"Nothing . . . I sort of got lost yesterday."

"Yeah?" Evert nodded. "Well, looks like ya made it back okay."

"That's not it."

"What's not?"

"I think I started to hallucinate. Creek talking, shadows . . ."

Evert stared. "It's easy to go a little crazy out here."

David relaxed, sitting back and drinking coffee. "Rattler almost got me too."

"You don't want to mess with them."

David took a deep breath, remembering his dream and looking at his cowboy friend. Who else could he tell about the dream? So he described the serpent monster, its tail transforming into a second head. "Funny thing is," he said, "I think I've seen that serpent before, somewhere . . . It was weird."

"Yeah, dreams always are."

Sure, David thought, but he expected to feel better, invigorated, not hazy nightmarish allusions. He had expected to think clearly in the clean, crisp mountain air, able to formulate a plan and a new life. But he felt adrift, frantic, desperately searching for the clarity.

After breakfast, he tried making a list - he had about 2,100 cash, a deed to the land . . . but the deed was good only if Susan didn't find out about it. Susan, he thought, trying not to think too much about her, not wanting to accept any possibility that he was lonely, that he missed her. If he did, then every move he'd made would be worthless, or worse, detrimental. Thinking of her made him feel like he was falling into an abyss. No, he thought, he would stay on his land for as long as it took to feel alive again, a new person; then he would live as that new person, a full and happy life. Maybe he would build a house in these foothills, or maybe in Montana. He would then have access to the mountains and daily rebirth if he needed it. But he still felt separated from his surroundings. David stared at his list, and threw it away. It wouldn't do any good until he could think clearly. He found

Evert sitting at the table, cleaning his rifle.

"What do you hunt?" David asked. He hadn't been hunting since he was a boy with his father.

"Antelope, elk, mule, deer."

David remembered the time his father shot a Canada Goose right after it landed on a lake, and his father saying how bad he felt about it, and feeling even worse when he noticed the wildlife preserve tag on it, but he tossed the tag into the water. "It's a question of which goose gets caught," his father had said.

"You comin' along?" Evert asked.

David followed him out, boots crunching on the frost-covered ground. He hunkered down on a ridge, crawling up next to Evert. Antelope grazed on the upward slope of the next rise and Evert took aim, then stopped and said, "Why don't you bag one first."

David looked at the rifle. "I don't have a license."

"Neither do I," he said. "And you're dead, so it don't matter."

The rifle barrel felt cold through his gloves as he lined it up on the antelope's flank. David held his breath, then jerked the trigger. The antelope ran, flowing like waves of prairie grass in the wind, running over the rise and disappearing.

Evert rolled onto his side. "You're too anxious."

Later, Evert shot a deer, and David watched him slice it open, blood everywhere. He looked away and spit. Evert said, "You want me to cut out the heart, so you can take a bite?"

David understood the allusion - Indian ritual, paying homage to the dead animal, eating its heart where its spirit lived - but he never liked watching his father gut animals. He sat and took deep breaths, his chest tightening, thin air raw in his throat. He stared at the blood-coated ground, the entrails strung across the sage like Christmas lights, and Evert with bloody hands holding a slab of deer meat.

That evening the meat sizzled on the barbecue while they guzzled beer and laughed about David's reactions to the gutting, then David grabbed the meat from the grill and bit into it, Evert telling him he might want to wait until it was fully cooked. The meat tasted lean, juices dripping, and David remembered when he was in Mexico, when he got sick from something he ate, probably raw meat, or meat not cooked properly. It had made his throat swell. Thought he was going to die, coughing and spitting blood. Scared the hell out of him. Now he swallowed and felt a lump in his throat, but he knew he was just reacting to the memory. This food was just fine, he told himself, and he guzzled beer, popping open another, washing down the deer meat. Suddenly, snow flurried from the dark sky.

One day drifted into the next and, as the holidays neared, Evert started to brood, cleaning his rifle more than necessary. They drank whiskey, played cards, and talked about right and wrong. David thought, *have I done anything "wrong"?* Wasn't it a matter of self-preservation, survival? Didn't everyone have to recreate themselves from time to time?

Late into the night, drunk, with David's eyelids drooping, Evert announced that he was going home. "Patch things up," he said, and promised not to say a word about David.

With Evert gone, the serpent dream returned, the serpent wrapping itself around his throat, strangling him, fangs bared, David waking, sweating and struggling to breathe.

# Chapter Fifteen

Sitting near the front of class, Susan tried to pay attention, but her thoughts kept yielding to the unusual sympathy card. She had ripped it up and stuffed it into the trash, but it wouldn't go away. Who would send such a thing? The possibilities narrowed quickly, forcing her to think about someone she wanted to forget, his words now reemerging to implicate him – "I don't give up easily." Was it something Kester Blucuski would write? If he could write at all, she thought, knowing immediately that it was an unfair assessment. She heard the instructor ending class, reminding them of their assignment, and Susan left, other students talking and laughing.

While the envelope had no return address, it bore a Columbia, Missouri postmark. She tried to recall if any of David's friends were from Columbia, or had moved there as she bought coffee in the university cafeteria and sat, paying bills before studying. Why no signature? Maybe a woman, a lover, maybe David having an affair?

A student sat across from her. "Whatcha' doin?"

Susan stuffed a check into an envelope, then looked up and recognized the girl, someone who liked to talk and treated everybody like a best friend. "Hi, Elizabeth."

Elizabeth picked up the checkbook. "You're married?"

"Not any more." She took the checkbook back, and opened it - David and Susan Brooks - she had stacks of unused checks with their names printed on them.

"Divorced?" Elizabeth asked.

"My husband died," Susan said, thinking, no reason to waste the checks . . . But did the bank even know about her husband?

107

She hadn't told them. Had she just assumed that her mother would take care of it?

"Oh, I'm sorry . . ." Elizabeth looked toward the lunch counter and pulled a crumpled dollar bill from her jeans pocket. "Doesn't that feel sort of strange? I mean, sharing a checking account with a dead person?"

Susan just stared. Elizabeth excused herself, and went to get something to eat.

Instead of going to the library as she had planned, Susan drove to the bank and asked questions about how checks were processed. She received only vague explanations, and the suggestion that banks do sometimes make mistakes. Eventually, she gained an account with only her name, Susan Brooks. She looked at it and frowned. Is *that* who she was? Susan Brooks?

At her house, she opened the door and looked at the few letters, mostly bills, on the floor. She sorted them, finding one with no return address. She ripped it open. The heading said that she should apply immediately for a second mortgage, excellent for home improvements. She stared at it, then threw it away, and opened the bills, thinking that the strange card had been a quirk, a one-time imposition, something to bury in her memory.

Slowly, over several weeks, Susan found some comfort in her daily routines, exercising after work, studying in the evenings. With each class, she gained more confidence - she *would* complete her degree in history. But she shifted its focus. She wanted to know more about early world civilizations, especially Pre-Columbian. Too long, Susan thought, she had ignored or denied her father's death as an influence on her life. Maybe this would be a way to understand and accept it. She would learn Spanish, recalling the few Spanish words her Dad taught her - *corazon, niña, bonita*. Eventually, she would go to Mexico, the land where her father spent his last waking moments, leaving his daughter to wonder why.

Leaves scattered around her feet in a cold breeze as she climbed out of her car, slammed the door shut, and hurried to her Spanish class. Black clouds churned in the sky. On the asphalt path to the building, two young men approached her and asked her to go to a party. She smiled and politely declined. With their propositions, however, she gained strength, pleased that they might have found her attractive.

She settled into her second-row seat next to the window. Lightning flashed, and she felt herself brace against the thunder. She reviewed her homework assignment, a dialogue.

*Yo soy un buen mujer.* I am a good woman.

*Que quieres?* What do you want?

*Yo quiero correr osamente peligro sin meido.*

She hoped that last line said, "I want to run daringly, but without fear." She worried about its accuracy - another flash, and thunder, the storm moving fast overhead. Her classmates tried to speak Spanish, sounding childlike, laughing at their own awkward attempts, like toddlers trying to run. But Susan's mind drifted. She could still hear her father's answers to her little-girl questions. Why were the Aztec so mean? His calm answer - they believed in ritual, common for their time. But nothing in her memory explained why her father had to die with the Aztec.

While driving in the dark, lights shimmering off the wet pavement, Susan thought about Jurgan's "checklist". She had been avoiding the hassle. But her mother pressed the issue, and Susan could think of no legitimate reason to put it off any longer.

When Jurgan arrived on the agreed upon Saturday morning, she still wasn't ready. She heard the doorbell just as she was climbing out of the shower. With hair wet, she picked the mail off the floor and opened the door, Jurgan smiling and saying hello. She led him into the kitchen and set the mail down on the counter. The top envelope had no return address. She flipped it over, outlines of a card showing through the paper.

"You okay?" Jurgan asked while she poured coffee.

"I'm fine." She looked at the postmark - St Louis.

Jurgan leaned over his forms, writing in names, addresses, phone numbers. "These questions may seem peculiar to you, but there is some logic behind them." He sipped the coffee.

Wanting to rip open the envelope, Susan left it on the counter and sat.

"To your knowledge," Jurgan said, "your husband had no addictions of any kind, such as alcohol, gambling, sex—"

"No. He didn't have an addiction to anything." She looked out the window, tree limbs swaying in the breeze, too close to the house, brown leaves spinning on branches and scattering across the ground. Could his passion for the outdoors be considered an addiction? "Did you and Mr Brooks have any problems - separation, suggestion of divorce?"

"No," she lied, "we were fine." Unless you considered his inability to talk to her, his impatience at her hiking, and her climbing, recalling their Rainier climb, near the top, when she felt she couldn't take another step and he grabbed her, literally pulling her up. Now she wondered if she would have found the strength to complete the climb on her own.

Jurgan checked the appropriate box on the form. "Sorry if this upsets you but . . . did he have any conditions that required medical attention, or monitoring?"

"No, I told you he stayed in shape . . ." Then she added, "You can search the medicine cabinet if you like."

"Allergies?"

"Not that I know of."

"Legal problems?"

"No."

As he went down the list, Susan felt that Jurgan wanted to know more about David than she did as his wife. How well did she know her husband? What did he gain from his escapes into the woods? At the beginning, when David pursued her, she remembered trying to avoid him. But he had been persistent. And she remembered feeling safe in his arms while staring up at the vast universe, the sky full of stars.

"Has he ever traveled abroad?"

"Does Mexico count? He went there once, before I met him." Jurgan printed on the form. Susan watched him, then added, "We talked about going there." The thought made her stomach knot. To her, Mexico was a place where people went and did not return.

"But you didn't go?" Jurgan asked.

"No."

"You uncomfortable with this?" he asked.

"It's okay, you're just making sure he's actually dead, right?" Then she added, "Since there's no body."

Jurgan finished his coffee. "Before we go on, is there anything you want to change, or add, now that you've had time to think?"

Susan exhaled. She was thinking about ways to get Jurgan out of her house. Then she remembered. "Mexico," she said. "David had a reaction to the food. Not just the typical tourist stuff, and it happened to him here once." She recalled the incident. David liked to try "exotic" food. They went to a new Thai restaurant. Susan complained that the food tasted odd, but he kept eating, telling her not to worry about it. Then, later that night, her husband clutched his chest, gasping.

Jurgan leaned forward. "What was it?"

"He couldn't catch his breath. Food allergy of some sort. But he called his doctor and got a prescription. That was the end of it. No big deal." But, she thought, David had been scared, and she had been terrified, barely able to drive him to the pharmacy.

"What was the prescription for?"

"I think Volmax . . . does that sound right?"

He sat back and wrote in the margins. "Just one more section . . ."

Susan got up and leaned against the counter, next to the card. "Does it have to be done now?"

Jurgan looked at the envelope. "You can open it," he said. "I don't mind waiting."

"No . . . these things make me cry."

He pulled the financial records' section away from the rest of the form, and handed it to her. "Fill it out when you can."

Once Jurgan had driven away, Susan ripped open the envelope, and stared at the front of the card - a nature scene, a brilliant photo of a couple, canoeing on a clear Ozark stream, big smiles, obvious love, floating peacefully. Inside, blank, except for the typewritten phrase. "He lives. In your heart, you know it." Like the first card, she tore it up. Then she changed into her jogging clothes and ran into the park, huge old trees with bare limbs reaching into the gray November sky. She ran fast. He lives? Maybe it was spiritual. Maybe the sender was referring to God, just the sort of thing a fanatic might do, send her anonymous sympathy cards trying to convert her. She looked up at the trees, the feel of snow in the air, and ran past a man with arms outstretched begging for money. Normally the beggars did not bother her, she had always been generous with spare change and pleasantries, but today they scared her, the holiday season fast approaching with nothing for her to give. She needed all of her money and she didn't feel all that pleasant.

She darted back across the avenue, into her neighborhood, and walked slowly up the sidewalk. She stopped and turned back to look at the park, feeling that some homeless soul had followed her. No one. The wind made her shiver. She turned to jog home and almost bumped into a man wearing an olive drab coat, knotted hair sticking out of his knit cap. Susan staggered back — Kester Blucuski.

## Chapter Sixteen

David hiked into the mountains, finding a little-used footpath leading to the source of Liar's Creek, a small waterfall near the top, water rushing and splashing over a talus slope, patches of snow glistening in the sunlight. He knew the sight was beautiful, postcard perfect. But he felt like he was in a jail cell, looking at the postcard. *No*, he thought, *I just need to go higher*. He climbed, but the unstable talus leaned with his weight, and he slipped on the wet snow as the sun beat hot in the afternoon. One huge, jagged slab tipped, and he jumped out of the way as it tumbled over, hitting with a loud crack. Gray clouds blew in from the west, blocking the sun, and quickly turning black over the peaks.

His fingers stiffened in the cold air and he wondered if they would ever heal properly. Even so, he would climb and keep climbing, pursuing his peace on the high ground. He slipped, hitting his forearm hard on a sharp edge. *Nothing will stop me*, he thought, heart pounding, expecting his adrenaline to push him toward lofty heights and some sort of spiritual reawakening. He kept going, curling his hand into a crack and shifting into the mist from the waterfall, standing on a ledge before a sheer rock face, wet, no way up but to climb through the icy water and cross, try the steep, loose talus on the other side. Snow swirled out of the black sky. The water crashed into a small pool before spilling out and down the mountain. He sat leaning against the rock face, and thought about his chances. He concluded that trying to climb through the waterfall would be suicidal. He still believed that another life waited for him in these mountains, that if he climbed higher, he would find passage. But not today, not here. He sat, staring at the route that lead him to this dead end. His breath turned into white puffs freezing on his skin. He rubbed his arms. Squinting, snowflakes melting on his forehead, freezing onto his eyebrows, he looked into the grayness and swirling snow, his wife filling his thoughts, suddenly there with him, her body wrapped warmly around his. His mind drifted sleepily - she warmed him, fit snugly into his body. His eyes drooped and he knew that if he stayed much longer on the wet, rocky crag, he would fall asleep, freeze to death. Suddenly, the wind chilled him, feeling cold on the inside as if the gusts were trying to carry away his soul.

Get moving, he told himself, and he began the slow descent, slipping and falling, the crack of rock hitting rock, stumbling back to the path where he hiked, limping, trying hard not to think of Susan and the home he once had.

Over the next few weeks, he tried several routes into the mountains, often reaching the tops of small rocky peaks, standing alone in the wind only to be confronted with thoughts of his wife. In his memory, her beauty haunted him. But *she* was not the ghost. It was he who had crossed into the world of the dead. Or was trying to cross, trying to cheat death, and find a new life. He thought of Savgren's pure mathematics and how his theories seemed so simple. But it was not simple. The calculations were simply devoid of emotion. And David had not calculated on missing his wife. He had not calculated that the mountains, where he had once felt safe, would now mock him with their cold winds, and snow swirling down the valleys, piling high over the old truck. One night, he fled the shanty, running out into the deep, moonlit drifts, and yelled, "Susan, let me go. Leave me alone," only to hear the yelps of coyotes.

After three weeks of being snowbound, he ran low on supplies. The only food he had left was powdered milk, cereal, and canned peas. He tried hunting in the snow-covered foothills, but didn't shoot anything. So he got drunk and sat next to the frozen creek, waiting as gray clouds surrounded him. A blue grouse ran out of the brush. He aimed, pulled the trigger and splattered the bird across the glittering ice glazed surface. He sat and stared for a long while, and grew weary, nearly falling asleep. A coyote nosed over the disemboweled grouse, gripped it in its jowls and started trotting. David jumped to his feet and tried to yell but he could only force a hoarse whisper. He aimed his rifle at the coyote, fired and missed, then fell, his bare neck scraping the ice crust.

David struggled to his feet, trudging through drifts, his breath misting in the cold, thin air. As flurries fell softly from the encompassing grayness, he remembered looking at the calendar not long ago, the days disappearing without much notice. He recalled his childhood and snow-covered subdivision streets. As an independent-minded twelve-year-old, he hiked wintry streets at night to escape the squabbling of his older brother and sister, and his parents' bickering. His father often came home late, seeking solitude, only to find his wife battling teenagers. While at the time it all struck David as hurtful, he later accepted it as normal. And now, for the first time, he fully understood and appreciated the warmth of his parents' home, especially during the holiday season.

Gray turned to black and the wind blew the snow slanting out of the sky. He struggled back to the shanty and, for a brief moment, he thought he heard music in the wind, and he suddenly realized that it was Christmas Eve.

## Chapter Seventeen

While sitting in the glow of the tree lights at her mother's house, Susan tried to stop thinking about Kester. Even with her heart pounding into her throat, she had been very polite, asking him, "What do you want?"

And he responded, "To see you."

Then she ran fast, looking back at him waving goodbye, not bothering to chase her, his voice raspy, promising that they'd talk again soon. But that had been weeks ago. Probably he meant no harm. Even so, she had trouble sleeping, double-checking the locks, even looking at alarm systems, but they were too expensive. Tuition was sucking her money like a vacuum cleaner. Now gifts bulged out from under the Christmas tree, and she was calculating their cost when her mother's friends came into the room, filling it with the smell of sweet perfume.

Susan forced a smile, listening to their incessant questions, not waiting for her to answer. "So Susan, who's the lucky man in your life?" No one, she thought, she studied a lot. "How's school this time around?" Fine. "You're young, Susan. Do you think I should live with my boyfriend first, or just go ahead and get married?" She looked at the old woman, long gray hair, thin smile, and bright, alive eyes framed by deep wrinkles.

"I don't know," Susan responded, wanting to ask the woman what to do after losing a husband.

Mrs Moore entered the room, proclaiming that it was time to open presents. Susan watched while they ripped the overpriced wrapping paper. She opened her few presents with care, one a figurine, an imitation Aztec artifact of a young girl. Her mother nodded and smiled. Susan thanked her, kissing her cheek, then gathered her things and eased quietly toward the front door. Who was the lucky man in her life, she wondered, while driving through the lost subdivision. Before she met David, she had lots of guys asking her out, but she couldn't sustain much of a relationship with them. There was always something about them that she didn't trust, but now she wondered if there hadn't been something wrong with her. Why had David been any different? Maybe it was his quiet approach toward a proposal that felt more like a mutual agreement or understanding. Were those moments the highlight of their relationship, a brief time never to be duplicated?

She drove up her cold city street devoid of Christmas, house uncluttered by trees, ornamentation. She rushed inside and looked for a party invitation she'd stuffed in with the bills, Elizabeth's Christmas party, at her boyfriend's, just a few minutes away. She looked at the invitation. Figures, Susan thought, that Elizabeth would invite her. Elizabeth acted as if they were long-lost pals and she invited everyone she knew to parties or "events", regardless of when she met them or how well she knew them. At the very least, Susan thought, the party might prove to be an interesting distraction.

Susan stepped out onto her porch, shut the door and locked it, then started walking up the street. She glanced back at her house, and thought she saw something - a shadow, a movement in the bushes. She thought about going back and getting her car. But she was already far up the street, ready to turn the corner. No, it was nothing, she thought. She was just being paranoid. But as she neared the party, music loud in the crisp winter night, she had the feeling someone was following her. Kester? Even though it had been weeks, he had said they would talk again. But when he didn't show up "soon", she'd forgotten about him, buried the reference and didn't want to think about it. She hurried to the party.

Having spent little time on her make-up, and wearing old blue jeans and her favorite sweater, Susan was surprised when she saw how formal everyone dressed. Elizabeth twisted and bounced to loud unrecognizable rock music, her newly poofed, crimson-streaked hair jouncing, and her black miniskirt pulling at her thighs which were wrapped tightly in black nylons. Susan shifted her way past young men reeking of cologne, wearing earrings, their hair greased back. In the kitchen, people stood, wearing colorful ties and baggy pants, and they watched Susan pour herself a cup of water and squeeze in a slice of lime. She sat in a corner, and looked at the clock.

"Susan!" Elizabeth called, pushing through the crowd. "I'm so happy you came." With her stood a young man in a white, starched shirt. "This is my boyfriend Bill, he's just fantastic." Then she disappeared into the other room.

"You want to dance?" Bill asked.

Susan folded her arms across her chest. "Not right now, thank you."

He sat next to her. "What do you do for a living?"

Susan searched the room for someone she knew, anyone, then finally responded, "I'm a student."

Bill leaned closer. "Oh yeah? You go to school with Liz?"

"Excuse me," she said, standing.

"You're leaving?" he responded, jumping up in front of her. "You can't go, you just got here. What are you drinking?"

Susan cringed, as Bill stood close, boxing her in the corner, his breath reeking of beer. "I have to go." The music blasted even louder, and Susan ducked under Bill's arm, then maneuvered through dancers who had been ignited by the music. She made it to the foyer, yellow lamplight reflecting on dark shiny wood, but Bill went around the dancers and blocked the front door. "You're in the way," she said. Then thought, what a jerk, and she thought about old dates - they either left when you wanted them to stay, or stayed when you wanted them to leave.

"Oh, come on, just because I'm Liz's boyfriend doesn't mean we can't dance?" He propped his arm on her shoulder. "She said I should make sure you had a good time."

"Leave me alone," she said. She looked at him and considered slapping him.

Suddenly, Kester appeared between them and knocked Bill's arm away, then stood facing him. "The lady wants you to *fuck off*."

Susan looked around the room, Elizabeth drunk and oblivious, dancing alone with her eyes closed, Kester smelling like auto exhaust, and the college boys converging on him.

Bill looked at the others, then said, "I don't think so, *asshole*." He shoved Kester, who stumbled back a step, smiled, then lunged, his hands pressing slowly around Bill's throat. Bill crumpled to the floor, eyes bulging, arms failing and flapping against the floor.

"Stop it!" Susan screamed, the sudden violence churning her stomach, her mind racing, *no this can't be happening*. "Stop!"

Kester let go, Bill coughing and spitting while the others stood gawking. Then he turned to Susan. "You want to get outta' here?" he asked.

"What? Are you friggin' insane?"

Kester looked at the young people. "Maybe," he said, "but I hope not." He pushed the front door so hard that it banged on its hinges. She watched him disappear into the dark, snow flurries swirling under the glow of Christmas lights.

Susan turned back to the crowd. Everyone was staring at her. "Excuse me," she said, then went inside, looking for Elizabeth, finding her leaning against the kitchen sink, drinking. "Would you mind," she asked, "giving me a ride home?"

"Huh?"

"Can you give me a ride home?" Susan didn't want to try explaining over the blasting music.

"Yeah, later."

"Now," Susan said, staring at her, taking her arm, and the

two of them went out the back door, circled to the front. "It's only a couple blocks," Susan said, as Elizabeth pouted over the steering wheel, and turned down Susan's street lined with parked cars from all the churchgoers, then stopped in front of her house. "Thanks," Susan said.

"I don't know why you couldn't have walked."

"Ask Bill."

Elizabeth drove away and Susan ran to her front porch, shadows startling her, snowflakes landing gently, melting on the concrete. She heard a thump. "Kester?" Damn, she thought, should've asked Elizabeth to wait, at least until she got inside. The cat scampered from a tree, meowing and rubbing against her legs. She stooped down, and picked it up, purring next to her face, then turned, and faced Kester, his dark form looming over her in the shadows. The cat leaped out of her arms. "Don't touch me," she said.

Kester held his hands out innocently and shrugged. "Glad to see you again too. Saved your life, helped you get rid of that jerk back there. And you still don't know how to be nice?"

Susan looked at the church. Should be letting out soon, she thought, maybe they would help her. "How did you find me?" she asked, stalling, only slightly curious.

"Easy."

"*Why* did you find me?"

"Just following doctor's orders."

She flinched. "What does that mean?" How crazy was he, she thought.

"My psychiatrist says I need to, let's see how she put it . . . something like, resolve my unattainable feelings."

She stared at Kester's dark eyes, big wet snowflakes swirling around his head. She shivered. "Did your doctor say you should send me bizarre cards and track me down—"

"Lady, when you talk like that I get *angry*. I don't know if you just ain't makin' any sense, or I *am* crazy."

In the dim porch light, one side of his face was contorted, as if in pain, and it made Susan want to believe him. If he was a sick man, maybe he didn't even realize he was sending the cards, or that they were . . . what? Socially inappropriate? Then she wondered how he was able to afford a psychiatrist. But she was shivering, her teeth starting to chatter. After the Canadian forest, she never wanted to be cold again. She needed to go inside. "Kester, can we talk some other time?"

He smiled, looking her up and down. "What's wrong with now?"

"I'm freezing."

"I can warm you."

She heard a car door. Church was letting out. "Please just go away."

He looked toward the park. "Still thinking about your husband?"

Susan felt her insides twist tight. "What about him?" she asked, then added, "He's dead."

"Maybe," Kester said, standing on the sidewalk while people in suits and ties and dresses climbed into their cars. "Either way, I can help you get over him." A police car stopped up the street, waiting for the church traffic to clear. Kester's eyes shifted. He stared at her, then disappeared into the wintry night.

## Chapter Eighteen

The wind clanked the stovepipe and sparks flew out from the wood stove as David shoved in another log. Outside, wind howled and rattled the windows, cold knifing through the walls, more snow drifting high against the shanty.

Sitting at the kitchen table, he hunched over a bowl of oatmeal, scraped out a glob, stuffed it into his mouth and tried to swallow. Next to the bowl stood a half-empty bottle of whiskey. The caramel-colored liquor glimmered in the dim light from the overhead bulb. He poured himself another shot and drank it, then rested his head on the table and shut his eyes.

David dreamed that his wife hiked ahead of him, heading to the source of Liar's Creek. She climbed onto the talus slope, fluidly moving over the rock, waving to him and calling, but he could not hear because of the wind. He leaped from one huge boulder to another, scrambling to keep up, eventually standing on a loose rock, just below her. Susan extended her arm, ready to help, but her brow furrowed and she whispered, "Are you leaving me?" But he had no answer, unable to speak, falling backwards and tumbling down the talus, then lying still, his head split, blood pooling around him.

David lifted his face out of a puddle of whiskey. The front door blew open, wind howling, white swirling into the kitchen. He staggered to the door, leaned his shoulder into it and shoved, the room suddenly silent.

In the past, aloneness meant peace and tranquility, but now he just felt lonely. Any conversation, a fight with his wife, would be better than this. Should have let her know why he was angry, and he should have questioned her feelings, explored her fears as well as his own. Too late for that, he thought. Why had he run? If he wanted to get away from his wife, he could have divorced her. At the right moment, he could have told her that they were not right for each other, that it had been a mistake. Was that sensible action more difficult than running?

As each winter day blended into the next, broken only by fierce wind and blinding snow, drifting to the roof of the shanty, David often went without food, staring into nothingness, trying to pinpoint a reason for faking his own death. But the more he thought, the more unsavory the action became. His wife collecting insurance money appeased him somewhat, but even that was fraudulent, verifying him as a criminal. Was there something in his own past that explained it? Once when he was a boy, he told his parents that he was going to "run away". Then he left for at least three hours and no one noticed. In retrospect, he figured they knew. They acted like it was no big deal, pretending they hadn't noticed him gone. Then he remembered his initial reason for running away. They hadn't given into his childish wishes. David now admired their insight. And each year he grew older, he appreciated how much they sacrificed of their personal time to have children and how hard they must have worked to raise them with a sense of right and wrong. Yet now he was losing his grasp on those values. Maybe he had done something wrong, but there was justification, wasn't there? He feared that if he logically searched for justification, it would become starkly clear that there was none. He worried about having children of his own, wondered if he could do it, thinking the experience too monumental - like climbing Everest without oxygen. Had he considered having children with Susan? Thinking about his parents now, and their unavoidable sadness at his "death" buried him in guilt. He sat peeling the label off a whiskey bottle. If nothing else, he thought, he had a good supply of booze.

Across the dim-lit room, Evert's rifle leaned next to the fire. David swigged more whiskey. Always look ahead, he thought, to the future. That's how he'd lived his life. Now he had no future. He had failed to make good use of Savgren's theories, unable to jump into another universe and create a new life for himself. He'd searched all the high rocky crags around his land and found no solace, no path to salvation. Perhaps, he thought, he needed to make a different transition, cross over to the world of the truly dead.

David stared at the rifle, wondering if he would feel the bullet. Or would it be too fast? Would it hurt? And then what? He held the rifle in his lap, running his fingers over the wood stock and the cold barrel. With arms outstretched as if he were diving into a lake, he held the rifle pointed at his forehead, but envisioned the bullet skipping off his skull. He aimed for his heart. The blood would fill the shanty.

Hands shaking, he held his finger over the trigger. But he couldn't do it. Which would be more cowardly, he thought, to kill himself, or to go on living? He set the rifle aside, opened the door and fell into the snow, stinging his skin, then staggered back inside, and passed out by the fire.

Waking to a gray dawn, he struggled to his bed, and lay on his back, staring at the paint peeling off the ceiling. He had only himself to blame, but still, he had to move on. "Get over it," he said aloud, his voice barely audible, sounding strange in the vacuum of the shanty. Suicide held no inherent truth, just eternal questions. He wiped frost from the inside of his window and peered out, a clear day, sunlight touching a high peak and David was filled with memories of Gannettt Peak, the highest in Wyoming, the sheer joy of standing on its snowy ridge, and then glissading down the glacier, spitting ice crystals in the glistening sunlight. Yes, he thought, Gannettt. Highest Peak. There, and only there, could he complete the leap, find his salvation, and begin anew.

David endured each dreary day, mentally preparing for his climb, knowing that he would have to watch the spring slip by, not be too anxious, and wait until summer. Spring climbing might get him snowbound on the high slopes. No, he'd had enough of feeling trapped like that. Summer held the best chance of reaching the summit.

David ate the last of his canned peas, the shanty feeling more and more like a prison. He was becoming weak, malnourished, but knew he would be okay, marking off the days as accurately as possible on a calendar that was several years old. In fact, as he looked at it closely, he noticed it was left over from the year he bought the place, the year he had climbed Gannettt with Savgren. Good sign, he thought.

Finally, in May, unsure of the exact day, David watched the snow start to melt, checking each afternoon and morning, discouraged when a spring snowstorm covered everything again. But the spring snow melted away quickly, and David dislodged Evert's old truck from a drift. Giving it too much gas, he slid into a boulder, the jolt slamming his head into the steering wheel. He looked in the rear-view mirror, and for the first time in a long while, examined his own face - the scar, new gray splotches in his black, frayed beard, hair knotted and long. His face ashen with black circles sagging under red eyes. Except for the new cut on his forehead - crimson blood dripping from his cheek - he looked like someone flat on his back in a wooden box. He smiled, thinking that he had come as close to death as possible without actually dying. Couldn't get any worse, he thought, then feared that it could. He took a drink of whiskey and tried to stay positive. Drinking helped keep the pain away. *Maybe, for me, this is the bottom.* Things would get much better from here on, he thought.

He drank whiskey all the way out of the foothills. When he hit pavement, he veered off the road, then jerked the steering wheel, and swerved back and forth across the yellow lines.

David parked in front of the Ram's Horn, got out, and slipped, mud splattering on his clothes. He stepped onto the wooden sidewalk, steadied himself on a post, then staggered into the bar. Not much worse . . . he would climb . . . Gannettt... again.

The bar was full of distorted faces staring at him from high stools, a dozen cowboy boots dangling in air. Evert was among them, wearing glass-studded cufflinks sparkling like diamonds, smoking a cigarette. David tried to say something, but couldn't, his throat too dry despite the whiskey, having not spoken to anyone in a long time, thinking that he needed a beer. Evert hopped off the barstool, grabbed David's arm, and said, "Let's get outta here."

# Chapter Nineteen

Often while driving past the state mental hospital with its brick turrets puncturing the sky and bars on the big windows, Susan wondered if Kester Blucuski stayed there when he wasn't wandering the streets and sleeping in the park. When she went jogging, she avoided people, especially the homeless, with their grocery carts full of junk, pans, clothes, aluminum cans, thinking that any one of them could be Kester. Usually the running released her fears, to be viewed at a distance, but recently they were staying with her, and the more she ran, the more restless she became. She feared Kester, but had he also provided a useful distraction, helping her avoid the bigger problems? Would she ever be able to sustain a relationship? When she completed her degree, what would be expected of her? She could pay her mother back for tuition loans, even though Mom wouldn't ask for it. Susan, however, felt a need to sever all obligations to her mother. She had depended on Mom for too much too long, and didn't want to owe her money.

Eventually Susan stopped going into the park altogether, and took long walks through the neighborhood, past the corner drug store, and the local tavern. "Maybe," Kester had said. Maybe what? Maybe her husband was dead? Of course he was. But "either way" Kester wanted to help? Anything Kester Blucuski said, she thought, had to be warped by his "unresolved" feelings. Maybe he just expected her to know the cards were from him, probably through some mystic connection. And that, most likely, she thought, was "normal" for the insane.

Susan sat in the front row of her World Civilization class, leaning forward, ready to question. She heard the classroom door squeak open, the clatter of desks moving, the sound of someone settling into a seat behind her.

Then she heard, "Mrs Brooks, hello." Jurgan waved. She watched the professor begin a lecture on Mesoamerican cultures. But she could feel Jurgan looking at her, and she turned around. He nodded toward the door.

She closed her notebook, shoved it in her backpack, eased out of her desk and left the classroom. He followed her into the hallway where she turned and confronted him. "What are you doing here?"

"Have you completed the forms?" Jurgan asked.

"Why are you so interested?"

"My job," he said.

"I don't believe you. All you're doing is prying into my life, interfering . . . You have no obligation, no requirements, no nothing until I make an official claim." She had more important things to do, she thought, like studying; Jurgan and his insurance forms nothing more than a nuisance.

Jurgan frowned, and shook his head. A young couple carrying armloads of books walked by, the girl laughing.

Susan walked down the hallway, floor shiny, motivational pictures framed on the walls, one imploring her not to be afraid of risk.

Jurgan ran after her, blocked her way. "All right," he said, "I admit it. You don't have to even talk to me really. But I am trying to help." He glanced out the window, then at his feet. "You have to believe that."

"I don't have to believe anything."

He grabbed her arms and shouted, "You're not listening."

She glared. "Let go."

"Okay . . . I just . . . it's personal." He eased his grip. "I need to work some things out."

"Like what? *Unresolved* feelings?"

"Something like that. You still don't have the money you

deserve. So I'm trying to fix it up. Look, it's tax season . . . What if I do them for you, free of charge."

Susan remembered her husband talking to her in the same way, with his arms outstretched, usually only when he tried to lie to her. She never thought it was a big deal, harmless lies like telling her he was stuck in traffic when he was having an extra beer with a colleague. She looked at Jurgan. "When are taxes due?" she asked. He told her, and she immediately felt her body go limp. It was too much.

"Look," he said, "I'll do your taxes for you *and* fill out the insurance form using whatever information I can uncover. All you need to do is help me when I need answers."

Susan flinched at the thought of Jurgan in her house, shuffling through all the files. But, while she didn't like the idea, it was better than having to do them herself. He stood waiting in the hallway, hands at his side, eyes attentive, and she decided to at least to get her taxes done.

Just a few days later, Jurgan sat at her kitchen table explaining a tax code that she understood nothing about. She interrupted him. "After this, we're finished?"

"Well, hopefully, there is one other thing."

"Always is, isn't there?"

"It's this breathing problem of your husband's. It sounds like a simple allergy of some sort but . . . we're having trouble with his physician and the pharmacy. We need to convince them to let us see his records without a death certificate. It's sort of a Catch-22. We can't prove him dead without looking at their files and they won't let us look at them unless we can certify him dead."

"How pleasant," she said.

"You could help. They might give you the information . . . as his wife, or widow."

Susan thought "widow" sounded strange, conjuring up images of old women and spiders. "What tax code says you need that?"

"None. This is for *our* records. We need to rule out all

possibilities." Jurgan sat stone-faced.

"Like what?" she asked.

"Someone having medical problems might consider taking their own life."

Susan looked away, the cat outside prancing with a bird in its mouth. She stood. "Find out for yourself." The last thing she wanted to do was dig into David's medical files. Would that explain his death?

Working all afternoon, Jurgan sat at David's desk. Occasionally, Susan peeked in to reassure herself. Once, he turned and stared at her.

"Need anything?" she asked.

"No," he responded. "Your husband left organized files."

"How does it look since I started keeping records?"

"Fine, I don't see a problem."

Susan was sitting at the kitchen table as Jurgan presented her the income tax return and the insurance form.

"There's another glitch," he said.

"Excuse me?"

"The deed to your Wyoming property . . ." Susan's body shook, and he continued, "It won't affect the return, but you should at least know where it is."

Susan set her coffee clinking onto the saucer. Wyoming property, she thought.

Jurgan leaned forward. "A ranch of some sort, maybe?"

Susan could feel her heart pounding, and her head throbbed, thinking, I don't know anything.

He reached across the table and touched her arm, his hand feeling like a claw. "You all right?"

"Yes, I'm fine." She looked at the bulletin board, the wilderness calendar with a photograph of glaciated mountains.

"You knew he owned it," he said.

Susan sat stiffly and glared at him. "Is that a question?"

"Take it however you like."

"I don't like any of it."

Jurgan leaned back, and looked at the forms. "All I'm trying to do is—"

"What?"

"It's okay if you didn't know."

"With no deed," she lashed back, "how do *you* know?"

Jurgan leaned heavily against the table. "There are clear payments in the first three months of the year. They were for a second property and they went to a bank in Wyoming. Also, in looking at previous years' tax records, there is a reference to the second property, the write-off for interest paid, maintenance, that sort of thing."

"There was no reason for me to go back . . . I kept records for myself after he left."

Jurgan stared. "You mean, *died*, after he died."

Susan grabbed the tax return. "Where do I sign?"

He pointed, and said, "Let me know if you find the deed."

After escorting Jurgan out, exchanging false pleasantries and thanks, Susan took a walk down the noisy avenue. As she passed the taxis lined along the park, she had an urge to get in, to sit in the back seat and let the driver take her away. She tried to imagine exotic problem-free places, and could think only about Wyoming.

## Chapter Twenty

The sunlight hurt David's eyes, and black spots floated in his vision. He crossed the street, horn blaring, car swerving to miss hitting him as he followed Evert to the real estate office.

"Shoot," Evert said, shutting the door. "Don't want people askin' too many questions, do you?"

"No," David slurred.

"Wasn't for all the snow, I woulda been up there sooner." Evert locked the doors, closed the shades, and went out for Mexican food. A few minutes later, he came back with the food, the spices reviving David, and beer cooling his mouth.

The phone rang. David looked at it. "You going to answer it?" he asked.

"Sure, if it's buggin' you." He swished beer in his mouth, swallowed, and picked up the phone. "Yeah," he answered, "this is Evert Carson . . . Ah . . . who'd you say this was? Hang on, let me check the file . . ." Evert held his hand over the receiver, "I think it's your wife." He made it sound as if they had merely stopped off at the local tavern on the way home from work. David sat stunned with salsa dripping from his beard. Susan's voice on a wire, a lightning-quick strike at him. Evert grinned. "Want me to tell her you'll be home soon?"

David paced across the dry wooden floor, thinking, maybe he should just pick up the phone and say – hello, Susan, I'm not really dead. We could do some hiking and maybe go climbing, get to know each other. He drank, then wiped his mouth with his sleeve. "I'm dead. Tell her that." David clenched his teeth and tried to imagine standing on the summit of Gannettt Peak, free from all concerns, and ready to start that elusive new life. No matter how he felt about his wife, how much he might miss her, she could not come along, would not stand on mountain peaks with him. She was behind him now.

Evert spoke into the phone. "Yes, ma'am, sorry, yes, right here . . ." David's heart stopped, then pounded hard. Evert continued, "Your husband purchased some land along Liar's Creek, the land I've been  watchin' over. If you'd said the Liar's Creek property, I'd known what you were talkin' about. Yes, ma'am, yes, that's right, yes I know the owner . . . that would be your husband. Wait, let me check." Evert held the phone against his chest. "She wants to know if we got a deed . . . you got the deed?"

David paced, ran his hand through his hair, sat, got up again and stared at the Wyoming map.

Evert said, "You got it or not?"

"Yes . . . I have it."

Evert stared at David, then spoke into the phone again. "Ah, I'll have to check through our files, ma'am. See if we kept it . . . but, why don't you ask him . . . Oh, I see, I'm sorry . . . Oh, I'm real sorry to hear that, ma'am . . . Will you be sellin' the land then? Hmmm. I'll look for it, and I'll call you back as soon as we come up with somethin'. Well, maybe you'll be comin' out to see it. Uh uh, bye, ma'am."

David stared at the sunlight through the closed blinds, specks of dust swirling as Evert walked past. "Is she coming?" David asked.

"Didn't say for sure. Probably. Don't know when."

David looked out the window at the muddy streets, wondering if he would have enough time. His chances of reaching Gannettt's summit increased the longer he waited. Summer was best. Foolish for him to try climbing before then. When would his wife visit Wyoming?

"I think if you're gonna leave," Evert said, "you oughta do

133

it soon. Don't worry about me, I won't say a word. People come and go all the time."

# Chapter Twenty-One

Susan set down the phone and listened to the empty house, as if voices from the past might provide answers. She heard a siren, and church bells. Sunlight beamed through the windows. Inside, nothing but the creaking of old floors. She tried to recall her husband saying anything about Wyoming. Yes, she thought, he had once. It had been uncharacteristic of David, asking her softly, tentatively, suggesting that they go there together. Now, looking back, she thought that he spoke with a hint of reverence. Or was it just her memory distorting the conversation? She couldn't remember her response. It was early in their relationship, before they were married. Probably she told him she'd consider it. But that was the last she'd heard about it. Until the funeral. She remembered Jack Savgren mentioning Wyoming at the funeral. What had he said? Something to do with climbing?

Calling Evert Carson did nothing to ease her anxiety. The property did actually exist. It would not go away, nor could she bury it. Logically, however, David had no reason to tell her about it; he never told her much about anything, especially anything that even remotely concerned the finances. She had happily let him deal with the money. But, in hindsight, that seemed to be a big mistake.

The phone rang, jangling her nerves. "Hello."

She heard breathing, then a heavy voice. "Mrs Brooks?"

"Kester?" She looked at the front door.

"Yeah, I'm close by. You want me to come over?"

"No," she said, then thought, was the back door locked?

"Then come see me. Tavern, just down the street."

Susan gripped the phone, her palms sweaty, wanting to hang up but unable to move. "Why should I?"

"We need to talk." He cleared his throat. "Things you should know."

Susan said, "Okay," and hung up the phone, then sat on the couch. She rubbed her eyes, exhaled, pushed back her hair, and stood, then thought she had to be crazy. But maybe Kester would leave her alone after this meeting. If he didn't, she would call the police, get a restraining order, do anything she could to keep him away.

She walked fast, turned the corner and saw the small tavern with beer signs glinting in the sunlight, torn screen door. She'd passed it many times. A tiny bell clinked as she entered, squinting, trying to adjust to the darkness. Two old men smoking cigarettes balanced on high barstools, ready to tip into oblivion. The barmaid wore heavy eyeliner smeared over her sweaty wrinkles, faded red hair thinning on top, and a silky blue blouse. Above her was a withered picture of the 1982 St Louis Cardinals World Series team framed by liquors, and she stood in front of plastic beer taps, cracked red and white.

Susan immediately felt out of place in her clean clothes, and she clutched her purse while searching for Kester in the foul-smelling tavern. He sat at a small round table, staring out the thick, tinted glass window. She eased carefully past the other tables, and sat across from him. He was cleaning his fingernails with a black-handled, wide-bladed knife. Two shots of Tequila waited. "I got you a drink." He put the knife away, bending down to sheath it next to his ankle, then drank his tequila. She took her glass and drank, the burning glow filling her body. Kester coughed, phlegm rattling from his chest, then scratched his beard. "Back then," he said, "only reason I met with that asshole insurance boy was to see you again."

Susan felt her stomach knot. "That's what you wanted to tell me?"

Kester scowled. "There's more," he said, then looked toward the old men at the bar. "I've done nothing good with my life. Except maybe saving you." He coughed again, holding his dirty hand over his mouth, then wiping it on his coat.

"Maybe you should see a doctor."

"Doctors cost too much money. Other people have money. I don't."

Susan looked out the window, the sunlight on the broken sidewalk darkened by thick, amber glass. "I'm sorry," she said.

"Sorry?" He glared. "What do I care? So what if people drive fancy Jeeps just to go to the *fucking* grocery store."

The bartender set two more tequilas on the table and waited. Susan paid for the drinks. "But you can afford a psychiatrist?"

Kester laughed, then wheezed, "Other people go to college. I do *their* college boy work for them. They pay shit for wages. Then they fire me when I tell 'em so." He drank. "Nobody appreciated me, except maybe that psychiatrist at the VA."

Susan sat straight. "You're a veteran?"

He shook his head. "Real easy to fool that psychiatrist. Bought a bunch of medals. Made up stories about being a hero. Now she won't even talk to me. Found out I didn't *qualify* for benefits. Wasn't who I said I was. But I coulda been, army hadn't kicked me out. Assault. Good one, isn't it? But my buddy said I was as good as him and gave me all the papers to prove it. He was a real pal then, and blew his brains out. Not such a bad idea. Except . . . now I got a purpose in life."

Clouds slid in front of the sun, further darkening the bar, and cigarette smoke hung against the ceiling.

"But," Kester said, "now I *am* a hero, ain't I? Saving you. They was real nice to me in Canada. Here they cut my benefits. Just because of the damn paperwork?" He leaned forward, his breath smelling of tequila. "When I carried you, feeling you on me, it was all I could do not to take you right there . . . I wanted you bad . . . I still do . . . why don't we just do it, get it over with; then if you don't like it, I'll leave."

Susan leaned away, wanting to run out of the bar, call the police like she should have done long ago. But she froze, took another drink, and recalled the last time she sat with Kester in a bar, the tavern outside Winnipeg, and the conversation about animals in the woods. She had yelled then, and forced the meeting to end, walked out. Had she run away from a lingering question, something lurking in her subconscious? "You," she said, "saw something . . . in the woods . . ."

He glared, then leaned back, shook his head, and mumbled, "It was a man."

"What?"

"You heard me."

"Did you see him?"

"Saw enough to know it wasn't no animal."

"But . . . a man? Running?"

He shrugged, reached across the table, and finished her tequila.

She stared at him. "In my heart," she said, "he lives."

Kester's eyes bulged. "Why'd ya say that?"

She remembered his anger the last time. "I don't know."

"Yeah, you do. Tell me."

"You sent me those cards, didn't you?"

Kester's brow furrowed. "I got no fuckin' idea what you're talkin' about?"

"But . . ." Susan stared into his bloodshot eyes. Was he lying?

Kester leered and touched her forearm. "Must be hard tryin' to love someone else, not knowin' what happened to the last guy." Susan stiffened as he rubbed her arm. "If he's alive, must be one hell of a bastard leavin' you for dead." Her heart pounded, and the dingy bar closed in on her like a coffin. "I find him," Kester continued, "I'll kill him for you. That insurance boy would have to pay up, wouldn't he?" Kester laughed. "Then we'd be rich, just like everybody else, you and me."

Susan jerked away and stood, dizzy, looking for a way out of the smoky darkness. She felt her heart fluttering in her chest, and thought she should say something, stop Kester from killing . . . Who? What should she say? Don't kill my dead husband? But what if he wasn't dead, the feeling sticking in her gut. But he *had* to be dead, she thought.

"Why ya leaving so soon?" Kester's voice rattled.

"Kester, I really appreciate . . ." She faltered, trying to find the right words to dissuade him. "Killing somebody won't do any good."

He shrugged, smiled, then said, "Maybe."

Susan turned away and fled the bar. She stumbled out, into the blinding afternoon, the sun blazing through the clouds. She ran past a couple holding hands, the woman pregnant, and the idea of people having babies struck her as odd. Had she ever assumed that she and David would start a family?

As she neared the house, she could hear a phone ringing, at first thinking the neighbor had his phone outside. But, standing on the front porch, she could hear ringing through the windows of her house. Then nothing. She opened the door and stepped inside. It rang again. She stood and waited, counting. Three. Six. Ten rings, and she finally answered it. She heard the "insurance boy" himself on the line.

"Susan?"

"Who else?"

"Right," Jurgan said. "You want to go to lunch. Have a beer, or something?"

"What do you want?"

He hesitated. "It's that Wyoming property—"

"What about it?"

"I contacted the real estate agent—"

"Evert Carson?"

"Yes," he said, as Susan gripped her phone, listening. "He can't find the deed, either. If you think about it, logically, there's only one other person who would have it."

She felt her face flush, again feeling that she had failed in her marriage, all her fault, responsible for her dead husband's actions. "Maybe David was going to sell the land, and took the deed with him to Canada."

"Sure," he responded. "And maybe he was one of those guys who had a dual life. . . they have entire families in different cities."

Susan looked out the window, an old man and woman tottering arm in arm, on their way to church. "He had a hard enough time with one wife," she said, then hung up. She sat on the couch, hands trembling. The phone rang again, loudly, rattling her. Why was it so loud? She didn't want to answer it, thinking it might be Jurgan again. The incessant ringing made her want to toss it across the room. "Hello," she grumbled.

"Susan? Is that you?"

She sighed. "Yes, Mom, it's me."

"Glad I caught you. I've got a great idea. Come to Cancun with me and—" jet noise roared through the telephone, "it's cheap."

"Just like that?" Susan thought about asking her for advice. But her mother would worry, offer to cancel the Cancun trip. "I can't go with you."

"What do you do with yourself? I hardly ever see you. You're always studying or working. I think you need to go out more."

"Not now, Mom."

"What about the insurance agent? Has he gotten your money yet?"

"No," she responded, then asked, "Why?" At first, she thought it strange that her mother would be asking about the insurance money, but then realized that it wasn't any different than what Mom had been doing all her life, helping her daughter, propping her up when Susan seemed ready to fall.

"I wrote a complaint. Our lawyer is ready if we need him.

But I'll send you another check if you're short on cash."

Susan leaned back on the couch.

"You need a vacation," her mother said.

"I'm going to Wyoming." Susan hadn't realized it until then, but the words slipped out easily enough. If nothing else, she needed to find out more about the property.

"Oh, that sounds exciting. You remember when we all went out there, as a family, to the Tetons and Yellowstone . . ."

"Yes, I remember." Susan relaxed, the memory soothing her.

"I'm happy that you're finally going to have some fun. Bye."

Susan sat staring out the window of her home, the sun sinking red over the trees, and she felt empty, trying to hold onto some semblance of normalcy.

A star appeared in the darkening sky, and she remembered their family camping in Wyoming, a bear lumbering into a stream and pawing at the water, a moose, and a wide green meadow full of wild flowers. Her father holding her hand, taking her barefoot into the cool grass, and pointing to a bright red flower. Indian Paintbrush, he said, and Susan picked it, only to have it wither in the car. When Dad died, Mom told her that he had become part of everything. Now, she tried to think of David as part of the mountains, as surely he wanted to be. Yet, she could not. Was he one of those men with dual lives? The idea was far-fetched. But she remembered reading about it. Maybe he had left her for another woman, maybe she had been inferior, done something wrong, was being punished, feeling just like she had as a little girl when Dad left. If she had tried harder, maybe she could have stood with her husband on mountaintops. She heard the clank of the mail slot falling shut, the thud of mail, late, but now a good excuse to move, to do something other than brood on the past.

On her way to the front door, with the room dark, she felt along the wall for a light switch, clicked it on, and saw David's hats still on the hat rack. He never wore them much, but liked to collect them - a *campesino* hat from a trip to South America, a baseball hat, a cowboy hat. They were so much a part of the house that she had overlooked packing them away. Susan picked up her mail, always half-expecting another odd sympathy card. When there was nothing, she felt let down, strangely disappointed. Couldn't even count on consistent insanity, she thought.

The phone rang again, and she grabbed it, "Hello!" Nothing. "Mother?" Then a few clicks and the dial tone. Susan listened to the buzzing sound, set the phone down, and waited a long time for it to ring again, finally giving up and going to bed, praying that she would sleep.

# Chapter Twenty-Two

David hung up the phone and stumbled out of the bar into the brisk Wyoming evening, with the full moon rising and stars bright. What would've happened if he had said, guess what, I'm not dead? Just drunk. He pulled out the Gannettt peak postcard, damp with beer, and looked at his drunken handwriting on the back, "Dear Susan, I —" then the long unstable line, ink bleeding across the card. He crumpled it up and threw it into the street. Couldn't give up now, he thought. Not when he had run this far. He climbed in the truck, started the rattling engine, and drove out of town, weaving across the centerline and swerving away from oncoming traffic.

Bouncing over deep ruts, he drove back to the shanty, then passed out on his bunk, dreaming about his wife on the side of a red cliff melting into blood. And women waiting for him in the back alleys of a Mexican border town. Tattoo artists with demonic faces and tiny pitchforks stabbing him. The serpent with its two heads pointing in opposite directions. And Susan in the past. Once, they had to wait on a ledge in the middle of a hundred-foot climb while the lead climber maneuvered past a difficult pitch. They waited forever, eventually climbing back onto the face of the cliff, Susan falling, dangling on a rope, swinging like the pendulum of a grandfather clock.

David woke, the mountains bright from the morning sun. He glanced out the dust-covered window at a tumbleweed, and thought about the high, glaciated peaks along the Continental Divide. Now that his wife knew about his land, each moment, each second that he stayed in Wyoming, increased his chances of being caught. He knew it was risky staying on any longer, but he clung to his deed as if it were his life, and set his sights on the highest peak in Wyoming. Gannettt Peak.

David sat at the table, rubbed his face, and looked up at Evert. "You want to climb Gannettt with me?" But his friend had no desire to climb, and David muttered, "Guess I'll go alone."

While gathering his gear, he remembered the camaraderie of past climbs. Now, making decisions alone, he thought only of the danger that lie ahead, but he was determined, pursuing that elusive new life.

At the trailhead, he strapped on his pack, and disappeared into the wilderness, the pack heavy but feeling good, pulling at his shoulders. Keep moving, he told himself, want to make this a fast trip, get into the wilderness, then out before the past caught up to him. Hiking furiously, curving up a trail through tall pine and meadows strewn with boulders, clouds floating near the treetops. He hiked into the evening, balancing on logs over swift streams, following the trail along Dinwoody Creek. He set up camp next to boulders piled against trees, and vaguely recalled the camp. Maybe he and Savgren had camped there, he thought, then wished the place would transport him back to that time.

Waking before dawn, he broke camp and followed the trail as it rose above tree line, ending at a moraine field and a wall of snow, the receding terminal of Dinwoody Glacier. He stopped near a small pool with a large chunk of ice floating in it, then sat watching the mountains cast long shadows down the valley. Even though he felt desperate to go on, ascend the glacier, he knew that he had to wait, make camp. Trying for the summit late in the day would be stupid, he thought, with rocks falling from ice melting in the afternoon sun, then trying to make it back in the dark.

Two climbers descended the glacier - ant-size dots - the only people he'd seen since starting. He had hoped to see a few more, thinking that maybe he needed people to identify who he would be. But not many climbers were out. Still early in the season. Any drop in temperature could bring a blizzard.

David stood expecting the climbers to stop, but they disappeared into the moraine. He doubted they even saw him. David sat on a rock and watched the sky darken and fill with stars, then a meteor flash by, disintegrating. He searched the sky for more, for some sign from the universe, from heaven, from anything, that this was a breakthrough, a passage to another life. Nothing. He collapsed into his tent without eating, waking late in the night, drinking water and shoving a handful of mixed nuts into his mouth. He was just an animal, he thought bitterly, needing food and water.

The next two days were overcast, mist and rain swirling out of gray clouds, trapping him in his tent, sitting alone for hours. He questioned his ordinary childhood, his marriage, and he questioned climbing mountains at all. What was the point? The answer *must* be, he thought, hidden in Savgren's world of mathematics, where numbers "explained" how one wrong move in an otherwise normal life could result in chaos. Could it explain his cowardly act in the wilderness? Running away from his wife? And therefore each subsequent act after that, nothing more than a chain reaction, each movement making it less likely that he could ever go back. Given an infinite set of circumstances, is there a high probability that everyone will become a coward? *Under what circumstances,* he thought, *can I become a new man?*

During the evening of the second day, the sky cleared, and he emerged from the solitary confinement of the tent. He watched the sun sinking toward the jagged knife-edge of peaks along the Continental Divide, then sat staring at ice in a glacial pool, a white iceberg in the flat, reflecting water. He stood at the cold water's edge and took off his coat and shirt, letting the cool air revive him. But that wasn't enough. He needed something to shock life back into him. He stripped and lunged into the icy pool, his heart stopping, recovering and gasping, crawling out and standing, shivering, the shadows creeping toward him. He stood in the open air as long as he could, watching the stars, avoiding any thought of his wife, then he finally climbed into the tent and slept.

He woke to sun glistening off the snow and blinding him, and started climbing, kicking steps into the ice-crusted mountain, stopping only to drink water, pushing himself past many false summits. At least he was moving. Not wasting valuable days. By noon, however, black clouds slid in from the west. The wind was sharp and cold, his eyes watering. He climbed until he could go no further, where nothing surrounded him, catching glimpses of other peaks through the clouds. But he felt none of the exhilaration of past climbs, wanting only to share the success with someone, anyone. He felt no spiritual awakening, no transition, no leap, nothing but the fear of being tracked down like an animal, and emotionally gutted. He sat on his pack in the snow and looked down the slope at his tent, a tiny speck of blue at the edge of the glacier. Lightning cracked across the sky, hail beating down on him, stinging. He crawled under a rock ledge and waited, climbing back onto the glacier when the hail eased, descending, and finally laying in his tent, sleet swirling out of blackness. Even in these conditions, he remembered that he used to feel in awe of nature's power, but the memory was a faint shell disappearing around his wretched self. He fell asleep immediately, waking a few hours later with the heavy wet snow sagging the tent so much it nearly touched his face. He spent a cold night burrowed in his sleeping bag, rolling over, covering his head, afraid to bump the sides, afraid the tent might leak or collapse. Waking again at four in the morning, he stuck his head out and saw stars, but the trail was buried. He needed to get out, knowing that time was crucial. Get out now, or be caught. By five, he had stuffed all his wet gear into his pack, and he started slogging through the knee-deep snow, wanting only to get away from the mountains he loved.

After hours of hiking, his feet wet and feeling frostbitten, he descended into a meadow where wild flowers bloomed red and yellow, and the sun warmed him. He ran, his soaked, heavy pack beating against his back. By late evening, after hiking continually, stopping only to eat handfuls of dry cereal, he started down a long series of switchbacks. At the bottom, he encountered hikers, saying hello to them, wanting them to respond and talk. But the hikers were in another world, laughing, gawking at him as if he were wildlife they'd never seen before.

Driving back to the shanty, David steered carefully around each turn, half-expecting to see his wife wanting to rip out his heart for his lies. But the shanty looked the same, no sign of trouble, and David washed up as best he could, then trimmed his beard, noticing the gray streaks. He put on clean clothes, lay on his bunk, and stared out at the sunny day, feeling detached, the scene ethereal, heat shimmering from the hills. He was drifting off to sleep when Evert arrived, talking about how good business was, then stopping mid-sentence. "By the way, your wife called. She's comin' out."

David stared. "When?"

"'Bout a week." Evert handed him a travel brochure of San Diego with a phone number written across it, and a name. "He deals in cheap real estate. Cuts corners." David stared at the brochure showing stucco buildings painted in pastel colors, clean streets, polished lights, San Diego as an urban paradise, nothing cheap about it. Evert continued, "He has a license you can use, only you gotta be a dead guy named Dave Cregan." David felt the new name sticking to him like a tight mask burning into his skin. He rubbed his face. "He has a job for you," Evert said, "unless you had other plans."

No, David thought, he had no plans. He looked at Evert, feeling unworthy of his generosity. "Why you doing this?"

"I need the money."

"Money?"

"He takes half your commission and sends me a cut . . . Pretty simple, ain't it?"

Simple, David thought, maybe it would be just as easy to sit in a lounge chair amid the sagebrush. When his wife got close enough, he would just smile, and ask her if they could talk things over, have a normal life. But allowing himself to be caught didn't feel right, again like he was an animal, to be tracked down and killed. At the moment, he thought, he felt like a rat, not even worth hunting.

Evert laughed. "You can take the old truck. See how far it gets you." Then he looked at David and asked quietly, "I told him you like to work hard - I wasn't lyin', was I?"

Perhaps, David considered, he could head east. The closer he got to St Louis, the harder it would be to turn and run. His momentum would force redemption. Then what? Maybe he could send Susan a letter, from a "friend", arrange a meeting on "neutral" ground. But, he thought, she would hate him, justifiably.

No, he thought, he would keep heading west, to the coast, where a future unfolded for him in California. He would become a dead guy named Dave Cregan and come alive again.

Late the next morning, David thanked Evert, and watched the cowboy real estate agent leave for work, David promising to stay in touch. Then he packed meticulously in sharp contrast to his chaotic life, folding his clothes into a suitcase, snapping it shut, and pulling it off the bed.

By noon, the sky blue, cloudless, he got into the pickup, shoved the stick into gear, and headed out, driving too fast, hitting the ruts hard. A jackrabbit jumped out zigzagging wildly, and he heard a thud. Just a varmint, he thought, ranchers kill them all the time. But he felt bad, unnecessarily sensitive, his heart heavy. While concentrating on the road ahead, he was unable to shake the feeling that he was always going the wrong way.

Coming over a rise, truck pointing toward the clear sky, then slamming back down, he hit the brakes and almost crashed into an oncoming truck. The other vehicle slammed into a ravine, the driver slumped over the steering wheel. David ran to him, opened the door, and shook him. "You okay?"

The driver coughed, then pushed himself away from the steering wheel and got out of his truck. He wore a cowboy hat pulled down on his forehead and gray streaks snaked through a black, ratty beard. Climbing back onto the road, the driver wheezed and coughed.

"Where you headed?" David asked.

"Up for some huntin'." He wiped his hand on his coat.

David stared, feeling that he knew him, but couldn't quite place it, didn't *want* to, so he looked at the road ahead, then the man's truck in the ditch. "Let's get you out of there."

They gathered wood and shoved it under the tires, then tied a rope to the back and pulled the vehicle down the ravine to a point where it leveled with the dirt road.

"Thanks," the man said, then extending his callused hand with dirty fingernails. David shook his hand, the man squeezing hard for a long time before letting go, then asking, "What was your name?"

David thought about telling him, but the request made him tense, jarring loose memories of a shadowy figure, a man with a thick beard and long knotted hair. David's heart pounded and his breathing felt constricted as he backed away, the man following him.

"Hey, I just wanted to pay you back."

"That's okay. You would have done the same for me."

"I dunno about that."

"Sure you would." David eased toward his open door.

"I don't think so." The man smiled. "You Brooks?"

David stammered, "No, I . . . that's not me."

"Damn," the man responded. "I was hopin' you'd let me hunt on your land."

"You're confused. My name's Cregan."

The man stepped closer, cleared his throat again, and said, "Blucuski. Kester Blucuski."

David looked at him, the black circles under the eyes, the dirty hands.

Kester bent over coughing. "Thin air playing hell on my

lungs." He cleared his throat and spit, smearing blood onto his coat.

David backed away. "You're fine," he said, reaching for the truck door.

Suddenly, Kester stood straight, pulling his thick, black-handled knife from a sheath strapped to his leg, the knife glinting in the bright sunlight. "Yeah, I'm just fine, but you ain't." David's hands shook and his mouth felt pasty. He stared at the knife, Kester rolling it around expertly in his hand, coughing, then smiling. "How do you kill a dead man, Brooks?"

# Chapter Twenty-Three

Susan watched the police officer in the sun, sweat on his brow, dark sunglasses, notebook in hand.

"You sure there isn't anything you'd like to add?" he asked.

"No," she responded, and considered telling him about Kester's threat to kill her dead husband, but thought better of it. They'd just think she was the crazy one.

"Okay," the officer said. "We'll find this Mr Blucuski. Warn him to leave you alone. He bothers you again, you give us a call right away. We'll take care of him."

Susan felt better, and thanked the officer. She watched the police car disappear up the street, and started to go back inside when she saw Jurgan. He had parked nearby and was walking toward her. "Another break-in?" he asked.

"Why? You want to raise my premiums?"

Jurgan frowned. "You're going to Wyoming," he said.

She had told the real estate agent she would be in Dubois on July twentieth but planned on arriving the eighteenth. Maybe, she thought, she would catch her dead husband "cheating" on her. "Carson tell you that?" she asked.

Jurgan raised an eyebrow. "He thought I was coming with you."

Susan was unable to recall any time in her life when she'd traveled anywhere by herself. Now she looked at Jurgan and said, "I'm going alone."

"Not really," he responded. "I'll be right behind you."

Susan looked away, the breeze stirring the bright green leaves, trees lining the city street, leading to the park. She could see people bicycling, running, children playing. She looked at him. He was waiting for her to concede. She had seen this before, men she dated expected her to submit to their wishes. Now, Susan thought, she just didn't want the hassle. Whether she wanted Jurgan to come along or not, she thought, he would be there, following her.

Jurgan said, "I'll pick you up . . ."

Susan called her mother to say that she would not be needing a ride to the airport, and Mrs Moore immediately asked, "Someone's going with you, right?"

"My insurance agent," Susan responded.

Her mother laughed. "That's one way to get your money."

Susan gripped the phone, fighting the urge to hang up.

"I'm just happy you're not going alone," Mrs Moore said. "I don't have to worry as much."

On the way to the airport, Jurgan drove fast, cutting in and out of traffic, then waited in line at the parking lot. Susan slung her pack over her shoulder and hiked through the lot while Jurgan struggled with his small leather suitcase. Once inside the terminal, they were delayed by numerous security checks, then they sat waiting at the gate. Susan had avoided any conversation with Jurgan, but now he shifted in his plastic seat, and asked, "You travel a lot?"

"No," she responded. She looked at him and wanted to suggest that he travel back to Canada and search the woods there. But talking to him at all felt awkward.

Sitting in the cramped airline seats, Jurgan leaned across her to look out the window, Susan smelling pungent cologne. He turned to her, their faces close. "Never been west of Kansas City," he said. "Have you?"

"Yes," she responded.

"With your husband?" he asked.

Susan stared out the window, remembering a different journey, north, the flight to Winnipeg, when she was still hopeful, thinking that the trip might ease the tension, and that maybe they could talk. But, she thought, it hadn't turned out that way, had it?

After landing in Riverton, Susan waited on the curb for Jurgan to arrive with the rental car, feeling the cool, dry wind and breathing in clean air. Soon they were heading northwest on highway twenty-six, along the tree-lined Wind River, then onto the open plains, full of brush, hardly any trees, not like Missouri, which was tropical by comparison. Susan liked the vastness, the sense of freedom. Jurgan hunched over the steering wheel and peered out the window. "Damn," he said. "Sure is desolate. How does anyone live out here?"

Easy, Susan thought, enjoying the scenery, full of childhood memories, her father stopping at historical markers, her mother urging them to keep going.

Then Jurgan sat back, and asked, "How's your friend Kester?"

Susan stiffened, glanced at him. But he kept his eyes on the highway, as if he'd just asked her about college, or if she thought it was going to rain. She hadn't said a word about Blucuski, hadn't heard from him since their meeting in the bar, since filing the police report. No more strange cards. She wanted to forget about him. She stared out the window, an elk in the distance disappearing over a ridge.

"You met him at that bar," Jurgan said. "Near your house."

Susan looked at him. "How long have you been spying on me?" Then she thought, he was no different than Blucuski, except Jurgan was better at being sneaky.

"Why did you keep it a secret?" He accelerated uphill - in the distance gray, jagged peaks, and black clouds to the north.

"Why should I tell you?"

He took his eyes off the empty highway and leaned toward her. "Because," he said, "I need to know." The road curved around a mesa, dirt slopes rising to the flat top, and the car veered onto the shoulder as Jurgan asked, "Did Blucuski see a man or an animal?"

"Ask him yourself."

"I tried." Jurgan sped down a long steep slope, braking. "Wouldn't tell me."

Susan smiled, then lied, and felt good about it. "Didn't tell me either." She owed Jurgan nothing, and she felt a deep distrust of him. Let him get his own information.

Jurgan looked at her. "Why did he want to see you?"

"Crazy stuff," she said, "about being in love with me . . ." Susan sat back in her seat, and looked out the window at the dry terrain: tumbleweeds, barbed wire, rock outcropping, a few trees in rock-strewn pastures.

Early evening, Jurgan drove past a campground into Dubois, slowing, hunched over the steering wheel, peering out at the streets and staring at people. They rolled to a stop at the real estate office, climbed out of the rental car and stretched, then went inside. The lone agent got up quickly to greet them.

Jurgan said, "We're looking for Evert Carson."

The agent looked at Susan. "That'd be me. Who are you?"

"Name's Jurgan. This is Susan Brooks."

"Pleased to meet you, ma'am." Carson glanced at the clock, then shuffled through papers. "I didn't expect you for another couple days."

Jurgan looked around the office. "Mrs Brooks wants to see her property."

Carson shrugged. "No problem." He walked out the door, climbed into his truck.

Jurgan ran to the rental car, yelling, "You want us to follow you?"

Carson stuck his arm out the window, waving them on, then pulled away from the curb and sped far ahead.

Jurgan started the engine, growling and popping in the thin air, the tires screeching as he pulled away. "Dammit," he said, trying to see past a car that had turned in front of them, "Where is he?"

Susan braced her hand against the dashboard as Jurgan edged toward the centerline ready to pass the slow-moving car.

# Chapter Twenty-Four

Kester lunged, knife scraping against the metal door.

David jumped to the side and dove, rolling off the road, down the steep slope on the other side, sage branch puncturing his leg. He ran, his leg bleeding, down into a gully, behind a clump of aspen, and looked back.

Kester stood at the road, staring, slashing the air with his knife, then he turned away and pounded the hood of his truck. He was gone for a moment, then came back with a rifle. He slid down the embankment, holding the rifle chest-high, and started walking toward the aspen.

"Brooks!" Kester yelled, coughing and hacking into the dry wind, rifle poised.

David dug his fingers into the ground, hiding in the gully, frantically trying to disappear. He peered out from a few scrawny aspen, thin twigs for branches. A bullet would slice right through them, he thought. He felt his leg bleeding, dirt sticking to the blood. He heard buzzing, then crackling like a dragonfly, unsure if it was an insect or, he thought, his mind on fire with this insanity, the noise loud in his ears. Got to get out of here, he thought, not enough cover. He rolled over, down the gully, onto his feet. Go, he thought, then heard the crack of the rifle, and he imagined the bullet hitting him in the back, tearing through his heart. He leaped behind a boulder, waiting, trying desperately to get his breath. He closed his eyes and remembered the cabin in Canada, thinking his chances had been better then, and he wished to God he could travel back in time, fight for his wife. He watched Kester scanning the landscape, the brush jerking in the wind, and he sneaked away from the boulder, following high sagebrush, praying he wouldn't be seen. The brush led over a ridge where the ground sloped into more aspen, and he started running, leg stiff. Behind him, he heard another crack, and he fell, then crawled. *Get up, away.* He ran past the trees only to find himself trapped by a steep thirty-foot cliff. He would have to climb it or turn around and face Kester's gunfire. He looked at the cliff, found an easy way up, and started climbing, blood oozing from his leg. Near the top, handholds faded away into smooth rock with only one thin crack. The wind died down as he leaned away looking at the difficult pitch. Hearing Kester walking slowly past the aspen, David knew he had to move, but his arms felt like lead. Couldn't hang on any longer. *Climb, you bastard.* He jammed his right hand into the small crack, and immediately felt two fingers go numb, the old injury from the accident. His hand slipped, and he pivoted out, dangling for a moment, Kester shouldering the rifle, aiming.

David jammed his good hand into the crack and felt his skin tearing as he pulled himself over the edge, bullets ricocheting, rock splinters cutting his face. He lurched forward, falling into dirt and scrub, and crawled away, the wind fierce on top. Kester would have to hike around the cliff, or climb it. Either way, David thought, it would buy time. He struggled to his feet and ran, limping, circling toward the road. He stopped and looked back. Nothing. Just the wind. The sun sinking into the mountains.

He limped, his truck not far. Then he saw Kester retracing their steps, running through the brush, stopping.

David heard the rifle, bullet zinging past, and felt sick to his stomach, climbing into the truck and trying to start the engine. Pushing on the gas, he turned the key, but the engine sputtered and died. *Come on*, he thought, *start, come on you piece of . . .* Kester staggered onto the road, then doubled over, wheezing. David turned the key again, but still nothing. "Goddammit!" he yelled, then leaped out and ran at Kester, tackling him, both of them rolling in the dirt. David felt fists pounding against his back, and he pushed away, sat in the dirt, trying to breathe, Kester kneeling, the rifle on the ground between them. Kester smiled, blood around his teeth, dripping from his mouth, then slowly pulled his knife in one fluid motion, lunging, the blade inches from David's gut. David grabbed Kester's wrist as they fell, knife plunging into dirt, David breaking free, crawling, stretching for the rifle, grabbing it by the barrel and turning in time to club Kester on the back.

Kester grunted, then lunged, both of them tumbling down the embankment, the rifle landing in the brush. David looked for it, but couldn't find it. *Where is it*, he thought, *has to be here*. Kester lay a few feet from him, still gripping the knife, moaning, rolling onto his side. Screw it, David thought, then scuttled back to the road, out of breath, and ran, leg stiff, arm aching, climbing into the truck, starting it, thumping and rattling, the engine grumbling to life, gears grinding. Kester crawled out, stood, and hurled himself at the truck door, knife scraping metal. "Shit," David yelled, pressing the gas pedal to the floor, swerving, but hearing a sickening thump against the back fender, looking in his rear-view mirror at Kester lying on his back, holding the knife up waving it at the sky, casting a long, crooked shadow on the rutted road.

Over the next rise, David saw Evert stopping and getting out, waving frantically. David drove alongside him, and tried to talk, his voice crackling and hoarse. "Might know who I am. Somehow, found me . . ."

Evert looked at him. "Christ Almighty, what happened?"

"Trying to tell . . . Kester . . . back there . . ."

"What? Who the hell—"

"I don't know how . . ."

Evert looked back. "Your wife's right behind me. I went ahead." David slumped against the steering wheel. Is this how he wanted it? Cut, bloodied, a wounded animal? Evert stared. "You better go. Unless you wanna be caught."

"What about Blucuski?" David asked.

Evert shrugged. "Like I said, I ain't no Jesus. Go. Or stay. Your choice."

He looked at Evert. He could accept being caught, but not like this. Not like an animal, and not while he still had a chance to get away, gain a new life. San Diego. A new life, he thought. Further west.

David drove away, each bump making him wince, coming to a fork, one leading straight to his wife, the other going nowhere. He shifted, the truck rolling back, then easing forward. He stared straight ahead and saw a small car, headlights shining into the purple sky.

## Chapter Twenty-Five

"Son of a bitch." Jurgan slammed on the brakes, then slowly eased over a deep rut. "You'd think the bastard would at least stay in sight." He stopped at the fork in the road, wind whistling through a crack in the window. "Well, do we turn or not?"

"I don't know." Susan folded the map.

"What do you mean, you don't know?"

"Go straight." She tossed the map behind her.

The wind howled, and black clouds slid over the high peaks. With the car's underbelly scraping rock, they drove toward Liar's Creek, suddenly coming upon Carson's truck blocking the way.

"What the hell?" Jurgan said, stopping, getting out.

Carson ran toward them yelling, "Go back."

Suddenly, Kester Blucuski staggered in front of them, gripping his knife, slumping to his knees. Susan shivered, and started walking to Kester, ignoring Jurgan's shouts to stop, the wind blowing a tumbleweed.

She stood frozen, staring at Blucuski. "Why are you here?" she screamed, waiting, watching him cough up blood. Did Kester break into her house looking for the deed? How would he even know about the property? It didn't seem right. Someone must have told him. But who? And why?

He crumpled to the ground, lying with his legs bent close to his stomach. She knelt beside him. "Why?" she screamed again.

Kester muttered, trying to say something, the wind taking his words like dust over the plains. Suddenly, he hooked his arm around Susan's neck, and pulled her close, the smell of alcohol and blood, his chest heaving, body convulsing. She shoved hard, trying to break free. Carson pulled at Kester's arm, bending it away, and she stumbled back, standing with fists clenched. Kester tore at his own shirt, his body twisted, mouth open, blood dripping into the dirt.

Jurgan turned away, holding a bandanna over his mouth. Carson put his foot on Kester and shoved - no response - then Carson disappeared down the embankment.

Susan stared at the stiffening body, and trembled, wanting someone to put an arm around her, make her feel better, but she had no one. She stood, slowly opening her fists. What was Blucuski doing here? She breathed in the smell of sagebrush and death, and stared at Jurgan's silhouette against the darkening sky. Only one logical answer, she thought. "You hired him," she said.

Jurgan wiped his mouth. "Yeah, right."

"How much were you paying him?" The wind blew her hair in her eyes as she faced him.

Jurgan responded, "I just said he could check it out . . . if he wanted. That's all. No big deal."

"You bastard."

"I didn't tell him to harass you. He did that on his own."

Jurgan turned away, but Susan grabbed his arm. "How much for this whole damn investigation? Why not just give me the money?"

Jurgan smirked. "That's what you'd like, isn't it?"

Susan looked at him, understanding fully that he believed she was in collusion with her husband. "Is that what this is about?" she asked. "You think I'm a crook?"

Carson climbed back onto the road, carrying a rifle. "Looks like he was hunting. Probably saw something. Decided to go after it." He looked at the rifle. "But this ain't his. Neither is that truck." Carson looked back down the road - flashing lights, the sheriff pulling up, stopping, and walking toward them.

160

Susan and Jurgan waited in their car while Carson spoke with the sheriff then came to their window. "Your friend Kester," he said, "cut up an old man, stole his truck."

Susan thought about Blucuski. Should she have done more to stop him? She had acted responsibly, she thought, filing a report. Jurgan was the one who used Blucuski. Let him deal with the mess.

"Did he kill him?" Jurgan asked.

Carson leaned over and looked at Jurgan. "Slashed up his forearm a little, but he'll be okay."

Jurgan nodded, then asked, "How long do we have to stay here?"

"Sheriff wants us back in town."

"Damn," Jurgan muttered.

They started the arduous drive back down the rutted road, the deputy passing, going to the body, flashing lights pitching like a ship in a storm.

At the sheriff's office, Susan drank coffee and stared at a jail cell while the sheriff asked pointed questions about Kester? Did you know him? Why did he come to Wyoming? Jurgan trying to respond. "He was looking for a man named David Brooks who owns—"

"But this Brooks, he's dead already, is that right?" The sheriff wrinkled his brow.

Jurgan responded, "Yes, that's right, in Canada."

"When was that?"

"Last year."

The sheriff turned to Susan. "And this Blucuski, you filed a report, something about him being in *love* with you?"

Susan looked away, the wind gusting, a giant tumbleweed flying down the streets of Dubois. "He was seeing a psychiatrist," she said vacantly, responding to the questions as if she were in the wrong place, wrong time. Should be somewhere else, but not sure where.

The sheriff shook his head, and turned to Jurgan. "And you're sticking to your story that you paid this psycho to come

161

out here? Find somebody who died last year?"

"No money," he said, "I merely suggested he could look—"

"Right." The sheriff snorted. "I got it. Nothing in writing. Evert, you make any sense of this?"

"Not a lot."

The sheriff let them go, and they headed back up to Liar's Creek, this time Carson driving slowly, allowing them to follow along closely through the black, windy night. Finally, they stopped, headlights reflecting off a long stovepipe sticking out of a small shanty with a narrow path leading to it. Between gusts, somewhere in the distance, Susan heard coyotes yelping. As Carson unlocked the door, she imagined her husband inside, next to a warm fire, smiling, saying hello, then introducing her to an athletic woman, able to hike and climb with David.

But the inside was drafty and dark. Carson turned on the bare light bulb dangling over the small kitchen table. Beer bottles lay on the counter, two plates in the sink. "I been staying here," he said, "taking care of the place." He opened an old icebox and set out beer. "Care for a shot of whiskey with it?" Without waiting for an answer, he poured whiskey for everyone and immediately downed his.

Jurgan asked, "Someone else been here?"

Carson frowned. "Not likely."

Jurgan leaned forward. "When did Mr Brooks purchase this . . . ranch?"

Carson took another drink and turned to Susan. "Pretty cozy, ain't it?"

"Were you my husband's friend?"

"Yeah, you could say that." He shrugged. "Sometimes I'd have to charge him for upkeep and the like. That's when I just moved in. Saved him expense. I told him about how good the huntin' was and that he should get out here." Carson rubbed his face. "He did too, came out a couple times. Then he musta met you and got distracted. . . I was real sorry to hear about your loss, ma'am."

Susan felt tears well up but fought them back. She was through crying about her husband. She just wanted peace of mind, a resolution that she now realized had been eluding her.

Jurgan leaned forward. "When was the last time you saw him?"

Carson shrugged. "Haven't seen him since the last time he came out here."

"When was that?"

"While ago."

"When?"

"Mister, you're startin' get on my nerves. You got a burr up your ass about something?"

The wind rattled the windows. Jurgan rubbed his temples. "Where are we supposed to sleep?"

Carson stood, and turned to Susan. "Excuse me, ma'am, I haven't been too mannerly. You must be tuckered out . . . damn, after today, I'm beat too." He showed them the two small bedrooms. "If you don't mind, I'll just stay here tonight. Show you the land in the morning." He unrolled a mat and sleeping bag for himself on the kitchen floor.

Susan fell onto the hard bunk near a rattling window, and looked out at blackness. She laid there a long while, pulling the covers over her, an oddly familiar smell, then passing out, dreaming that her husband knocked on the door. In the dream, she opened the door and let him get in bed with her. He was making love to her. While not wanting him to stop, she resisted, suddenly realizing that her husband's hands were grimy, that he had a black beard streaked with gray. She woke with a start, worried that someone might have heard her. Susan lay awake for a long time, listening to the storm, rain pounding the shanty. His spirit was out there, somewhere in the night, she thought. Tomorrow she would say her goodbyes, push David's death firmly into the past and get on with her life.

# Chapter Twenty-Six

The dirt road became nothing more than tire tracks before finally disappearing into the sagebrush where David stopped and got out, the wind beating against him, lightning cracking. He had no idea where he was. He knew only that he was in trouble. He remembered hiking with his father, lightning striking treetops, snapping limbs, his dad laughing, telling him not to worry, and they marched bravely through the downpour, David wanting to believe his father could hold up his big hands and block thunderbolts.

David backed the truck into the sage, hoping it wouldn't puncture a tire, then pulled back onto the dirt, looking for another route. Kester Blucuski, he thought, why had Kester tracked him down, remembering the hunter in Canada, and the name in the newspaper, the man who carried Susan out of the woods to the hospital. David recalled leaning over his wife in that cabin, a moment now receding into the past at light speed, yet . . . forever present. Had Blucuski not been there, had David woke Susan from her nightmare, what would have happened? There was no way to know. No way to go back and nullify the moment, go back and divert Kester before he became entangled in their lives.

David drove into the storm, waves of rain pounding down and turning the road slick as ice, truck sliding sideways into the sage. He frantically tried to steer. The rain eased and he rolled onto rocky ground, coming to a split in the road. Which way? Frantic, the thought of Kester's knife carving into his heart, making him sweat, David gripped the steering wheel, pressed hard on the gas, and veered left.

He drove through the windy black night, feeling like he was gaining altitude but aware only of his headlights, and the rain. He saw a small yellow light in the distance. Nearing it, he felt like he had been there before, not fully recognizing the landscape until he drove the truck, sliding down a hill, braking and fish-tailing next to the shanty.

Evert was rolling up a car window, shutting the car door, the yellow light going out. David parked, got out. Evert stepped forward. "What the hell are you doing back here?"

"Don't know," David said. "Blucuski?"

"Dead," Evert responded, then looked back at the shanty. "You comin' in? Or you going to make me get all wet?"

"She's in there?"

"You bet she is."

David stared at Evert, the wind picking up again. He *could* step back into his old life, go inside, huddle by a warm fire, try to straighten out the absurdity. Or he could drive away, down the treacherous road through blinding rain. With Kester dead, he thought, David Brooks was still presumed dead. He could become Dave Cregan and start over. Kill Brooks once and for all, and become a different person, someone who might settle into a "better" life. Wasn't that the plan?

Starting over would be easier, wouldn't it, and why not take the easy route? That's what everyone did anyway, wasn't it? Faced with tough choices, people took the only path that worked for them. And once the decision was made, all other possibilities disappeared. In such a world, was there any room for regret or redemption?

David turned away, rain pouring out of the blackness, and drove away from the shanty, down the crooked road.

# Chapter Twenty-Seven

Sunlight blazed in a deep blue sky as Susan woke groggy, the mountains starkly gray, snow-capped in the morning light. She came to these mountains looking for her husband, not really expecting to find him alive, although the possibility nagged at her. She did expect to find out more about him, make peace with him, having lost him without really knowing him, why they were married. She lingered in the kitchen, waiting for Carson and Jurgan, finally waking them and rushing them through breakfast and outside. If anywhere, she might understand her husband by seeking the high ground. That's where David would be, at least that's where she hoped his spirit might still linger in the wind and cool air. There, in the mountains, she wanted to finally rid herself of those vague feelings that David was still alive.

They hiked along the creek, then up a steep ridge, Susan keeping up with Carson while Jurgan trailed far behind. They followed the ridge as it rose higher into rocky crags, finally stopping at a cliff with a clear view of the Continental Divide, sunlight glistening off snowfields. Susan sat alone on a rock ledge while Carson walked to the other side of the ridge overlooking the foothills. Susan remembered vacations with David. She always wanted to stop and look at the wild flowers while he hiked faster, pushed on harder, as if he were running from her. Looking back on it, she thought, she should have confronted him, asked him to slow down. She recounted the trips: the Ozarks, Great Smoky Mountains, and the White Mountains. Then they climbed Mt Rainier. She had never felt so physically beaten in all her life. Was it after that trip when they started arguing openly, even though they'd been courteous before?

Jurgan slogged up the incline, then sat next to her, sweat dripping from his face. A drop dangled on the end of his nose. "What's the rush?" he panted. "Not a damn thing out here."

Susan stared at the snowy peaks. "My husband liked it."

"How do you know?" Jurgan looked around. "He told you?"

Susan knew what he was trying to imply, that she had been here with David, knew about it all along, knew that David would "hide out" here while she collected the insurance money. She looked at him. "You're an asshole."

Jurgan eased back from the edge of the rock. "Carson give you the deed yet?"

"Why?" she asked. "You want to buy the place?" Then she stood. "How long are you going to follow me around?" Having Jurgan in her life would always remind her of her husband. If she wanted to forget, and live, she would have to get rid of him.

Jurgan frowned. "As long as it takes."

Susan shook her head, turned away, and hiked over to Carson. She stood next to him and looked out at the high rolling foothills, and a herd of tan and white antelope.

Carson reached into his coat pocket, pulled out a thick, crumpled envelope full of papers, and tapped it on her arm. "I guess you'll be wantin' this?"

She looked at him, then opened the envelope, the deed, with its notary circle and legalese, almost as good as a death certificate. "What was my husband like?" she asked.

"What do you mean, ma'am?"

"You can live with a person and not know a lot about him."

Carson looked at her. "He liked to climb mountains, liked to push it. Ambitious person, probably too much for his own good. But you knew that."

"Yes," she answered, "he could be hard on himself."

"And he liked spendin' time alone . . ."

"He went on business trips, but that was work. I went with

him everywhere else." She remembered the way they fit so easily into each other's arms. But that was at the beginning. Toward the end, they avoided each other. She thought of David standing alone, along the ridge, gazing up at the peaks. "Did he have girlfriends around here?"

Carson laughed. "Not that I know of."

The sun felt warm on her legs, and she picked a crimson Indian Paintbrush.

"Maybe," Carson said, closing one eye against the sunlight, "things will work out for you."

"You talk like he's still alive." Susan dropped the flower. "Is he?"

"You were with him," he responded. "You believe he's alive?"

She stared at the horizon, the boundless country. "No," she said, "I can't."

# Chapter Twenty-Eight

Unable to shake the feeling that someone was still after him, David waited for the Northbound "Tijuana trolley" as it rolled through San Diego subdivisions, on its way downtown. Almost every waking moment during his drive to the West Coast, he felt like someone was following him. He ate in his truck, parked in the shadows, and slept at rest stops. He spoke as little as possible, avoiding vacationers, fast-food employees, anyone who tried to be friendly. He watched people but always quickly averted his gaze when they looked back. Now, in San Diego, standing next to the steel rails in a chilling breeze, he stared at three Mexicans who spoke rapid Spanish and laughed. He remembered going to Mexico years earlier, the people in the small towns smiling and waving at him as if he were a celebrity, and he wanted to climb one of the volcanoes surrounding Mexico City. His wife, he recalled, had not been enthusiastic about the climb.

The bright red trolley rolled to a stop, sparks popping from the wires. David climbed on and sat near an exit. The Mexicans sat near him, and he listened to their voices blend with the sound of the clattering metal wheels on the track. He could comprehend only stray words like *gringo, tonto,* and *verdad,* their tone harsh, and he knew at once that these particular Mexicans were not anything like the campesinos he remembered. These people were rough, probably would knife him for his money, or just for fun, see the blood flow. Several stops later, worrying that *he* was their "stupid gringo", he got off at the north end of the line, downtown San Diego, the Mexicans also getting off, and walking behind him. He passed a coffee shop, went inside, and watched the laughing Mexicans pass.

Behind the café counter, a deeply tanned woman stared at him with big brown eyes. A cheap, silver-plated necklace full of charms circled her neck, one charm at her throat, a serpent with another head instead of a tail. Like his dream, he thought. She asked him if he wanted coffee.

"No thanks," he mumbled and hurried out.

Looking up between buildings, he could see clear blue sky and a thin cloud tailing over the summit of a skyscraper, and he felt relieved knowing the possible origins of his serpent dreams. In Mexico, he must have seen the pendant. His memory had been distorted by time, and illness. He had thought about it while barbecuing fresh game in Wyoming. And now, he remembered stopping in the small Mexican town for food, eating tortillas filled with sinewy meat and grainy rice. Later, he saw raw flanks of red, bloody meat hanging from rusty hooks, flies buzzing around them. It had been a strange experience, lying in the hay of a campesino's home, feverish, his insides churning with Montezuma's revenge, then being hit hard by what he later discovered was an allergic reaction. Could hardly breathe. Made him want to know more about Montezuma. He even read a little about the Aztec, now trying to recall what he had read.

David pulled out a slip of paper from his shirt pocket, checked the address, and walked a few blocks. He stopped in front of a real estate office that looked just as Evert had described it - a small dark hole in a big building. Desks were crammed together side by side with a narrow passage to the back. Upfront, a secretary who looked at him.

"Hello," he said, "my name's Dave Cregan. I believe I am expected." Evert's "friend" stood from behind a desk, walked over and immediately slapped David on the back, then talked about money and how to make it, giving him books and a stack of paperwork, including a phony real estate license with Cregan's name.

"Cregan used to work for us," the office manager said, "before his heart crapped out."

"Won't somebody notice I'm not him?"

"Nah, he worked in the LA office. Besides, this is the West Coast, agents come and go."

Later that night, David sat on the floor of an empty apartment, drank beer, and gazed out the window, his view constricted by nearby buildings. Jets roared overhead, descending into North Island Naval Air Station. They flew in low, coming off the ocean like huge, mechanical seagulls. Once, at the aerospace company, he worked obsessively on those jets. But now, he unrolled his sleeping bag, laid down on the hard floor, and stared into the blackness.

David woke, gray morning light filling his unfurnished apartment, his arm stiff, fingers numb. He stood, staring at the bare floor. Cregan. He could no longer be Brooks, and he would never again work in aerospace. Someone might mistake him for David Brooks. But who was Cregan? He made coffee, and studied real estate books, maps, and appraisals.

Before meeting his first clients, Dave Cregan put on a suit and tie, trimmed his beard, and combed back his hair, the thin, crooked scar running between his eyes. The scar had healed into a pale line, but had not disappeared as he had hoped. During the meeting, he rubbed his fingers, and looked from the man to the woman, a young Mexican couple who shifted easily between English and Spanish. They were the first of many as Dave Cregan worked long hours, often taking the deals no one else wanted, owners who cussed him out, demanded he give up his commission, divorcing couples who labeled everything *his* or *hers* and shouted at each other while he was trying to sell their home.

After several months, he stopped worrying that someone might track him down. Other than an insane person, who would want to? Why should they? He had given up everything. And in dealing with the small ethically indifferent office, he was paid in cash, no official record of his earnings. But he wanted a "normal" life, and respectable work. And he was beginning to resent the fifty percent cut out of his earnings, Evert getting only a fraction of it.

On several deals, he worked with a woman named Barbara who represented the other clients. She was also the office manager of a competing company. Barbara told him that he could do better. "If we worked at the same place," she said, "we could see a lot more of each other."

David sat across from Barbara, ivy snaking across her large desk, touching the off-white, peach-trimmed walls. She handed him application forms. While reading the forms, he wondered about his social security number. Should he use Brooks or Cregan? Then he worried about taxes, and leaving an obvious trail. "Can I fill these out later?"

She frowned and sat straight in her expensively cushioned chair, her dark hair just touching the lapels of her gray suit. "Sure, but I need someone to do a closing for me tomorrow. Can you do it?"

David stared at the ivy winding its way around her lamp. "I think so."

"I'll get you started," she said, "but then I have to leave for another deal."

That evening, he drove to his old office, and searched the files for Cregan. The man was divorced, kids grown, wife bought an RV and roamed around with her "lover". No social security disbursements. Then he searched the Internet, but with each click and scan he encountered increasingly useless information, and no way to legally change the social security number. He found case after case of fraud, but in all of them people were trying to take *out* money. No one paid *into* the system. Feeling relatively safe, David completed the form using Cregan's number.

The next morning, driving through dense fog, he arrived at the title company an hour ahead of schedule and read through the papers. Nothing unusual. Should be easy. The couple purchasing the house was putting twenty percent down and they had already paid five thousand in earnest money. He flipped to the mortgage company's settlement statement. Typed clearly at the top of the page was the borrower's name and address. They were from St Louis. He stared at the name, Len Riggs, transferred by McSoren Aircraft Company, the same company where David had worked. Had he ever dealt with Riggs? McSoren was a big company, but David had contact with many of its employees. The door swung open. He jumped, the papers falling to the floor. Barbara entered. "You're here early," she said. "I'm impressed."

He looked down the hall. She was alone. "It looks fairly straightforward." He picked up the settlement papers.

"It is, but be careful, the guy's an engineer. A stickler for details."

David was trying to remember all the engineers he'd met when Len Riggs and his wife arrived. Riggs looked vaguely familiar - closely cropped hair, and the way he tapped the pencils in the front pocket of this white shirt. But it could be any one of many engineers.

"So," Riggs said, "looks like we have a lot to cover here." He flipped through the papers, looked at Barbara and asked, "You think it's okay?"

She nodded and said, "Looks good to me."

"Well, I know this sounds bad," Riggs said, "but I feel a little uncomfortable with Barbara leaving."

David stared at him - the hair, nose, everything beginning to suggest that they had met.

"Mr Cregan is very qualified," Barbara said, "and I've looked it all over carefully."

"Okay," Riggs responded, then began reading. Barbara excused herself, reminding David that they would meet later.

Riggs read every word and scrutinized every point, handing papers to his wife who signed them and waited for the next. David sat and stared, occasionally forcing a smile. When he did speak, he cleared his throat. About midway through, Riggs leaned back, stretched, and took a postcard out his front pocket, looked at it, then showed it to David - a warplane taking off from a test facility in Maryland. "You know anything about warplanes?" Riggs asked.

David hands shook and he put them under the table. "Not much."

Riggs tapped his pen on the desk. "Well I don't know a damn thing about all this paperwork. Could you explain it to me?"

"I could . . . but I would bore you to death."

Riggs laughed, and started flipping through the papers and signing them.

His wife asked, "Are you from San Diego, Mr Cregan?"

"No. Not originally."

"Where are you from?" she asked.

"Chicago."

"Really?" she said, smiling. "Len is from Chicago."

David stiffened, having been to the "windy city" only a few times. He listened to her talk about Lake Michigan, the near-north side, the Museum of Natural History. Riggs handed the rest of the paperwork to his wife, then sat stone-faced. Not knowing if Riggs was looking at him or not, David blinked and said, "Looks like a good deal."

"Have we met before?" Riggs asked.

"I don't think so."

"Where'd you say you were from?"

David hesitated, then said, "Chicago."

"Maybe that's it."

"It's a big city."

"I used to love flying over the lake."

His wife signed the last paper, and the deal looked as if it were going to end mercifully. But, while they were shaking hands, Riggs squeezed hard. "You ever work for McSoren?"

"No."

Riggs stared. "You look like someone."

David tightened his handshake. "Don't we all?"

"Yeah, guess so." Riggs let go, and turned away, the door shutting behind him, and David exhaled, rubbed his face. The door opened again and Riggs rushed back in. "Wife left her purse." He grabbed the handbag, glancing at David as he left.

David got into his car, started the engine, then leaned back and closed his eyes. *Riggs didn't recognize me, didn't recognize Brooks*. But, he thought, the fear welling up from his gut disturbed him. *Haven't I made the leap yet, into this new life? My God, he thought, I have a new name, job, identity. What else will make me forget the past?* After a few minutes, he remembered his "date" with Barbara, and he hoped that she might be the missing component to a complete life. He shoved the car into gear and drove to a bar near the beach, Barbara in her gray suit sitting at a window table, looking at her watch. They had a few drinks and watched the rolling surf, and Barbara talked about enjoying her success and making lots of money, but it wasn't everything. They left the bar, took off their shoes and walked on the beach, the breaking surf surging around them, the gulls screeching overhead, the ocean glimmering deep blue, in constant turmoil, small whitecaps in the distance. She plodded through the sand awkwardly in her knee-length skirt, carrying her shoes in her left hand, leaving her other hand free to be taken. She asked if he preferred dinner out, or at her place. But he didn't care.

While driving onto the highway, he watched the darkening eastern skyline. He followed Barbara into an apartment complex, a maze of streets until she finally parked.

"Maybe I should go," he said, feet illuminated by landscape lights.

"Why would you want to do that?" she asked.

"I don't know . . ."

She took his hand and led him inside. Her apartment smelled clean, bright pastel furniture and thick white carpet. While pouring wine, she said, "It's been a while since I had anybody over."

David set his wine on her glass table. He felt like a cheating husband, even though the new Dave Cregan was an unmarried man. But what sort of man would he be? He didn't feel good enough for Barbara. Need more time, he thought, had to shake all remnants of Brooks. "I . . ." he said, "I'm tired."

"So am I," she said, getting up, glancing toward the bedroom. She stood close to him. "We had fun. Didn't we?"

"Yes," he said, "but . . ." He walked to the door, then stepped into the hallway. "Maybe some other time," he said.

David shivered, always surprised at how cold the nights could get in San Diego. He drove South toward his apartment, but felt compelled to keep going, and he passed his exit, heading for Tijuana, where he belonged, mingling with strippers and prostitutes.

# Chapter Twenty-Nine

While drinking bitter, cold coffee, Susan stared at her research paper on Aztec Civilization. She wanted to know why her father had studied the Aztec who were advanced intellectually yet shrouded in bizarre, brutal ritual. She looked out the back window at long shadows slanting across the sparse lawn, and the yellow leaves clinging to branches. She flipped through a book and found Chacmool, a man with legs and arms bent backward, holding a plate. Shuffling through her notes, she found a quote from an archaeologist, "We learn about ourselves by digging up the past . . ." Her dad used to say the same thing. What had she learned digging up the past in Wyoming? The cat leapt from the window sill and purred against her legs. "Wasn't much to learn," she said, petting the cat, "was there?" But, she thought, even though she had learned very little about her husband's past, she had gained a resolution for herself. He was dead.

But she couldn't help thinking about those cards. Had Blucuski sent them? She had not received one since their meeting in the bar. She would never know why he chose those words. She had always assumed the "he" referred to David. Or maybe Kester himself. But it could just as easily refer to her father, the words now resonating in her own heart. Suddenly, her marriage made sense, referring her continually back to her childhood, her father walking with her in the woods, making her feel important, like a grown-up when he asked her which way they should go, honestly asking her opinion. Decisions she had been reluctant to make ever since her father died. No one, she thought, ever fully gets over the loss of a loved one.

Accepting the death of her husband was difficult, but she felt relieved having done so, knowing that she had already taken many steps toward becoming a whole individual. But now, she became painfully aware that she had never accepted her father's death, and the complete silence of the house suddenly overwhelmed her. An old car rattling up the street brought relief, interrupting the quiet. My dad, she thought, what made him leave his little girl to visit godforsaken places? Susan squeezed her eyes shut, a little girl again, insisting that he *can't* be dead. *Please God, I won't ask for anything ever again.* She remembered yelling at her mother, why did you let him go? After that, Dad's little girl felt at fault, crying for a long time.

Now, Susan lay on the bed watching the room turn gray, then dark, and she listened to an ambulance, then the creaking of the house, contracting in the cooling night air. She remembered as a teenager, and a young woman, feeling okay for a while. She was never alone, but always lonely.

The night took forever to pass into a gray Monday morning, Susan slipping in and out of sleep. The Wyoming deed, she thought, eliminated all doubt, and now she should submit the insurance claim, cash in on David's corpse.

Susan paged through her notebooks and found a pamphlet. She'd been carrying it around for weeks, afraid to fill it out, but also afraid not to. She stared at the pamphlet, photographs of sprawling Mexico City, other photos of snow-capped volcanoes. Another of an Aztec god. She studied it, then flipped through her notes, finding a description of Huitzilopochtli, the war god, a god that required human sacrifices. Did horrible bloody carnage appeal to tourists? But another photo showed the university where she could learn the language, and she wanted to go, earn credit toward her degree, and understand why her father went to Mexico. But she didn't have the money. Should that stop her? She grabbed a pen and filled out the form. Then she headed for her mother's to ask for another loan.

Susan drove past trees bulldozed over, huge trunks snapped, sharp wood sticking up like spears, into the last remaining wooded area where her childhood home stood surrounded by destruction. She found her mother in the bedroom, wiping dust from a frame, carefully packing photographs into a box. Susan looked through the photos, pictures of her father standing next to a grass hut, hand in his thick hair, smiling. She found one that must have been taken shortly before his death. He stood with his arm leaning on the shoulder of a short man with a broad smile, small round stomach and ruddy face. "Who's this?" she asked.

"That's Professor Menendez. If you're going to Mexico City, you must see him." She handed Susan a letter. "Give him this."

Susan read aloud, "I hope this letter finds you in good spirits . . ." A jet roared low overhead, rattling picture frames on the walls. Susan frowned, and said, "Mom, you need to get out of this house."

"Don't worry about me." She patted Susan's arm. "Go to Mexico."

# Chapter Thirty

David parked at the border and got out, the night hazy and yellow. He followed a wide sidewalk, drawn by the smell of burning meat and tortillas, and smoke wafting over the Tijuana "river", a concrete waterway resembling an open sewer. The sidewalk led him zigzagging up over the sewer-border, past brightly colored murals, swirling scenes of bloody revolution, to a street lined with dirty yellow taxis. He stood, hesitant to walk up the dark street crowded with peddlers. Young American tourists wearing jeans and knit shirts climbed out of the taxis. They carried full shopping bags, bottles of tequila, and started walking back across the border, a different route than the one David had taken. For a moment, he thought about running up the street, into the dark Mexican world. But he had just come from such loneliness and misery in Wyoming. He came to San Diego for a new life. If he wanted to visit Tijuana, he thought, he'd better do it as a tourist.

He joined the shoppers and followed them, passing spotlights illuminating a huge Mexican flag, snake writhing in the eagle's talons, then through Customs, the agent singling him out, pulling him aside, asking him to empty his pockets. David watched the others leave while he handed over his wallet with Cregan's name on an expired, temporary driver's permit. The customs agent looked inside the wallet, held it close to his nose, then handed it back and let David go. Relieved, he hurried to his car, determined to reinvent himself as Dave Cregan, and form a relationship with the nice-looking, professional real estate agent, his colleague.

The next morning, he phoned Barbara and apologized for leaving her apartment so soon, forcing himself to act normal, the way a good, honest man might ask a woman to dinner. But over oysters and shark steaks, Barbara said, "I just love the weather here."

He swallowed shark and blurted out, "You wanna go to Tijuana?" He stared at her, hoping that she could help carve out his new identity. Her response would help give him direction. If she said yes, then Mexico would be a part of Dave Cregan's memory.

Barbara's eyes widened. She chewed her food, wiped her mouth and said, "No one has ever asked me."

David looked out the restaurant window at the sun still relatively high over the Pacific and he poured the last of the wine. "Let's do it then."

"Now?"

"Why not? It's early."

She gulped her wine, and they walked a few blocks to catch the trolley, boarding with other tourists heading south. They got out following the wide sidewalk winding up over the Tijuana river, this time David noticing that someone had painted giant apelike footprints, leading into town.

Taxi drivers swarmed, their voices rising in an incessant question, "Taxi? Taxi?" Vendors sold plastic rings, gold-plated pendants, and greasy tortillas. Old women begged, children sold Chiclets, and middle-aged men sat with shirts and tequila bottles propped on exposed bellies. An old woman with tattered rags hanging from her arm opened her palsied hand near Barbara's legs.

They walked up a hill past a Mexican flag hanging still in the sunlight, the smell of gasoline and leather in the air, dust perpetually floating, then turned a corner onto a street full of tourists swarming in and out of shops, past huge donkey piñatas, painted green, white and red. Barbara held his arm as David maneuvered through the crowds, steering them into a shop full of leather goods where she bought a belt studded with turquoise. They went to a restaurant and ordered margaritas, sitting at a glass table on a veranda with ornate black iron closing it off from the street, the waiter wearing a starched white shirt splattered with grease. The drinks came in huge round glasses full of ice and tasted alcoholic and metallic. Despite having eaten dinner earlier, Barbara ordered tacos, wanting to taste real Mexican food. David took two bites, the meat sinewy and moist, and washed it down with the margarita, then chewed an ice cube, tasting Tijuana dirt. The taste lingered and he recalled his previous experiences in Mexico, and he stared at red meaty juices pooling on his plate. Then he looked at Barbara who didn't even touch her Tijuana taco even though she was the one so interested in trying real Mexican food. Maybe, he thought, it was all a little too real for her. If he were going to gain a new life, he thought, he would need to follow her lead, he would need a little superficiality.

Barbara pulled him into several shops, purchasing trinkets and clothes, and he bought them drinks at bars along the way. They were headed back when she stopped in front of a narrow door leading into a dark bar, then turned to him, her face flushed. "I've heard about these kind of places," she said. "Let's go in?" They sat at a tiny round table a few feet away from a stage. From the jukebox, horns blared. A short woman with small breasts and large thighs danced and stripped down to her G-string.

A few sailors came in hooting and howling. One of them climbed onto the stage and, kneeling before the stripper's gyrating thighs, tried to stick his face into her crotch. She clamped her hands over his ears and pulled his head into her belly while more sailors and a few college students filed in from the street, the smell of wet hair and stale beer filling the bar. A tourist wearing a green knit shirt draped loosely over his potbelly leaned near Barbara and splashed beer on her. She turned to David and said, "Can you believe this place?"

David sat between her and the tourist, while the sailor crawled on his knees, chasing the stripper. People stuffed into the tiny bar, howling and laughing while the stripper danced, pelvis protruding forward, waddling across the stage toward the sailor, then sticking her finger behind her G-string. The sailor tackled her, straddled her, and unbuckled his belt. The bartender grabbed him by his waist and hurled him off the stage onto his buddies.

Barbara clutched David's arm. The tourist leaned close, staring at them. David turned and said, "What do you want?"

"Sorry . . . I . . . It's just that you look like someone . . ."

"Everybody does," he responded.

"Your voice sounds familiar too."

David cringed, looking at the fat, balding man with facial features that resembled someone he knew a long time ago.

"Where you from?" the tourist asked.

"Nowhere." David drank his beer.

Finally the tourist said, "I'm originally from St Louis . . ."

David stared up at the stage, hoping for a distraction. Need to get out of here, he thought.

"Name's Vic Stephenson?" He held his hand out to shake.

David took it reluctantly. "Good to meet you," he said, then turned away.

"I know," the tourist said. "Yeah, has to be - you're David Brooks, right? Remember me?" He beamed, eyes squinting.

Chest tightening, David finally recognized the man. They hadn't seen each other since the first year they'd gone to college, but in high school they had almost been friends.

"Hey, it's me!" Vic said again, holding his arms out and smiling.

David's mind raced. Did this old classmate still live in St Louis? Didn't he realize that David Brooks was dead?

"Oh, come on. I know it's been a long time, but you *have to* remember me . . . I transferred to college in Tulsa, got a job, met my wife there."

David gasped, the crowded bar suffocating, closing in on him. "I don't . . . know . . . you..." He had to deny it. Think Cregan, not Brooks.

Lowering his voice, Vic said, "I don't think my wife would like this place." Then he turned to Barbara. "Hello, we're only going to be here another day. Why don't you two meet us tomorrow?"

David managed to inhale a deep breath. "Look . . . I don't . . . know . . . what you're talking about." He stood and grabbed Barbara's arm. "Let's go." His face felt very hot, the taste of Tijuana tacos lingering. He swished beer in his mouth, but the bar reeked of sweaty human flesh, and he had to get out. Pulling Barbara, he knocked into Vic the tourist.

"Hey! Watch it! Man, I'm sorry for the mistake . . . You just looked a lot like him."

Outside, the streets glowed in the darkening evening, neon flashing and sidewalk video machines beeping. Street vendors offered him serapes and girls. Then more beggars, children selling trinkets. Spanish fused with English, making the streets hum with incomprehensible jabber. David's throat clogged and his lungs felt as if they were collapsing in on themselves. He heard a crash. He had been dragging Barbara. She had been resisting, hitting him, screaming, "Let go, you bastard, let go of me!" One of her packages had dropped to the street and shattered, a crystal statue of a businessman. But now it was in pieces, reflecting the neon of Tijuana.

"Barbara . . ." he said, taking a breath.

"What's wrong with you?" she asked.

He looked at her pleading eyes and let go. Breathe slowly, he thought, terrified of the familiar, horrible feeling - throat swelling, his heart pounding hard trying to compensate. If he didn't calm down, he would hyperventilate, maybe pass out. Had to calm down he thought, staggering away without her.

She caught up to him. "Wait! You can't leave me here."

David grabbed her arm. "Let's go," he wheezed. "Now."

# Chapter Thirty-One

Susan was sitting alone at the airplane window, peering down at the rust-colored cloud of pollution hanging over Mexico City. She imagined the great Aztec city of Tenotitcitlan, five hundred years ago, the clear lake and its causeways, the intricate temples, and their artistry. She looked at her notes, reading "prisoners as victims ... but for many rituals, Aztec warriors sacrificed themselves as they did in battle - life flowed from death."

After landing, the student group boarded a university bus, weaving through traffic, past modern skyscrapers and ancient adobe dwellings, women in bright, modern dresses. Susan felt it all swirling by in a hubbub of activity, the bus finally pulling into the university's courtyard with its Mexican flag, green, white, red, and Aztec symbol. A young man leaned next to her and said, "The green is for hope, white for purity, and red . . . I'm not sure."

"For the blood of national heroes," Susan said, and thought, the blood nourished the gods and gave energy to everything in the universe. She carried her luggage across the courtyard along with the others, finally settling into a narrow dormitory room with a girl who asked, "Who do you think will be our professor? What did you think of the bus ride? Where's the bathroom?"

To Susan, all the questions were inane, annoying. But as she settled into her bunk, she realized the youth and innocence of the girl - a phase that she had missed entirely. Perhaps she would have asked the same kinds of questions, then called home as soon as they landed and told her dad how exciting it all was.

The next day, after their campus tour guide walked them around the entire campus and droned on about classes and expectations, Susan skipped dinner, and entered the heart of Mexico City, searching for Menendez. She wandered through streets crowded with businessmen, and ended up on a narrow sidewalk with brown and white row houses. She asked people along the way, "*Por favor, donde es esta casa*? Where is this house? Please."

When she finally knocked on a tall, narrow door, she felt faint, having eaten nothing, the cool evening making her shiver. A woman wearing an apron opened the door and looked at Susan holding the letter of introduction.

A man appeared, Susan immediately recognized him from the photo, looking the same, except older, gray streaking his black hair, wrinkles fanning up from his mouth and wide-set brown eyes. He took the letter, started reading, then looked at her and laughed. He spoke perfect English. "Susan? It's you?" Menendez put his arm around her. "You will stay here. This is my wife. My children are grown and gone. We have plenty of room."

While his house would certainly be more comfortable than the dormitory, Susan did not want to depend on anyone for anything. "No," she said, "I don't want to impose."

"No, niña, not an imposition," he protested. "I would be in debt to you if you stayed."

She looked at him. Turning down the offer would be an insult to his hospitality. "What about getting to class?" she asked.

He laughed. "You drive a hard bargain, niña, but I will also provide transportation. Now, you must stay."

Susan sat in a big easy chair, and looked around the room, small but filled with mementos, swords crossing on the wall, carved pre-Columbian figurines on tables next to Virgin Mary statues, a large shelf encased in glass and filled with artifacts. Menendez disappeared into the kitchen, and Susan stood to look at artifacts, but was immediately drawn to a wall filled with photographs, her dad as a relatively young man, maybe about Susan's age now.

Menendez reappeared, standing next to her. "Your father loved to go anywhere new, any chance of finding a simple artifact and he would go." Menendez shook his head. "I'm sorry I was not with him at the end."

Susan's mind drifted, thinking about the ending. "No," she said, "do not blame yourself." She had gotten over feeling guilty about her husband . . . but not about her father, at least not fully. She had been just a little girl when it happened. Now, she felt more capable dealing with such complex feelings.

She slept in the bed her dad used when visiting Menendez. She remembered being frightened at night and climbing into bed with her parents, the warmth, the shaving cream smell of her father. She held onto the pillow, and slept soundly, waking, ready to explore Mexico.

Menendez himself drove her to the university in an old Buick, through the city, talking the whole way about what a lousy driver he was, dodging cars that appeared from nowhere. They almost crashed, Menendez gesturing and cussing in Spanish. When Susan got out of the car, she joked, "Maybe a taxi next time?"

"Si, si," he responded and drove off, leaving Susan to wonder if he'd make it back okay. Then she turned and walked up the red-bricked path into the university courtyard, past the glorious Mexican flag, eagle with the snake writhing in its talons. After a week of intense study, she joined three other students attempting to climb Ixtaccíhuatl, one of the volcanic peaks that protected the ancient city of Tenochtitlan. They rode in the back of a flatbed truck, over narrow roads with deep gullies. While bracing herself against the jarring bumps, Susan checked her equipment, ice axe, crampons, and rope. One of the other climbers nodded and smiled at her, yelled some encouragement, then turned to his friend and said something Susan couldn't hear. But she knew they were concerned about her coming along. The third climber, a strong young woman from Colorado, had stated it openly, "Are you sure you can do this?" Susan repeatedly assured her. But now as they came to the end of the road, and climbed out of the truck, standing at the base of the immense peak, she gasped in the thin air, closing her eyes, her head spinning in the blackness. She remembered Mount Rainier, her husband pulling her up the final slope. This time, she was on her own, on a mountain that he had wanted to climb.

Susan kept pace with the younger climbers, but then started to lag. They were going too fast, she thought. They were too anxious. She stood and scanned the rock-strewn slope curving around a steep edge, sparse white clouds in the distance. She drank water, and continued, catching up to the others at the melting snow line. They all sat and strapped on crampons. One of the young men was struggling to breathe, and Susan handed him water. Then she stood and started onto the snow slope without them. She could hear them yelling for her to stop, too dangerous for her to lead, but she felt strong. Maybe, she thought, with something to prove. She kicked steps into the hard-packed snow, pausing every twenty feet, then continuing.

With her pack weighing on her, each breath a gasp, the thin dry air stinging the inside of her nostrils and making her throat sore, she stopped. The sun beat down unmercifully, and she smeared sunscreen on her sweaty brow. She looked behind her, the others slowly following the footsteps she had kicked into the snow. She leaned on her ice axe, and looked up at the clear sky, the sharp ridge ahead, one side black rock with ice waterfalls, the other a steep snow slope. She felt for the first time that she understood her husband's love for mountains. She had a direction - up, and only up. Like her studies, the only thing that mattered was to keep going forward, higher, never looking back. As the others arrived one by one, Susan clipped them into the rope, and she led them along the ridge, slowly, steadying herself with the ice axe, finally reaching the top, sitting in the snow and pulling in rope as the others joined her, hugged her, and laughed. Susan stood, adrenaline surging through her body as she watched a thin plume of smoke rising from neighboring Popocatepetl.

After several photographs, they began the descent, each step tense, Susan knowing that the way down would be nerve-racking. But on the lower slopes, oxygen filling them, they started glissading. At the trailhead, they camped, sat around a fire and sipped brandy. The others joked about how they would have quit, but couldn't leave poor Susan going to the top alone, so they followed.

Taking classes at the university, visiting museums, having to speak the language every day, Susan became fluent on a basic level, always ready to try abstract, philosophical conversations. Spanish required gestures, and emphasis, and the Latino men often gathered around her, listening to her descriptions of "Estados Unidos". A few wanted to marry her, and she learned how to decline tactfully.

She began to understand more about her father, gaining a picture of him as a man who loved exploring the highlands and looking for evidence of past civilization. Menendez helped, telling her, "A man needs the right balance of solitude and family, and your father's work in this country was his solitude. But he loved you, more than anything."

During a Christmas party, after singing "Silent Night" in Spanish, then in English, Susan sat drinking tequila with Menendez and his cousin, a campesino from a pueblo not far from Mexico City. The cousin told stories about farmers finding artifacts while tilling a field.

Menendez laughed, and turned to Susan. "Your father and I used to chase down countless stories. Always it was nothing."

Susan looked at him. "But you went anyway, right?"

He drank. "We were much younger."

"I've never been," she said, eyes wide, eager to explore the highlands.

Menendez shook his head. "Your father would be proud, but—"

"I could go alone."

He laughed. "All right, niña, if you want to, then we shall go."

Menendez equipped a group of students with picks and shovels, and they all rode a bus that was full of campesinos carrying chickens, squawking and stinking up the vehicle. Susan stuck her head out the window, preferring the dust, as they wound into the high country, getting out at a town where Menendez's cousin provided burros. Susan rode her burro, into the farmlands, burro sweat foaming on her legs, stopping at a cornfield. Supposedly, here, while tilling the field, the farmer had discovered the lost grave. Now the corn was high, crisp, and it cracked as they knocked it down.

Susan watched as Menendez directed them to cordon off the site, then he lifted a pick and swung hard into the sun-baked earth. Susan took her turn, digging, feeling faint but refusing to rest. Eventually, she dug into dark, loosely packed dirt. She knelt and started clawing through the dirt, feeling pieces, broken, tiny clay shards of what might have been Aztec artifacts. She showed them to Menendez, and asked, "What does this mean?"

"This tomb has been looted," he responded. "It is more common than you might think."

On the way back, the bus sped along a narrow dirt road, on the edges of sheer drop-offs into deep gorges. Menendez turned to her. "One day archaeologists will be digging up thousands of buses from dried-up river beds," he said. "When they find my skull, they will wonder what creature possessed such a fine container for brains."

"You are a smart man," she responded. "I admire you."

Despite waving it off as nonsense, he sat straight, and smiled.

Admittedly relieved that they made it back to Mexico City safely, Susan helped unload the bus, put away equipment, then slept so soundly that she woke with a sense of regret. It was her last day in Mexico and she had wanted to stay up late the previous night. She imagined drinking and toasting and talking with Menendez one last time.

"So you must return soon," he said, Susan standing in the airport terminal with the other students. She hugged Menendez goodbye, pretending for a moment that he was her father. Flying out of always-sunny Mexico, Susan didn't feel prepared for February in St Louis, landing, wind howling and whistling through doors, waiting for luggage, people hurrying everywhere, moving too fast. She phoned her mother, but no one answered, so she carried her suitcase outside in the bitter cold, and waved down a taxi.

Wet snow swirled out of the gray sky as she lugged her suitcase up the front stone steps, and unlocked her door. Inside, the mail was stacked on the table. Susan unpacked, took a shower, and had just settled onto the couch to look at the mail when the phone rang.

"Susan," her mother said, "sorry I missed you at the airport. How was your trip?"

"Great. Menendez sends his regards."

"Good man," she responded. "I've got some news."

"Okay . . . " Susan opened the electric bill.

"I'm getting married."

Susan leaned on the edge of the couch, stunned, unable to grasp what her mother was saying.

"You'll like him, he loves the outdoors, and he's *fun*."

"I didn't know you were dating." Her own voice, she thought, sounded as if she were objecting. She should be happy, excited, but the announcement had caught her off guard.

"Are you okay, Susan? You don't . . ."

"What?" She tried to hurriedly sort through her feelings so that she could be positive. Her mother, she thought, the one person who had been there for her all these years. No, that was okay. She didn't need anyone's help anymore.

"Well, you don't seem to have a lot of friends. It's just that I worry about you."

Susan quickly listed her "friends". Elizabeth, whom she hadn't heard much from, only sporadically since Wyoming. Who else? Jurgan? Her mother was right. She had no friends.

"There's more. David's mother called me . . ."

"And?"

"His dad passed away."

Susan tried to remember the man, but couldn't picture him, and then felt again her own father passing, and her eyes moistened.

"One last thing," her mother said. "Your insurance agent visited me the other day. Maybe he isn't as bad as we thought."

Susan's stomach tightened. "What did he want?"

"He said he made a mistake. Wants to help you get your money." Susan heard a jet roaring over in the background, and her mother yelled, "Bye, I love you . . ."

While listening to the dial tone, Susan stared at the mail, and saw a big envelope, a wedding invitation. Must be from Mom, she thought, since she didn't know anyone else who would invite her to a wedding. She opened it, then read, "The parents of Elizabeth Ann Crawford . . ." She scanned down, "to William H Baxter." Elizabeth's boyfriend, the one she met at that party. Susan had tried to forget that night, Bill coming onto her, then. . . . Better call Elizabeth, she thought, tell her to back out, wait until she was older. But it was typical of Elizabeth to invite her. Even though they had barely spoken to one another recently. Elizabeth thought everyone was her friend, and would be disappointed if any one of them didn't come to the wedding. Susan filled out the RSVP card, number attending - one. She looked at it and thought, was that it?

One? She had become her own individual, but can anybody ever be wholly complete by themselves? Suddenly, it seemed like everyone was getting married except her, and she wasn't anywhere close to doing that again.

She found a small envelope with no return address, ripped it open and read a photocopied letter stating that if she didn't send it on to at least ten people, she could be paralyzed in an automobile accident. She ripped it up and threw it away. Near the bottom of the stack, she found a business envelope with no return address, St Louis postmark, and opened it, unfolding another set of insurance papers, and a plain white paper, with words in neat, bold type. "Mrs Brooks. Even if he's still alive, I'll accept your claim. Please call me, Jurgan."

Susan felt her heart flutter as she dialed the phone and listened to his voicemail. She looked at the insurance papers, all of them filled out for her, waiting for her signature, notes telling her to sign in three places. Then it would all be over painlessly. But why now? Was his investigation over? She looked at the envelope with no return address and the St Louis postmark, and the blank paper with the typed message, the syntax vaguely familiar. She tried calling again, but got voicemail again. Then she stared at the phone, anxious to talk to someone. Not to seek advice, but to hear someone else's voice. She had no friends, she thought, then picked up the phone and made a business call, checking on her property. Had Carson rented it, she thought, she could use the money.

# Chapter Thirty-Two

Across the border, David breathed easier, the swelling in his throat subsiding, able to ask Barbara if she was okay. But she turned her head away, and wouldn't talk. At her apartment, she slammed the car door, and told him that they weren't right for each other.

David drove out to Point Loma, a massive abutment silhouetted in the night like a behemoth. He followed the winding road to the end, then walked down to the water. Far away from the rocky shore, he could see a green light from a boat, floating like a firefly. Music carried through the air, broken by the waves crashing over the rocks, cold spray hitting his face. Maybe if he swam into the ocean, he thought, for fun, and did not drown, it would prove that God was forgiving. Or he thought, it would mean he was "lucky". Savgren might explain it as neither. Mathematically speaking, they all would be random events, swimming, tidal waves, rescue boat within range to save him, or not. Neither God nor luck had anything to do with it.

Back in his sparsely furnished apartment, he glanced at the steady red light on his answering machine, showing no messages from anyone, then stood leaning on the open refrigerator door, staring at the leftover pizza, and he wondered if it was right for him to eat while people starved. He lived, while others suffered and died, to what end? Slumping into his small, secondhand couch, he stared at the floor. Just out of reach lay a book about the Aztec. Interesting stuff, he thought, but felt too tired to read at the moment. He turned on the TV, eventually falling asleep and waking to the sound of morning news, the sun shining hot through the windows. Right and wrong, he thought, could be relative, couldn't they? When is it okay to hurt someone for the greater good of all, or when does faith justify killing? He pulled the curtain shut and sat, the TV showing a construction crew using jackhammers to break away the walls of an apartment building. Inside the building, a 900-pound man was suffocating under his own weight. The fire department used a forklift to haul him out. Movement, David thought, meant life. If he was going to survive, he had to move, not sit and stagnate like the 900-pound man. Aztec warriors, muscular healthy men, believed in movement as "life energy", the movement of the sun, and of blood rushing through their veins.

David changed into running shorts and T-shirt. Outside, the sunlight hurt his eyes. He shuffled into the street and started jogging, each stride feeling like a struggle to live. His muscles ached, and his feet felt heavy as lead, but after the first mile, he ran easier, and moral questions felt less burdening.

Back in his apartment, he sat staring at his phone for a long time before calling the Dubois real estate office. No answer. Past office hours. He called information for a home phone number. He let it ring for a long time before a woman answered.

"Evert Carson please," David said, then heard a clunk and muffled voices. As he sat, still feeling strong from his run, he calculated what he would ask Evert, anyone suspect anything, any challenges to his new identity.

"Yeah . . . hello."

"Evert, it's me, David."

"Huh, oh, Dave, how ya been?" Evert sounded drunk.

"Have you heard from . . ." He didn't know what to call her, his wife? Ex-wife? Widow? But Evert knew, speaking with sudden clarity.

"Yes, I've heard from her, I hear from her all the time. She lets people use the place up on Liar's Creek, rents it out .

. . fishin' . . . huntin' . . . you know. I gotta send her a check now that you mention it."

"Oh . . ." David looked at the blank TV screen. "And you're back with your wife?"

"Seems so, don't it? You going to call yours?"

David hesitated, held the phone, wondering what to say. Was Evert proof that one could return to his wife, without recrimination? Return from a drinking binge, maybe even an affair. But, David thought, after what he had done, how could he go back? "I just wanted to know what she was doing . . ."

"Right."

"How is she?"

"Fine," Evert said, "she's a nice gal." David tried to remember all the things that made Susan a "nice gal" while Evert went on, "But I wish ya could do something about that insurance dude . . . he's a pain in the ass."

David grimaced. "Still?"

"He keeps sending stuff out for me to sign, and when I don't, he calls me up. Hell, I don't owe him a damn thing." The line crackled and Evert asked, "You there?"

Gripping the phone, David suddenly felt as if someone else were listening. "Yes," he said, "I'm still here."

After hanging up, David stared at the wall. He remembered the day he bought term-life from Jurgan. The small event felt like it happened a lifetime ago, but he remembered it clearly, the aggressive agent taking him off guard, David succumbing to the slick sales pitch, distracted by his longing for Susan. If not for the timing, even a minute one way or another, maybe he wouldn't have any insurance. Now he sat and shook his head. Why hadn't his wife collected the money yet? All along, it remained in the back of his mind. Knowing she would have the money made it easier for him to run. Less guilt. She would get something for her grief, cash in on his "death". But the thought of her grieving disturbed him. How much did she grieve? How much did she miss him? She either didn't love him much, or she did and he caused her pain. Either way, he felt bad.

David drove to a bar that charged ten dollars for a small Vodka Tonic. The view was almost worth it, sun slowly turning red, shimmering and merging with the ocean. After two drinks, he got up to leave when a young woman with long sun blonde hair sauntered in and sat on a barstool near his. She smiled prettily, white teeth set against a dark tan, ordering a drink. He kept glancing at her. Silver earrings inlaid with jadestone dangled from her lobes, and her eyes were large and unusually pale green. She suddenly stared at him and said, "Are you waiting for someone?"

"No." He looked in his wallet.

"I'm not either," she said, turning toward him and asking, "What color are your eyes?"

"Can't you tell?"

"Hmm, very blue," she said. "Are they really yours?"

"Whose *would* they be?"

"They could be cosmetic."

"Contact lenses?" he said. "I don't need them."

"Lots of people don't need them to see . . . Lenses can make your eyes any color you want. Look at mine. They're top-of-the-line." He leaned close, searching for her lenses. She said, "They're breathable . . . really lifelike."

He stared. "I can't see them."

"Even cosmetologists have trouble telling the difference between them and the real thing."

"Are you a cosmetologist?" he asked, hopeful. Someone who lived and worked for the superficial might help him, establish him as Cregan, a surface being who never worried about suffocating in the depths of his own thoughts.

"How perceptive of you . . .You should try the lenses. They're great. You can change who you are whenever you want."

"It's not that easy." God knows, he thought, feeling dejected, he had tried.

"Too bad," she said, smiling. "If you had green eyes, I would ask you out."

Just beyond her blonde head, he watched a plump man in plaid shorts enter the bar. David put on sunglasses and stood. Seeing that the man in shorts wasn't Vic the tourist, he scanned the room, searching faces.

"Don't leave," she said, touching his arm.

David sat and used the rest of his cash to buy them drinks, finding out that everything with Janice could be, and often was, cosmetic. He had difficulty deciphering what was real. She worked for a place called Second Looks, Inc. and the optometrist there was a good friend of hers. And she convinced him to try green lenses.

Feeling uncomfortable about inviting her into his messy apartment, David agreed to meet Janice, then she would drive him to get the "new eyes".

"Will I see things differently?" he asked, looking at her while she drove casually, one hand on the steering wheel, arm hanging out the window.

"Hope so," she said.

He wondered what she meant by that, then figured that he probably appeared glum at times.

David leaned back in the optometrist's chair and let Janice place the lenses in his eyes, stinging, feeling like pieces of gravel, but tolerable, tears flowing down his cheeks. After a few days, he hardly noticed them.

The thin film of green made all the difference to her. She apparently liked the person she saw in him, his eyes, his nose and scar, his closely cropped, graying beard. "I think older guys are sexy." She had a red streak in her blonde hair, which hung to one side and fully exposed her gold earring. "You have a sense of intrigue . . . What sort of secrets are you hiding?"

"My eyes are blue," he said.

David followed her to concerts and cosmetologist parties. She liked the way he was able to socialize with her superficial friends. However, he used earplugs at the concerts, the lyrics incomprehensible anyway, except one he'd heard before, a remix of "don't touch me, I'm a real live wire; run, run . . ."

After several weeks, David began to feel completely, irrevocably severed from his past. He was someone else, some perpetually tanned native of California, like Janice. He felt as if he might be "normal", able to fool himself for amazingly long periods of time. Maybe she was just the sort of woman for him. As Dave Cregan, he might be able to make love to her. He would not be a man cheating on his wife.

One evening, David joined a few of Janice's friends at her apartment, and he drank several beers before switching to margaritas. When her friends left, David started to follow them out. "You shouldn't drive," Janice said, blocking the door. He stood unsteadily, looking into her eyes. She took his hand and led him to her sofa, facing toward the shoreline. They sat and watched the lights from airplanes circling in a holding pattern over the ocean and downtown. Janice leaned into him, tilted her head up, and they kissed briefly, then again longer. She looked at him and said, "I was beginning to think you didn't like me."

But he did. He liked her soft lips, the feel of a woman, something he had not felt in a long time. They slid to the floor, Janice taking the initiative, guiding his hand onto her breast, unbuckling his belt, telling him that she wanted him. He closed his eyes, the smell of her perfume familiar, too much so, and he almost whispered Susan's name. Opening his eyes, he looked down to find Janice kissing his chest, her blonde hair spread over him. He wanted her, but felt like he was an observer, watching someone else's life. Janice took off her clothes. She rolled a condom onto him before straddling him. He watched, holding back, while she rocked up and down moaning. Then he let go into the prophylactic barrier.

With Janice asleep next to him, he eased off the sofa, went to the bathroom, then put on his clothes. He got a blanket and laid it over her. She opened her eyes, and murmured, "Don't go."

"It's okay," he said, leaning over, kissing her head.

While driving, he felt empty, and he told himself that he was Dave Cregan, San Diego real estate agent, no one else. He lay in bed, eyes open to keep the room from spinning. Eventually, he fell asleep, and slipped into a series of dreams, jumping erratically from one scene to the next. His father hiking ahead of him in the woods, David as a little boy running to catch up, happy to grab his father's hand. Susan sitting on a boulder and crying somewhere in mountains with deep, green ravines.

He woke late, dressed slowly, and was about ready to leave, get some food, when the phone rang.

Evert's voice sounded more distant than ever. "Dave?"

"What's wrong?"

"Your dad . . ."

David slumped into a chair. "What?"

"Heart attack . . . He didn't make it, Dave."

"When?" he asked, as if that made a difference. But, he thought, *how could my dad die without me feeling something, some passing of the spirit, some soulful cry in the night.* But why would Cregan feel anything?

"Few days ago. Just now found out myself. Your wife called . . ."

"But he was in good shape," David said, his head pounding, stomach in knots, a warplane roaring overhead. "I don't understand."

"Nobody ever does."

David left his apartment, thinking that he shouldn't be surprised. Part of life. An everyday occurrence. Keep it simple. No need to feel anything. But he felt awful, and worse knowing what his father must have felt after David's supposed death. They hadn't stayed close. During his adult life, they rarely spoke. But it was his dad. And he had good memories. No. Can't be. Please, he thought, the agony rushing in on him, feeling despicably guilty. Had Dad grieved for his son? Of course he had. There was no doubting his father's sorrow. David fought back tears. Keep it on the surface. Besides, that was David Brooks, not Cregan's dad. Cregan had no father, no connection to human emotion. Cregan lived a purely superficial life where nothing hurt, and no job was bothersome, Cregan worked to get drunk, maybe try some drugs, and go to cosmetologist parties. He was not Brooks. He was Cregan.

He rode the trolley to the border, and started walking through the bustling Tijuana streets. Leaving the downtown "tourista zone", he explored the "suburbs" of Tijuana where huge gullies separated shanties bunched together on dirt slopes, ready to slide down on top of one another at the first heavy rain. Pathways twisted up and down the hills past chicken coops and clothes lines, pale blue and pink stucco walls. So many ragged children caged in schoolyards, all kicking at one frayed soccer ball.

He sat on a bench near a church. David looked at the small, adobe church with the wooden cross on top, splinters in the hot sun, and he remembered when he lost an important aerospace manual, praying to God that no one would ask for it, swearing that he would be a better person. He found it a day later under his bed. The manual had fallen from his nightstand. Then he thought of his friend Savgren, the pure mathematician, how Savgren's wife became pregnant - had her baby cut from her womb - how Savgren prayed while the baby died in his arms. Later, David listened to him quietly explain the genetic probability, a one in 50,000 chance. Could've happened to anyone. Just one of those things. David's own prayers about finding a stupid manual paled in comparison to Savgren's loss. Was it all random? A chaotic world of random suffering and death?

A breeze swirled dust around David's legs and into his contact lenses. Up the trash-littered road, an old woman in black climbed steadily toward him, her cloak up, blocking the sun. He watched her laborious steps. When she'd finally made it up the street, she pulled down her hood, revealing long gray hair and a deeply wrinkled face. He gazed into the blue sky, but was forced to look at her when she asked, "*La hora*?"

Then in English, "What time?"

"*Esta es* . . . It's three o'clock," he responded, suddenly embarrassed to speak Spanish. He showed the old woman his watch. She nodded and smiled at him, showing black gaps between her teeth, then went on her way.

The question from the old woman felt like a knife stabbing his chest. When she smiled, he felt as if the knife twisted. La hora - the hour - the day, the year, his life - how many years since *la hora de la muerte?* He stood and searched for the woman, wanting to help her climb the next street, and in return, ask that she take away the pain. But she had disappeared into one of the countless shacks teetering on the edge of extinction. His eyes hurt, but when he rubbed them, his hands felt dirty. He wiped them on his shirt.

A boy ran up to him, selling trinkets, holding up the tailless, two-headed serpent dangling on a silver chain. The boy, with his round, smiling face was oblivious to David's tears. Was sorrow so common here, a natural expression, to weep at simple requests? David bought the necklace. The boy thanked him and ran away.

# Chapter Thirty-Three

Susan didn't expect much from Carson, but she felt better knowing that he was sending a check, and just talking to someone. She felt obligated to tell him about David's father, but Carson hadn't known the man.

Susan signed the insurance forms, stuffed them into the envelope and walked to the corner mailbox. She pulled the mail slot open, then looked up at the nearby bar, and remembered her meeting with Kester, his twisted grin and dark eyes. She dropped the envelope into the mailbox, clanging shut, Kester's words coming back to her, "Got no fuckin' idea what you're talkin' about." Maybe he didn't send those cards, she thought.

Susan opened the mailbox door and peered in, wondering if the post office would let her dig through all the mail so she could take back the claim. But what then? She would look it over, make sure it was filled out properly, then just drop it back into the mailbox. Still, she had the feeling that she had acted too soon. Something still lingered in her subconscious that needed to be flushed out. If not Kester, then who sent the strange cards?

For the next week, Susan buried herself in Aztec studies, reading about their views of the dead, and responsibility, losing herself in her work. But her mother's wedding interrupted her solitude.

She drove past a big wooden sign, able to read only a couple of phrases, "Airport expansion . . . tax dollars . . ." then past stacks of broken trees, lying like twisted cadavers, their thick trunks snapped and splintered, arriving at the last remaining oasis of trees with daffodils lining empty lots and sunlit leaves turning pale green. Her childhood home stood crumbling, but brightly decorated, with yellow balloons and red ribbons. While she parked, a jumbo jet flew over, forcing her to put her hands over her ears.

Inside, all the big furniture was gone, and chairs lined the walls. A band had set up their instruments in the middle of the living room. Susan stood with a group of people gathered around her mother and the man who would now be her "stepfather". She listened to them promise to love each other, then a jet rattled everything, and they kissed, her mother turning around, grinning, and telling everyone to have a good time, "Wreck the place if you like." The band started up, playing to the roar of aircraft flying low - old people dancing, a few married couples with children running and screaming happily. Susan stood next to Mom and watched her stepfather dance with children. "In some ways," Mom said, "he's like your father, don't you think? Of course, nobody is the same, but I like him."

"Do you love him?" Susan wasn't sure what formed the basis of a good marriage, but love had to be part of it.

"Very much . . .." She faced her daughter. "What about you, Susan?"

"Oh, I like him just fine . . . "

"That's not what I meant. When's the last time you went out with anyone?"

The room suddenly struck Susan as quiet. No jet noise. Flight patterns must have changed, she thought.

"What about Jurgan?" her mother asked.

Susan glared. "What?"

"I think he likes you, maybe you should give him a chance."

Susan excused herself, and went outside where men were laughing and spray-painting the house with big black letters. Just Married. Good Luck.

A few days later she received a letter from Menendez. It read: My dear nina, I have great news. Something that will surely bring you back to visit. I, Professor Rodriguez Alfonso Menendez, have made a very important discovery, and I want to share it with you. Your father would have wanted it that way. In the highlands between Puerto Vallarta and Guadalajara, I have discovered a partially buried, previously unknown, and potentially significant temple of the Aztec. The weather and a recent earthquake have contributed to revealing this ancient temple. And I invite you to view it. What do you say to that? Please come down in August. We will be ready then, I think, to do some initial research. All the best from my family and friends.

Susan read it over several times, then she labored over her return letter, telling him she would try to join him. Then she looked at her checking account, entered in the check from Carson, and another loan from her mother. It would be difficult, but she could return to Mexico.

Later that night, lying in bed, Susan thought again about the sympathy cards. If not Kester Blucuski . . . maybe her husband was tormenting her from the grave. Then she thought about Jurgan, his letter, the death claim, expecting him to call as soon as he got the signed papers. But he hadn't, she thought, finally falling asleep.

She woke groggily, dressed and found Jurgan's letter shoved in with junk mail ready to be thrown away. She stared at it, "even if he's still alive". On blank paper - no letterhead. She folded it up and put it in her purse, then called Jurgan, the secretary telling her that Mr Jurgan would be in soon. "Thank you," Susan muttered, deciding to visit his office.

Susan parked in front of a tall building, the lot lined with trees. She entered the lobby and read the directory next to the elevator. The sudden uplift and stop made her feel light-headed as she stepped out and looked down a long carpeted hallway with the smell of fresh paint. She opened a pine-colored door marked Jurgan Insurance Company in gold letters.

Inside, Jurgan was tapping on his computer keyboard, the

screen changing, then he turned. "Mrs Brooks, good to see you."

Susan unfolded his letter and handed it to him. "What's this all about?" she asked.

"I don't understand," he said.

Susan stared at the paper. "Why didn't you use company letterhead?"

"I ran out." He walked around and sat on the corner of his desk. "After this is over," he said, "maybe we can go out for a drink . . ."

Susan looked at him, noticing his thin lips. Arrogant bastard, she thought, he truly enjoyed his job. If not her husband, nor Blucuski, then who? Who else had any stake in her husband's death, and how she felt about it? Of course, even the word choice was similar, Jurgan not bothering to disguise that. *Must've thought I was stupid.* "*You* sent me those cards."

He stared at the floor, shook his head. "If I did, I would never admit it." He looked at her and laughed. "You *are* talking about those peculiar condolence cards, right?"

"But why would you . . ."

"Not that I would know, but it seemed like a good idea. Might have made you panic, then you'd lead us to your husband." He shrugged. "Didn't work, did it?"

Susan glared, her fists balled up, wanting to say something, but unable to speak. How could anyone be so calculating, she thought, with such disregard for anyone else?

"They were poetic," he said "don't you think?"

"Fuck you." She stormed out, slamming the door, running down the hallway the wrong way, turning to find Jurgan blocking her. She pushed him out of the way, ran past the elevator, down the steps, and out to her car, squealing tires as she sped out of the parking lot.

## Chapter Thirty-Four

Wearing the serpent necklace against his chest, David walked back across the border; his throat felt parched and swollen, his breathing erratic. He recovered, and inhaled, taking slow measured breaths. Nothing to worry about, he thought, didn't eat anything, and he couldn't have a reaction to the air, could he? Was there something in the history and culture of Mexico that made him gasp for breath? He smirked. Could be. After all, doctors weren't gods. They only made calculations, guesses like everyone else. Except, he conceded, they could dole out medication. Sometimes medication helped.

That evening, he dug through his belongings, eventually finding the prescription bottle he'd stolen from his home. Seemed like yesterday, he thought, looking at the faded label. Taking it in the first place was lucky - David Brooks stuffing the empty prescription bottle into his pocket - as if he knew Dave Cregan would need it.

He explored the possibility of ordering the pills through the Internet, but was confronted with endless personal questions and numbers - too much revealing information floating around Cyberspace. So he drove to the drugstore.

Standing under the scrutiny of the pharmacist, he held his hand to his throat and explained in a hoarse voice that he was on a business trip. He needed more pills, at least until he got home.

The pharmacist took the faded bottle and keyed in the refill number. "Yes," she said, "there's a match." She stared at the computer monitor. "It's kind of old."

He coughed, then took a deep breath.

"Just a minute," she said. "Okay, we can give you a refill, enough to get you back, but then you'll have to see your doctor." He paid her in cash, but then she said, "Just sign here, Mr Brooks."

He took the prescription from the counter and stared at her. "Brooks?"

"Yes, you are David Brooks."

"No," he said, "there must be some mistake. My name's Dave Cregan."

"Okay, wait." She looked back at the computer, but the other pharmacist was using it.

"I've got to go." He backed away. "Can you just make the necessary changes?"

She frowned, and he fled the pharmacy, clutching the bag close to his chest as if someone might be following. He had his drugs, small pills to pop the moment his throat started to swell. Now, he thought, he could explore deeper into Mexico and look for some explanation in the chaos and suffering. Why had he run and why had his father's heart stopped beating?

During his visits to Tijuana, he bought more trinkets from downtrodden street vendors, gave coins to old women and dirty kids. He spoke clumsy Spanish. He drove down the Baja coast, camping alone and watching the sky turn red, melting with the sea. Upon returning from these trips, he would wrap his arms around Janice and hold on.

Sometimes, he felt well balanced, and other times he felt like he should read everything he could about mental illness. He decided to try herbal medicines. He thought they made a difference, allowing him to be efficient at his job, and more responsive to Janice. But he wasn't sure.

One night, he woke with music reverberating in his head, *can't sleep, bed's on fire.* Janice rolled over onto her back and pulled him on top of her. He waited until he was sure she'd had enough, then he allowed himself a release. He never said her name and, while holding onto her afterward, he did not say anything. She stroked his hair but instead of falling asleep as she usually did, Janice sat up, and asked, "Why do you always hold out on me?"

"What do you mean?"

"I don't know . . . You're holding back . . ."

"No," he responded, "I don't think I'm holding back anything."

"You *are*, Dave." She leaned against the headboard.

"I'm just that way . . . It's nothing."

"You aren't sharing . . ." She shook her pillows. "I tell you how I'm feeling about things, I tell you all sorts of things . . ."

He stared at the glowing red numbers of her clock radio. You mean, he thought, like how you're going to wear your hair at the next party? But he kept silent. Hairstyles didn't interest him. But, he thought, they could be important to someone else. For a moment, he almost gave in, almost told her that he felt compassion for Tijuana beggars, that he felt mostly boredom at concerts, that he had a secret he could never tell her. "What do you want me to say?"

"I don't know . . . anything . . . what about your parents, you never talk about your family, what are your parents like?"

He opened his mouth to say that they were "regular" parents and that his father had died recently, but the question made him flinch. My father, he thought, the man who worked hard, the man who would never admit to being sick, exhausted, or defeated, who was, in hindsight, a damn good dad. And now he was gone forever. He looked at Janice and wanted to say, I loved my father, and my mother is probably going crazy right now without him but I can't talk to her or help her.

"Janice," he said, "we're doing fine." He wrapped himself around her, and hung on, feeling oddly that if he did not, he'd spin off into oblivion.

Janice leaned into his arms and whispered, "Things can't just stay the same, even if we do nothing."

As she drifted off to sleep, he remained awake. He leaned over to kiss her but stopped, remembering all too vividly kissing Susan in the same way, while she slept.

Slowly, he eased out of bed. Janice was right. There was never any real status quo. He would have to kill the memories, those times early in his relationship with Susan when they "connected", memories of his childhood, his work, his friends, everything. He would have to embrace his new life, commit himself to the cosmetologist, forever sunny in San Diego.

After deciding to fully become Dave Cregan, doing whatever it took to create a new past, steal a different social security number, *anything*, he crept into the other room and dialed Evert's number. Break the only remaining contact, he thought. In Wyoming, it was well past midnight.

"Are you crazy," Evert asked, "always calling in the middle of the night."

David hesitated. "Have you talked to her recently?"

"Yeah, just the other day. She's fine, asking how business was doing, that sort of thing, nothing special."

He held the phone, unable to speak, feeling like he did in Wyoming, unable to pull the trigger. Regardless of any decisions he tried to make, he couldn't break from the past, kill off David Brooks. It wasn't that easy. Would he be forever stuck between two worlds?

David fell asleep on Janice's couch, and dreamed that he was in the Tijuana suburbs where the old woman asked him for the time. "The time?" he questioned, then said, "The time is three o'clock." The woman smiled and said, "*No, la hora es la hora de muerte.*" The hour of death. But the conversation was in slow motion, as if it had been three o'clock in the afternoon, on that day, for several months. Then the old woman's face transformed into the smiling face of a young woman with blue eyes and long hair. She stared quizzically into his eyes. He felt he knew her. Susan? Yes, it had to be. She turned and ran downhill, her black robe flapping around her legs as she ducked in and out of alleyways, leaping over gullies. She hurled herself headfirst over an adobe wall that was lined on top with broken glass. He chased after her, pushing off the top of the wall, slashing his hands wide open. On the other side, she stood with her back to him, facing children playing soccer. He grabbed her arm, his blood smearing her robe. But it was the old woman again, glaring at him in horror and trying to pull away. He released her and suddenly the old woman sang, "*No me toques, soy un alambre verdadero; matador psicotico, correr correr correr, correr para siempre*." He recognized the lyrics, but they sounded odd, then he realized that the old woman was singing in Spanish. Waking, David could not remember any of the Spanish; yet he understood it in his dream.

The old woman had mocked him with her wisdom, telling him to go ahead and run forever - but he couldn't. And that was the paradox. He decided to do something he was incapable of doing. He would always be plagued by his past. He had tried hard to jump cleanly from one life, one universe, to another, but had failed. Mathematics and physics, he thought - they always pushed the boundaries of practicality. He smiled wryly. Not surprising that his expectations far exceeded his ability. He could see clearly what he'd known all along. He, David Brooks, had expected to reach high peaks in all aspects of his life all the time. Had he loved Susan beyond what he could expect in return? Or had he merely fallen in love with his expectation of what she could be? Focused only on her potential. Susan, after all, had suffered the death of her father at a time she was ill-equipped to deal with it. He knew first-hand now what it felt like and he was an adult, at a time when such loss was "normal", at least statistically. And even then it felt awful. Susan, on the other hand, had to cross a great chasm, overcome the loss of her innocence, her childhood, before ever climbing to the mountaintop and shouting for joy, the sheer exhilaration of success, and life.

David stared at Janice's glass table and saw his reflection, the face on an aging, brooding man who couldn't force himself to smile. No wonder, he thought. He had expected his life to be one exhilarating moment followed by another. No wonder he'd been disappointed. In reality, it was an existence all too easily disrupted by pain and loss, and fear. And now, he feared his self-created purgatory spiraling into a living hell.

David stood, and went to the kitchen, the floor cold on his bare feet. His future, he thought, glancing at the shut bedroom door, did he have any control over it? Could he glide over the surface knowing that catastrophe lurked beneath? He picked up the phone, walked past the couch, and stood looking out the window, airplanes landing, the shoreline, waves surging up the beach, and a seagull floating on a wave. He could not believe in Cregan. He tried, but it had been impossible. Faced with that realization, he felt lost. He had to believe in something? Something that would gain him redemption . . . forgiveness. God? Jesus Christ perhaps? But crucifixion seemed too noble a sacrifice. His transgressions suggested something more horrible than crucifixion. Perhaps the answer lay in Mexico, a land that tugged at his now racing heart, pumping blood energetically through his body.

Janice woke, went into the bathroom and called to him, suggesting that they spend the day in her apartment, watch movies, and talk. While she took a shower, he called Evert again. Only one woman could forgive him. "Where is she now?" he asked.

"How should I know? You call her."

David shut his eyes and heard his father's advice: "Better to just tell the truth, take what's coming." He gripped the phone. "Evert, do one last thing for me, will you? What are her plans? Find out what you can. I need to see her again."

# Chapter Thirty-Five

At Elizabeth's wedding reception, Susan sipped her drink carefully. Would she always be alone? Not that she minded. She got along fine. So what if she was alone? But, as she watched Elizabeth dance, dress swishing across the floor, and the disc jockey playing "Time is on my side", Susan remembered her own wedding. She remembered feeling safe in her husband's arms. But only at the beginning. Later, she felt tense, unable to understand what he wanted from her, unable, she now knew, to give herself wholly.

When the music stopped, Elizabeth came over and sat next to Susan. "I wish you'd try to have some fun."

"I *am* having fun."

"But you aren't dancing with anyone? You should have brought your friend Jurgan."

Susan looked at her. "Why would I do that?"

"Well, he *told me* you might ask him."

She felt her stomach tighten. "Was he bothering you?"

"We got to talking, that's all. And you two went to Wyoming together, I just thought . . ."

"I like being on my own." Susan watched a couple swinging each other around while the music played.

"I don't know if you ever knew this, Susan, but I admire you. You're independent, and smart . . . Well, I think I can be that way too." She looked down and spilled champagne. "Even as Bill's wife."

Susan felt a little embarrassed under the weight of the admiration. "Thanks," she responded, "I'm sure you two will be just fine."

Susan walked outside, the spring air, cool and moist. She looked up at the sky, the moon, and dark clouds, a flash of lightning in the distance. She could admit that her marriage had been in trouble long before their accident. David wanted to spend all their vacation time climbing mountains or exploring wilderness. While she enjoyed it, she always felt she wasn't what David wanted her to be. She knew that. But more importantly, she wasn't what she, Susan Brooks, soon to be Susan Moore, wanted to be either. Maybe, she thought, by taking back her name, her father's name, she could correct some of her mistakes.

Determined to have fun, she went inside and immediately saw Mike Jurgan standing in the lobby. She heard thunder and watched him walk toward her.

Jurgan smirked, and said, "You look good."

Susan shook her head. "Can't you just leave me alone?"

Elizabeth burst through the doors, looked around and saw them. "Hi, guys. Mike, I thought I saw you come in." She stumbled and almost fell into his arms. "You know I would have invited you . . . I just thought . . ."

"I know," Jurgan said, "you thought Susan would bring me along. Me too."

Elizabeth's face flushed as she looked at Susan. "Bill and I are going to Puerto Vallarta, we're going to loaf around in the sun, do some snorkeling . . ."

"Sounds like fun . . ."

"Aren't you going to Puerto Vallarta also? For some sort of archaeology thing?"

"Yes, I'll just be passing through, I—"

"Susan, you work too much. I mean, you *could* stop in and say hi, maybe spend a day with us, instead of always working. I'm sure Bill wouldn't mind. I mean, we've been living together and we already went to Florida."

"I don't know . . ." Susan responded.

"I'll expect to see you."

Before Susan could protest further, a bridesmaid rushed in

and grabbed Elizabeth's hand, pulling her back to the party. Just like her, Susan thought, to want people around her all the time. In a way, she wished she could be as enthusiastic about people. She wondered if that was enough to keep from feeling lonely, and she tried following them, but Jurgan blocked her way.

"Look," Jurgan said, "I'm just trying to tie up some loose ends, that's all."

"*What* loose ends?" As far as Susan was concerned, he had no business bothering her, and weaseling his way into her life by sucking up to Elizabeth. And her mother, of all people.

"No big deal," he said, "some computer mix-up, I'm sure."

"So what is it?" Susan asked impatiently.

"It's nothing really," he said, eyes shifting. "I don't want to upset you."

Susan heard rain. "Tell me then, and quit acting like I'm not smart enough to understand it."

He frowned. "A refill number . . . somehow, someone in San Diego used your husband's prescription refill number . . ."

Susan felt her stomach turn. "What does that mean?" Like a sudden recurring illness, she felt David's spirit lurking in the air.

"It means I'm great at cracking computer systems," he responded.

"Good for you." Susan thought she smelled stale beer on his breath. Wouldn't surprise her if he drank too much when he wasn't harassing her. "All right. Who do you think stole the number?"

"Could be whoever broke into your apartment?"

Susan thought about the missing jacket, other odd things. "But why would . . ."

"You tell me."

"Maybe," she said, "someone dug it out of the trash. Like you."

"Yeah, maybe."

"So what happens now?" she asked.

"I go to San Diego. The guy used a different name, Dave Cregan. Like I said, it's probably a computer mix-up. This Cregan character refilled his script, and they entered the wrong number or something. Who knows? But it won't take long. It's going to be nothing, I'm sure. After that, the investigation's over."

She stared into Jurgan's eyes. Was he lying again? She turned and started walking toward the door, hearing him yell, "I'll let you know if I find anything."

Susan drove on the highway, rain pounding out of the night sky, huge truck roaring by, nearly blowing her off the road. The storm let up as she parked in front of her house, and she shivered as she climbed out of her car into the rain-soaked night. The streetlights were out, and she rushed through the dark, hurriedly unlocking the front door and slamming it behind her. She got ready for bed, but knew she wouldn't sleep. She sat in front of the TV, a breeze billowing the curtains in front of the screen, and the air chilled her. She had become used to the idea that her husband was dead. Yet, this other David needed a prescription with the *identical* number?

She tried to escape by watching a cop show. In the show, the dialogue focused on *the payoff*. Disgusted, she turned off the TV, the light reduced to a silver dot, piercing like her memory, the insurance money like a thin cord tightening around her neck. She needed to sever the cord and let David drift away for good.

She phoned Evert rousing him from his sleep, his groggy voice over the long-distance mumbling, "No, David had never mentioned San Diego," and he couldn't understand why Jurgan would want to go there. "Oh, you're going to Puerto Vallarta? That's good, never been there myself, seems like it'll be good for you. Yes, I'll try to sell the ranch, sure, if that's what you want."

Telling Evert to sell the place in Wyoming felt good, but there was more. While it eased her anxiety, it also compelled her to go into the basement and confront the debris from the past, piled in a dark corner. David's clothes, books, papers, stacked haphazardly waiting to be organized or maybe thrown into the dumpster. Or burned. One bare light bulb, glaring too bright, cast annoying shadows. Susan opened a box of old paperbacks, shoved it aside, and opened another, this one full of letters.

She sat on the basement floor and sifted through the letters. Several were from friends: Jack Savgren enthusiastically calculating expenses for a climb in Chile that never happened, an old note from Evert Carson trying to convince him to go hunting, and romantic correspondence between David and old girlfriends. And then, there were those written to her. She remembered stuffing them in the box with the others, wanting to get rid of all their memories together.

She looked for the letters sent shortly after they were married. David had gone on several short business trips to Patuxent River, Maryland, where he had been working on a new fighter aircraft for the Navy. Susan remembered the trip. Important stuff. When he was in St Louis, he worked overtime, up to sixty hours a week. She shuffled through the pile and found a postcard. "Met some friends in D.C., visited Western Maryland, very nice country, looks like it would be good cross-country skiing. Love David."

She found a letter dated later in that year. "Dear Susan: The weather is gray and I drove to a place called Calvert Cliffs expecting to find a good climb. But the cliffs were nothing more than 50-foot mud walls. I almost tried to climb them anyway, but figured I'd be buried in mud. Instead, I drove up the road and visited a Nuclear Power plant. Great nature experience. Love, David."

Then another postcard, a picture of tourists lining up at the Washington Monument. "Sick of this BS. We've got to go somewhere - looking forward to Rainier. I wish we could just go climb mountains, and all that. L—-, David."

Susan held the two postcards side by side and stared at them. Somewhere in the span of that year, David had gone from "loving" her to just "L—-ing" her. She sat and tried to recall what had changed, and her response to the changes. Had he been trying to pull away from her? If so, why not just say so. The more David worked the more he wanted to work. He flew in from business trips at all hours of the night, tired and irritable. She looked closely at the postcards, then threw them onto the dirty basement floor. Despite her own misgivings, she had tried hard. She stuffed the letters back into the box. Climbing out of the damp basement, she fought to bury the good memories, before they were married, and for a while after. What had changed? Or, had anything? After the initial thrill of romance and satisfaction of being married, satisfying her mother at the same time, she'd begun to drift. Or was it David? For a while he took responsibility for their marriage, trying to manage it the same way he would a guided missile. Their marriage had *not* been "fine". But it hadn't been hopeless either. Had it? Were they doomed from the start and the fire in the forest just speeded up the inevitable?

Exhausted, she fell into bed, pulled on an extra blanket, and went to sleep. She dreamed she was digging somewhere. She wasn't sure where, but the light was dim, and she was working hard, sweating - large fern, hanging moss and vine, jungle plants. Her shovel hit something; she knelt down and started clawing at the dirt, and she found a small green box shaped like a coffin. She opened the box, and it was full of dollar bills. She scooped up the bills, and uncovered David's face, deep furrows in his brow, eyes sunken and dark. David's face lit by moonlight. *Goddamn it, Susan, don't just sit there.* "What do you want?" *I don't care. Paddle.* "Tell me what's wrong."

Susan twisted in her bed, but the hole she had been digging was now deep and wide and steps spiraled down into the earth. She climbed down the spiraling stairs, circling around and down endlessly. Deeper, she went, and the pigment of her skin changed to a ruddy, light brown color; she became shorter, black hair, black eyes - sandals on tired feet, heavy poncho-like dress. A monotone voice coming from inside her spoke: "The Aztec woman had to rise on her own merit, or body . . . But she had her place. A woman might escape as an individual, but she was drawn back to it as a species . . . the sole aim to produce children." Susan resisted the pulling of the earth, the spiraling stairway, clawing and crying, trying to climb back up. But the stairway opened into a palace where she stood as an Aztec surrounded by naked plebeian men and women who slowly disrobed her. One man stepped forward and Susan began licking him, sucking and pulling with her lips, feeling him swell, then pulling her lips away and calling a plebeian woman, ordering the woman to touch them both, while Susan guided the man into her. Susan woke to find her own hands massaging, and her own finger thrust in, her body curled. Wanting the illusion, she sought sleep again, and she came several times, then drifted off - the man in the dream merged into her, and she became both man and woman. Aztec high priest. She stood gripping a knife with both hands, raising it high over a man, who was tied across a stone with his back bent, chest ready. Susan lunged down, and the man became David, screaming, the knife puncturing, rotating, carving. Susan sank her hands into the blood and ripped out the beating heart.

She woke gasping, sweating. Hot. She pushed off the heavy covers and climbed out of bed, opened the window and went into the kitchen for water. It was morning. Thank God, she thought, as she pulled on her workout clothes and headed for the park. Walking furiously for the first eight minutes, she eventually slowed and analyzed her dream, rationalizing enough to forget it. Obviously, she had been working too much studying Aztec culture. That, and her anticipation over Menendez's important discovery. And David, because of the weddings, the money, the postcards in the basement. And the sex, of course, because of the total lack of intimacy in her life. While she had experienced doubt about her future, she never felt any less a woman. Perhaps part of the dream was merely her desire for sex getting mixed up with her need for equality. Finally, feeling in control again, she slowed her pace, turned around, and headed back to the house.

## Chapter Thirty-Six

When David spoke with Evert again early the next morning, he felt as if he were waking from a deep sleep, his life speeding up suddenly.

"She wants to sell your property," Evert said, "and things don't look so good."

"What do you mean?"

"The insurance dude must be on to something . . . he's going to San Diego . . . Guess you'll have ta lay low or—"

"What about Susan? You find out anything?" He gripped the phone.

"Yeah, she's on her way to Puerto Vallarta, I think to meet a friend."

"What about a hotel, or a cell number just in case you needed to get a hold of her . ."

"No, Dave, she doesn't have a cell, and she called in the middle of the night, just like you. That's all I could get without sounding like I was going to rob her goddamn house while she was gone."

David set the phone down and found Janice on her balcony, lying out in the sun. She stretched, body arching, legs drawn up. He stood over her, hesitating. "I'm going to Puerto Vallarta."

She pushed sunglasses into her thick hair. "Are you asking me to go along?"

"It's business," David said.

"Really?" She sat upright.

David felt uneasy at her piqued interest, her eyes full of curiosity, the look of a woman ready to find out something she didn't want to know. He looked at her. "Personal business . . ." he said.

"Sounds mysterious. And you can't tell me?"

"I could, but . . ."

"You just don't want me to go."

"No, that's not it," he protested, feeling as if he'd inadvertently lied to her.

"Don't you trust me?" she asked.

David thought about that a moment. Did he? Did he know how she might react if he told her about his past? "Sure," he said, "I trust you."

"Okay then." She stood. "Ask me."

David looked at her, the jealousy in her tone building. He tried to calculate probabilities, predict the future. What would happen if Susan found out he was alive from another woman? Getting forgiveness for death seemed easy by comparison.

"Any other time, I would—"

"Sure you would," she said.

"Look, Janice, it's just that I have to do this alone."

"Do what?" Tears welled up. "Just tell me. Are you going with someone else?"

"No, I'm not—"

"Then why can't I go? You do your 'personal business' and I'll swim in the ocean."

David looked at her. No matter what he said, she would want to come along. He felt sure of that. And she wasn't going to give up easily. He envisioned a horrible, long argument, and break-up. As Dave Cregan, he tried to maintain a superficial relationship with Janice, but he now realized that was impossible. If he said no, she might even follow him to Puerto Vallarta, or start digging into his life. He had no idea how deep her jealousy might run.

"Please ask me," she said.

"Okay . . ." He hadn't counted on Cregan's identity becoming intertwined so completely and inexorably with someone else's life. "Come to Puerto Vallarta," he said, acting like Dave Cregan. "Should be fun."

Janice looked down, then came over to him, wrapped her arms around him and kissed. He responded half-heartedly, his thoughts carrying him back to his wife, Susan, their weekend trips to the Ozarks, the stark winter sky and her warmth, her lips touching his, pulling back, the space between them filling with desire. He remembered coming home from an east coast business trip, finding her asleep, curled around her cat. While he had resented it then, he now felt regret that he wasn't honest when he woke her in the middle of the night, didn't just come out with it then - he'd lost his job. He needed her. But why didn't he? Why couldn't he tell her? Would she have offered any support? By then, they had already started sliding toward dissolution. He wished they could have explored their fears and expectations together.

Janice let go, and he could feel suspicion lingering in her voice. "I'll go pack," she said.

# Chapter Thirty-Seven

The wrecking ball swung into Susan's childhood home, walls crashing down, wood bending, snapping, metal scraping, the roof collapsing. Her mother turned to Susan. "I'd feel so much better if you had someone."

"Mom, *you* said it was okay to be alone. You did it for years, remember?"

"I just want you to be happy."

Susan watched the dust rising from wreckage, then thought, happy? What was that? Her mother and stepfather climbed into a brand-new RV, the big vehicle swaying as it rolled through the obliterated subdivision.

While driving, Susan thought about Aztec women, how a few of them gained important positions, the most important being that of high priestess. In a way, she thought, she had journeyed a difficult path, and had arrived at an important juncture in her life. As she pulled past the church and parked, she felt her heart beat fast at the thought of Menendez's "important discovery". But then she also thought about Jurgan in San Diego, and his plans to "catch up to her" in Puerto Vallarta. Thoughts of David still haunted her, now, long after she had fully accepted his death and moved on, and no matter how hard she tried not to, she imagined Cregan as her husband.

Susan packed carefully, meticulously folding her clothes, making sure she had books, briefcase, pens. She stood on the front porch. If Dave Cregan was her husband, hiding, then he had left her - purposely. If he had done that, then surely he would have left clues. Everything in the days after David's death was a blur. Thinking about it now, with a clear mind, she was afraid of what she might find . . . But something about her checking account had been bothering her for a long time, something out of place, not in the right order.

Leaving her luggage on the porch, she went back inside, and down into the musty smelling basement, still a mess, the scattered postcards - dust everywhere, the bare light bulb coated with dirt. She rummaged through the stack of boxes and eventually found the box full of canceled checks. Carefully flipping through the checks, she focused on the numbers, skipping to later ones, then back to the earlier numbers. She found the one she wanted, and held it up to the light. The 4000-dollar check dated August twelfth. Just a small piece of paper, yet heavy in her hands. She studied the front carefully, then flipped it over. Yes, it was David's signature endorsing the back. The ink was faded, but it looked like it had been stamped August twenty-second, which at first didn't appear unusual, since it matched the bank statement. But the stamp suggested someone had cashed it *that day*. If David cashed the check, she thought, then he could be alive, maybe in San Diego. The teller stamped it wrong. That was it. Susan studied it further, turning it over, putting it back and pulling it out again to see if it would look the same. Finally, she put it away. She couldn't believe that David would live a lie for so long, give up everything. Leave her. No, she thought, couldn't be possible. He wouldn't do that, telling herself over and over that it was all a terrible mistake, the evidence . . . coincidental . . . nothing more than a series of terrible mistakes.

# Chapter Thirty-Eight

Soon after they arrived in Puerto Vallarta, David told Janice that he needed time alone, and he walked the beaches, stopping at each hotel and methodically asking for Susan Brooks. But after endless "no's", apologies, and shrugs of indifference, he gave up, and sat, staring at the rolling blue waves and glistening sunlight.

"Get any personal business done," Janice asked, lounging in the beach chair next to him, her feet in the wet sand.

"No," he responded, trying not to lie. He didn't want to tell any more lies, if he could help it.

"Are you going to tell me when you do?"

"Yes." He sipped a chocolate liquor that she had ordered for him.

"And then you'll tell me what it's all about?"

"If you still want me to."

She stood and ran into the water, the surf rushing around her legs. David scratched his beard and sat back in his chair, the sun bearing down on him unmercifully. Through his dark reflecting sunglasses, he watched people stroll up and down the quiet beach. He thought about Susan. He recalled that evening at her mother's house, the warmth, the wine, Susan's apparent indifference. David now understood, having experienced his own loss, that she had never accepted her father's death. She'd been just a girl when he died. Must have broken her heart, he thought.

Finishing off the liquor made him feel a little better. He squeezed suntan lotion onto his reddening chest and watched sun-blonde and skinny Janice run from the water and sit beside him. A seagull skimmed the waves. "Why don't we do something different?" he suggested.

"Like what?" she asked.

He flipped through a brochure. "Climb some pyramids, or go for a tour of the city."

"You can't be serious? Those slums are filthy." She tilted her head back and laughed. "And climbing pyramids? Just the thought of it makes me want to cool off. Hey, let's go swim. It'll make you feel better." She grabbed his arm and tried to pull him to his feet, but he resisted.

"You go ahead."

Janice pulled wet hair away from her face. "Is touring the city part of your business?"

"No," he responded, then muttered, "I don't think so."

"Don't think so? Or don't really *want* me to come with you?"

"I just made a suggestion, that's all."

Janice stared, and appeared confused, then sauntered down the beach, the warm lap water rolling around her feet. If he could remain Cregan, he thought, could he love her? He looked at the brochure, the photographs of pyramids, and artifacts, one of them a small photo of an Aztec pendant, his two-headed serpent. He thought about his encounter with the rattlesnake in Wyoming, then the serpent dreams. Why an Aztec image? He felt sure he had seen the serpent years earlier. Otherwise, why would it have emerged from his subconscious? But why that one? Did the two-headed serpent mean something to the Aztec warriors? Good or bad? Two lives, like his? Or was it mere coincidence? In a purely mathematical, random universe, anything was possible, and coincidence likely. But, on the other hand, he knew from his conversations with Savgren that even random events seemed to flow toward order. And ever since that dream, the serpent reappeared everywhere. Probably, he thought, he had become fixated on the image. Maybe like people who notice children with the same name as their newborn, or the way separated lovers hear their lover's name whispering from the lips of strangers. Now, he stared at the brochure, and read more about the Aztec. Perhaps, he thought, the ancient culture would provide a key, an entry back into his life as David Brooks. Brushing sand off, he stood. He watched Janice dive into a rolling blue wave, then headed up the beach. At the hotel, he scribbled out a note: "Went to look for ruins."

# Chapter Thirty-Nine

With Menendez and his team close behind, Susan hiked up a steep hill anxious to see beyond, expecting a lost Aztec temple, teeming with the ghosts of long-dead high priests.

"Slow down, niña," Menendez said.

She looked at him. "Can't I be the first to see it?"

"For you, it will be the first time."

"With no people," she responded. "I want to see it as you did, as my father might have."

"Of course," Menendez said, "I understand." Then he added quickly, "You will be careful? Don't touch anything. Don't step on anything."

Susan smiled, and followed a narrow path through low scrub brush scratching her legs. At the top of the hill, she looked over treetops at an expansive ravine. Nothing, she thought, exhausted after the thirteen-hour bus ride over steep curving roads, and the haggling with the local officials about payment for keeping the area secure. And now, so close.

Menendez stood next to her. "We must cross this ravine, then just over that ridge . . ."

"How did you find such a place?"

He smiled. "I listened to a campesino's story."

Susan hiked the narrow path for hours through the highland forest, up over the next ridge, again expecting the lost Aztec temple to unfold before her. Again nothing but treetops.

"We will be there soon," Menendez said.

Susan descended into the ravine, the slope steeper than any of the others, full of loose rock. "Be careful," Menendez shouted, "the path ends at—" She didn't hear the rest while

229

digging in her heels at the edge of a cliff hidden by the trees. She heard white water roaring over rocks, but could not see past the treetops. She leaned over the edge, the cliff dark red, then looked back at Menendez who shook his head as if he knew what she was about to do.

Susan looked at the cliff, remembering rock climbing with her husband, Rainier, Ixtaccihuatl, now fully understanding the mental game. Climbing was a measure of confidence, and she felt confident. She grabbed a small tree and lowered herself over, shoving her hand into a crack, stepping on firm ledges, feeling her heart pump hard as she looked down and realized how high the cliff rose out of the forest. She climbed, a few of the holds breaking free, rock falling, but she easily reached the bottom where she could barely see the sky through all the trees. A small river was carving itself into black moss-covered rocks, white water surging around them.

Menendez stuck his head over the edge of the cliff and called down, "Are you all right?"

She waved, but got tired of waiting for the others, so she hiked upriver, finding a place to cross. She leaped from rock to rock and, on the other side, at her feet, she noticed broken shards of pottery, then a few feet away, a small four-headed artifact. Incense burner, she thought, then looked up and could hardly catch her breath. Small artifacts lay on the ground, most of them broken, but some that looked whole. Steps rose up a steep slope, half-buried. She climbed, following along the steps to the crest of the hill, amazed at the view - bright red cliff now crimson from the setting sun, forested mountains and, looking north, a view down a steep canyon, then an expansive valley. Susan knelt, pushed her hands into the cool earth, trying to visualize what lay beneath it, and thought about her father. In all the photos, he was smiling, and now she understood why. Exploration in itself was alluring, exhilarating, and the actual discovery was like riding a wave, riding high and happy, the rush of the wave breaking, white water, settling onto soft sand. She knew now the extent of her

230

father's love, not just his "work", but for everything surrounding it, the whole process of learning about ancient history. She could almost hear his words echoing up from the valley below: "Soon, my best little girl . . . soon you will want to come with me." Susan now closed her eyes and felt her father's spirit, the air itself like his hand caressing her cheek. She opened her eyes, moist from tears she didn't know were there, and understood how her past guided her future.

# Chapter Forty

The Greyhound bus was provided by the hotel and, like all the other gringo tourists, David first glimpsed the city beyond Vallarta's high-rise hotels from the bus window. The so-called ruins turned out to be fake, placed near the sandy beaches. At first, he was fooled, believing that a wall sticking out of the ground was an excavation in progress. But he grew skeptical when their guide led them past a diverse collection of ancient artifacts strategically placed along a paved path. Speaking in English, the Mexican tour guide explained what little he knew about giant Olmec heads and their characteristic thick, down-turned lips and flat noses. David tapped the side of a six-foot head and listened to reverberations from the hollow inside. Further along the path there was a freshly carved fresco of Mayan jaguar gods, then feathered serpent heads jutting out from an "Aztec" wall. Near the exit, there was a gift shop with hundreds of replicas - pottery, effigy vessels, fertility gods. All the fakery made him sick. He was tired of it. He reached into his pocket and pulled out his serpent pendant. He looked at it thinking that it was more authentic than the replicas still under glass in the gift shop. He slipped the pendant over his head, the serpent now dangling from his neck, feeling cool against his chest.

David wandered into a shaded area, and into a small museum where at least a few pieces might be authentic. A Death Mask. Odd, David thought, to be called a "death" mask when it looked so lifelike, fragments of polished jade carefully crafted into its face, long nose, and dark obsidian eyes. The mask was in excellent condition, except for a small crack running between the eyes and across the forehead. He touched his scar. When, he thought, could he rip away his own mask, the face of Dave Cregan, and piece together what remained of Brooks?

The ride back to the hotel was fast, the bus swerving in and out of traffic. In his hotel room, he found Janice, drink in hand, sitting on the edge of the bed, watching TV, the rapid, unintelligible Mexican words filling the room like static.

She turned to him. "Did you have a nice time?"

"I left you a note."

"You told me the tour wasn't important."

"No," he protested, "I asked you to go along."

"But you didn't tell me you would go anyway, and leave me alone all afternoon."

David shrugged. "I screwed up," he said. He remembered arguments with his wife starting like this. Would he be doomed to making the same mistakes? "I'm going to take a shower."

In the bathroom, he leaned on the sink and stared at his reflection, his fake green eyes, scar. His serpent necklace around his neck. He could no longer live like this. Even if he didn't find Susan. Standing in the warm shower, he watched dirt swirling down the drain. The longer he stayed with Janice, the more lies he would have to live. And a life of lies was as hollow as the Olmec head. Returning to the room, he found the lights off, candlelight flickering over the hotel's special lobster dinner, and Janice waiting in a soft white nightgown.

He drank wine silently, while tasting the hot butter on the chewy lobster, eating side dishes, thinking again, as he had since arriving, that the food would be all right. Hotel food had to be sterile, he thought, otherwise, tourists would avoid the place. Still, he worried that any food prepared in Mexico might make his throat swell shut. He took a pill each day, just in case. And now, he wasn't sure if the medication or the dry air and sun made his mouth feel parched all the time.

Janice looked at him, her skin sunburned and tight. "I would

233

have gone with you," she said, "but I can't stand those buses, the people who ride them don't bathe, and you'll probably get sick just breathing the air; at least on the beach you get sea breezes."

"Hotel bus," he said. "It was clean." He drank water.

"Are you better now?" Janice asked.

David looked at her and sensed tension in her voice. Maybe he was the tense one, he thought, his shoulders hunched up, holding in all his feelings like he had with his wife. He wanted to talk, but not with Janice. Where was Susan?

"Commitment," Janice said. "It just happens . . . If we are going to be together . . ." She stood and walked over to him. She wrapped her arms around his neck, kissed his ear, and slid her hand under his shirt.

"No," he said.

"It's okay," she responded.

David pushed against her shoulders. She moved his hands to her hard breasts. She backed him onto the couch, kissed him heavily, pulling on his lower lip with her teeth, her lithe body moving rhythmically against him. David felt disconnected, his body not his.

# Chapter Forty-One

Susan had hoped to dig more, but Menendez and his small team seemed to take forever, painstakingly marking the perimeter of the site, which left only enough time to scrape a layer of dirt from the first quadrant. On the way out, he paid local *federales* to guard it from looters. Menendez and his team returned to Guadalajara while Susan took the arduous bus ride back to Puerto Vallarta, arriving mid-afternoon. Tired of sitting for hours in the cramped bus, she walked through downtown, then into the South hotel zone where a hot, dry wind blew along the beach while the sun shimmered off the blue Pacific.

Susan had debated whether or not to visit with Elizabeth in Mexico. But it seemed almost rude not to. After all, the bus station was not far from the hotel, and they would be there at the same time. And Elizabeth, with her social exuberance, would be disappointed if she didn't join them, make it a party.

She found her young friend on the veranda shaded by a table umbrella, her nose smeared with zinc oxide. Behind her was the Azetlan Hotel jutting up into the clear sky. A group of tourists played volleyball in the white sand and sun.

Susan was sweaty and covered with dust as she set her pack down and sat with Elizabeth who said, "My husband's in bed with a hangover." A waiter set down drinks and politely asked, in English, if there was anything more they needed. Elizabeth handed him ten American dollars and he left.

"What is this place?" Susan asked. "Some sort of tourist club?"

"All of Vallarta is like this."

"Not all of it." Susan pointed behind her. "Go that way and you'll find a real Mexican city." But, she thought, those were her own values. Elizabeth and Bill had a different concept of fun.

"Right, but we're here to relax. That's not a bad thing to do sometimes . . ."

Maybe, Susan thought, but felt anxious to get back to work. She could at least gather information at the museum in Puerto Vallarta. Or, she thought, she could spend the last of her mother's loan, pay her back after selling the Wyoming property. Then she could stay here longer, even go back to the site alone and look around, count the steps, dig a little. Menendez might get mad at first, but would get over that quickly. He wouldn't mind. She would be careful. He wouldn't be ready with a bigger, more experienced team in at least a week. After that, the place would be crawling with people.

After checking into her room, Susan walked with Elizabeth along the long, wide beach curving toward the next high-rise hotel. By evening, Susan's skin was getting red, and she didn't want to smear on more of the oily suntan lotion. Her white room smelled of disinfectant, giving the illusion of cleanliness. While showering, she drowned a cockroach. She had trouble getting to sleep, and woke shortly after - the smell, the white room feeling like a hospital - déjà vu - the hospital in Winnipeg. Where was David? She felt like he was out there in the wilderness.

The next day she went scuba-diving with Bill and Elizabeth. Susan liked the idea of diving into the silence of the cool Pacific. Beneath the shimmering surface, she felt a different sort of aloneness. In her own world, Susan dove deep along erratically-shaped coral reefs, enthralled by the fish and the brightly-colored rocks. Twisting her body to fit into a small gap, she dove underneath the coral. Bright colors swirled around her as fish darted. Regulator bubbles were suspended by the reef before sliding through imperceptibly small openings. She looked behind her, then in front. She could not have possibly come through that way, she thought, the reef surrounding her. Elizabeth and Bill. Where were they? She heard clanking, the sound of her own tank hitting the coral. She could feel her heart pounding through to her back, against the tank. She followed a school of silver fish through a big opening, no reef, just a vast expanse of water. Allowing her body to drift, with the sensation of peaceful nothingness, she sank. She felt in control, sinking deeper and watching, studying the various fish, shades of light, wondering if any artifacts might have been thrown into the sea. She smiled. What a wonderful country, she thought, able to hike into the rugged, mountainous highlands one day and the next day, explore the ocean.

Someone gripped her arm. Bill was pulling her toward the surface. Popping free at the top, she yanked the regulator from her mouth to protest, but sucked water into her throat. She coughed and spit, and they dragged her onto the beach, stripping off her heavy tank. Bill's face was white, and he yelled, "Jesus, what the hell were you thinking?"

Susan coughed. "*I* knew what I was doing," she said, "but you obviously didn't."

"We were scared," Elizabeth responded. "You looked hurt."

"I'm fine," Susan said, thinking that their concern was a little extreme. She watched a seagull dive into a wave. "I've had enough fun for today," she said, and carried her scuba gear back along the beach.

After a short taxi ride, Susan got out in front of the museum, with thick round pillars, wide stone steps. She met the curator, and he led her to an oppressively tiny office, wishing her luck, and shutting the door. One narrow ray of sunlight from a round window lit the corner of Susan's work. She moved a large stack of excavation records and hunched over an open ledger.

Each artifact was listed, its size, location of find, and a short comment regarding its possible significance. She turned the pages carefully, running her index finger over the location-column, then pouring over the relevant entries and devouring the information. Menendez's temple could be the heart of a small city, she thought, a trade center between Tenochtitlan and Monte Alban. She also found many entries for "laughing heads" and "Chacmool". As she scribbled them into her notebook, she thought about people traveling narrow pathways, six hundred years ago, through the forested mountains of the western highlands. Closing her eyes, she leaned back and saw her dead husband hiking feverishly on one of those pathways, slipping and falling into a canyon.

Susan pushed away from the desk, the office suffocating. She closed her notebook and escaped to the cool, cavernous museum. "Damn," she muttered, having avoided, until now, thinking about David, the small inconsistencies about his death, and Cregan in San Diego. Now, however, she felt him alive again, as if he were searching for her - she imagined them both in the past, David an Aztec warrior searching for the high priestess. Like her dream. She emerged from the building into the brilliant three o'clock sunlight.

# Chapter Forty-Two

For David, Puerto Vallarta felt like other Mexican cities - crowded streets, vendors selling ponchos, belts, jewelry, hailing shoppers with tortillas flapping in grubby hands, the sweet smell of bloody meat sizzling on portable grills, the smell of the trodden earth itself wafting up into a swirl of mingling odors all seemingly at odds. Similar to, but not, the Mexico he'd known in Tijuana. These people were proud of their heritage, the streets vibrant and full of activity.

He explored the city on foot, walking down narrow stone streets and alleys, parched white adobe row houses, fat women standing in doorways with chubby babies perched on their hips. In the center of town, the marketplace, a bus careened around a corner and nearly crashed into a tortilla stand, Mexicans jumping out of the way. He stopped and examined the leather wares of a bronze-faced man, the "tan" developed over generations of struggle. David yanked off his cheap plastic-coated belt, gave it to the man, and bought a new leather one. He liked the feel of authenticity. While slipping it through the loops, he scanned the busy square. A small park with a statue of a man on horseback shone white in the sunlight filtering through the trees. Shadows danced in the breeze while he watched a woman, an American, on the other side of the park. She was holding up a blanket, examining it in front of the shopkeeper. Susan, he thought, and moved closer, standing near the statue. She wore a long, faded white dress and a scarf pulled tightly around her head, tied at her chin, keeping her hair from blowing across her face. She spoke rapidly, in Spanish, gesturing, then suddenly threw her hands up in disgust and walked away into the milling crowd. The shopkeeper chased after, shouting a lower price, but she did not turn back.

David followed her, knowing that the woman was Susan, but stunned by the fluency of her Spanish. Another bus came around the corner with its tire up on the sidewalk, then thumped back to the street. As it lurched into gear and accelerated, the woman ran out of its way. David stopped short, thinking she would be hit. But the bus passed and she was on the other side of the street, bargaining with another vendor over another blanket. David held his hand to his forehead and squinted. Moving along the sidewalk toward the street, he struggled past *campesinos, mujures y niños*, speaking in embarrassed Spanish, "*Perdon, perdon.*" He reverted to English. "Excuse me, sorry, pardon me." An afternoon lunch crowd of businessmen in black suits and ties, and shiny shoes, blocked his way. He started across the street and a taxi zipped by. Taxis were faster than buses, harder to see.

He picked up the blanket she'd held, and looked up and down the narrow, shadowy street. *Any* long white dress in the shadows could be hers. He threw the blanket back onto the table, and started off one way, then stopping, his eyes feeling tight and dry. He could feel his heart pumping as he ran, walked, hoping to see her again. She stepped out of a shadow, turned toward him, looking past him, her face visible only for an instant, but clearly Susan. She walked into the crowd, David trying to follow. He searched the street, went inside a few shops, and asked for the woman "*con una falda blanca*". Eventually, he gave up and headed back toward the square, the breeze cooling his sweat and chilling him, stopping to buy a serape.

Walking back, he struggled to understand what he had just seen. His wife, the woman he had known, seldom went anywhere alone; she lacked ambition, and did not speak any foreign languages. But the woman in the white dress was

240

Susan. No question. And she was speaking fluent Spanish, venturing alone into this Mexican city.

As he returned to the center of town, the sun was sinking and the shadows lengthening. Wrought-iron tables and café chairs remained in sunlight, a favorite spot for tourists. At several of the tables, men and women in neatly pressed shorts and windbreakers sat tiredly with their shopping bags full. Then she appeared again, her skirt flowing as she floated into an empty seat. David felt cold and pulled the serape around his shoulders. He had to confront her, seek her forgiveness, gain redemption, and life. He would return from the dead. He touched the serpent pendant next to his heart, and slowly walked toward her, seeing her joined by a man wearing long, pressed pants, a jacket, and sunglasses propped on his head. Then another woman showed up and the three of them headed for the opposite side of the square. Regardless of the outcome, he thought, *I must act. Now!* He ran into the square only to have Susan and her friends climb into a taxi and speed away.

David searched frantically for another taxi. Eventually one pulled up, and he jumped in the back seat.

"*Ah . . . Yo quiero . . . ir . . . el otro taxi*?"

"Heh?" The driver turned toward him.

"*Derecho*," David said emphatically, pointing straight ahead and speaking very slowly. "*Otro*. Taxi."

He wanted to add "you idiot", but knew that *he* was the idiot, not the driver whose face suddenly glowed with the pleasure of understanding. "Ah, *tu quieres segui el otro* taxi." He floored the gas pedal, the vehicle screeching and airborne for a second, then speeding recklessly. Slow down, David thought, slow down. They rounded a corner and were engulfed by a sea of traffic, taxis, buses, cars filling the narrow streets. David gripped the seat while the driver slammed on the brakes, the left fender scraping a bus. He felt his heart sink, knowing that he had lost her again. This time he would not give up; he would not run. No matter what, he would find her.

The bus driver got out and yelled in Spanish. David watched them wave their hands in the air, scowl at each other, then the bus driver shook his head, spit, and walked away muttering to himself. The taxi driver sulked on the way back to the hotel. David did not blame the driver for losing Susan. He understood that the driver was only trying to eke out a living. And he gave him a big tip.

As he walked into the brightly-lit lobby, he felt out of place, as if everyone was sure to question his grimace and his bloodshot eyes.

"Excuse me," someone said in English and David jumped, turning quickly to see the hotel manager.

"Yes."

"I'm sorry. I did not mean to startle you. But there is a letter for you at the desk."

David watched the front desk clerk pull out a long white envelope, then he sat in one of the leather chairs that circled the perimeter of the lobby. He looked up at the ceiling with its arches and pillars reflecting pink light from the sun sinking into the sea, then opened the envelope and found one sheet of hotel stationery, the letterhead and design - a red-eyed serpent in a perfect circle, eating its tail. At first he did not recognize the handwriting, soft curling waves of blue ink, but the message was clear. "David, thanks for some good times but you were getting to be too much work. Maybe we'll try again someday, who knows? Maybe you'll share some of your secrets. L—- Janice." He rushed upstairs to their third-floor room, and surveyed the mess - bedclothes bunched up, wet towels draped over the headboard, his clothes indiscriminately strewn about. David was unprepared for the feeling of loss, his fake life devoured by the other head of the serpent. He had existed, shared thoughts, no matter how shallow, and even laughed in his alternate reality. *Any* time spent with Janice had been a commitment. He owed her some explanation, some consolation, not wanting to leave any more broken lives in his path to redemption.

David looked out the window and saw Janice with her suitcase, sitting in a lounge chair, on the hotel's long patio, sundress tucked under her long legs. He ran down the spiraling stairs, out the back door and walked along the beach, toward the patio.

The sun hung on the horizon ready to slip into the ocean while a breeze chilled the evening air. Several tourists were watching the sunset. He recalled Janice talking about sharing the event with him. A man wearing a bright green shirt and carrying two drinks sat next to Janice. David stood on the beach watching, voices from the patio like pieces of broken civilization, tumbling in the surf, lapping onto shore.

They stood, Janice moving away quickly, the man going back into the hotel. David called for Janice to stop, as the molten edge of the sun finally disappeared into the Pacific, leaving only the red glow. "Oh," she said flatly, "it's you. Didn't you get my note?"

"Yes, I did, but . . . Look, Janice, I understand why you would leave."

"Yeah, sure you do." She shook her head. "I don't know when to believe you. I don't know you. I didn't even know you were from St Louis. That's pretty basic, isn't it?"

David looked at her. His life with her was gone, like a boulder removed from his chest, but leaving an empty space. "You'll be okay," he muttered, trying to assure himself more than her.

She scowled. "Are you married?"

"Yes," he responded, "I am, but—"

"I don't know what your problem is. And really, I don't care." She pushed through the doors and ran toward the lobby.

David shivered, sure now that, as he suspected, the man on the patio was the term-life agent Jurgan. Lights from the highrise hotel created a yellow glow fading into the darkness. Exhausted and hungry, he went inside, past the restaurant, people laughing and the aroma of sopapillas spilling out into the night. Pausing at the restaurant entrance, he felt the warm air from the huge room with its lights dimmed, plants twisting around pillars and reaching the ceiling. He climbed spiraling stairs leading to the third floor and as he approached his room, Jurgan appeared at the other end of the gold and red corridor.

David froze, feeling like an animal in the headlights of an oncoming truck, staring at the insurance agent in his jogging shoes, pressed slacks, camera. Then he ran back the way he had come, onto the dark beach, white surf surging over the sand, running past the next hotel and up into the street blaring with traffic. Taxis pulled to the curb, then departed, swarming around an open parking space. He waved his arms frantically and one of the taxis took him away. If he was going to be revealed as the miserable impostor that he was, it must come from him. If Jurgan told her, he would be a criminal caught, trying to weasel forgiveness to save himself. He had to find her first. Then he could answer her inevitable questions. Jurgan would twist the truth to get whatever he wanted. David could no longer lie to her. He would try to prove his worthiness, regain a shred of integrity.

He stopped at hotel after hotel, asking for all Susans, pounding on the desk when a clerk refused to reveal names. One clerk looked at him and said, "Susan Chambers." Had she married, he thought. Not likely. Evert would have told him that one. But he found himself wishing she had been unable to start a new life without him, just as he had been unable. Whether she was married or not, he had to see her, whatever happened after that was all right. He described Susan as an attractive woman and the clerk responded, "Yes, yes, I think I see that." But as David's pulse raced, the clerk talked about a white-haired woman. He moved on, asking for, and finding a Susan Moore. She had discarded his name. Wouldn't the Susan he married have kept his name?

David stood in the lobby, and stared at the stairs leading to her room, then down at his hand shaking. Should he just rush upstairs and bang on her door, looking crazed like this, like he felt, his eyes popping out of his head and his heart pounding, clothes dirty, a Tijuana beggar? And, he thought, who was this Susan, this woman who was no longer his wife? Now Susan Moore? But, he thought, not the Susan Moore he had married. The woman in the white dress was independent, confidently alone, and she appeared to know where she was going and why.

# Chapter Forty-Three

At the airport, Susan watched Bill hook his arm around Elizabeth's neck, pulling her into the terminal, his hand clutching a red bull statue with black horns, then they merged into the crowd of other tourists. Relieved to be alone again, Susan also felt empty, almost wishing she could be more like Elizabeth, happy with her husband, and always ready for the next good time. Then she shook her head and thought she was being naive. They would probably get divorced, like so many other marriages. Better to be alone, she reasoned. Lifelong marriage reserved for only a select few.

During the taxi ride back to the hotel, Susan read over her notes. One more day at the museum, then she would visit the archeological site by herself. Then home. Wherever that was, she thought, feeling increasingly disconnected from St Louis.

Returning to her room, she found a message from Jurgan: "Meet me for a drink."

Susan's gut tightened. Jurgan must've found out something about Cregan. Maybe it was Jurgan's presence in Puerto Vallarta that she had sensed, and maybe that was why she imagined her husband as an Aztec warrior slogging toward the temple. She wanted Cregan to be just another coincidence.

She waited at her hotel's long wooden bar with ceiling fans slowly swirling overhead. Jurgan arrived disheveled and anxious, his smile forced, camera slung over his shoulder, ordering tequila. He leaned close, and said, "I think it's over."

Susan glanced around the lounge where couples were talking and laughing. The bartender set down two shots of tequila. She drank, and felt a warm glow, for a moment the doubts falling away. But they returned quickly. What did he mean, he *thought* it was over? *What* was over? "Did you meet Cregan?" she asked.

Jurgan shrugged. "He left for vacation."

"Then how—"

"He's vacationing in *Puerto Vallarta*."

She looked at him. Too much of a coincidence, she thought. What were the chances of that happening? "So you came *here* and found him?"

"Drink up," he said. "You know, since you *did* file a claim, it would be fraud if—"

She glared. "Dammit, did you find Cregan or not?"

"No," he said. "I didn't actually meet him."

Susan stared. "Then how do you know?"

Jurgan leaned his elbow on the bar, his face cupped in his hand, eyes bloodshot, hair tousled. "I had a long talk with his girlfriend."

"Girlfriend?" The images of her husband alive in a dual life returned. Did he reject her, she thought, for another woman?

"Yes," Jurgan continued. "His *girlfriend* described him to me. But . . . obviously, he wasn't your husband. Only an outside chance anyway. I never took it too seriously. Just being thorough."

"You don't sound convinced," she said.

He shrugged. "Everything else fit. Then his girlfriend kept telling me how much she loved his *green* eyes. I told her bull crap! Did she think I was stupid?"

"I'm sure she loved that."

"Who cares? I wear contacts. Eye color can be fake. But then she told me she was a cosmetologist, a professional . . . so I guess she'd know." Jurgan touched Susan's arm. "Your husband's eyes *are* blue, correct?" She nodded. "Still," he said, "it doesn't feel right. What am I missing?"

"I don't know," she responded.

"Maybe I was wrong about you." He squeezed her arm, leaned forward abruptly and tried kissing her, his lips touching

247

hers. Susan pulled away, stood, glared at his grinning, tequila-laden face, then she grabbed a napkin from the bar, and fled, wiping her mouth as she ran up the curving stairs to her room.

Susan thought, wasn't too surprising that he'd want to screw her. Jurgan had been deceiving and manipulating in everything he'd done. She remembered his head in the dumpster behind her house. She should've pushed him in.

She shut the door to her room, and remembered Jurgan explaining his black eye — messing around with someone else's girlfriend. Probably the girl hit him, Susan thought. At least this time he made sure the other guy, her husband, was dead before trying anything.

She lay on her back staring at the stucco ceiling. She thought about Bill and Elizabeth. Compared to Jurgan, Bill seemed fairly innocent. Maybe they would be okay, lifelong partners. What about Susan and David? Given a better chance in the beginning, she thought, what would have happened to them? She drifted off to sleep, dreaming of fish darting in and out of a reef. She dove deeper and deeper until she found a cavern, following it, twisting and curving, entering a chamber where she found papers - insurance forms, land deeds, canceled checks - all bound by rope and stacked high to the chamber ceiling. The rope broke and the white papers swirled around her in a whirlpool - the ocean draining into a dark hole. Suddenly, reaching through it all came two arms, reaching for her, and she was drawn into the swirling vortex - the swollen face of her husband emerging, eyes pale green receding into blackening sockets. She tried to swim to the surface, but David held firmly to her leg, her mouth open, crying out "No," water pouring into her lungs. Somewhere, she heard loud, steady pounding.

She woke lying on her back, choking. Someone knocked on the door.

"*Senorita, esta bien*?"

Susan responded weakly. "*Si, si, esta mala suelo, nada mas.* Bad dream, nothing more."

Then the voice spoke in clear English. "Are you Susan Moore?"

"Yes." She opened the door.

"A message for you." A young porter handed her an envelope.

Susan sat on her bed and stared at the envelope, Aztec letterhead, serpents coiled into circles, all devouring their tails. Jurgan? Who else? But why didn't he just deliver his own message? She started to open it and noticed that her hands were trembling. She set it on the nightstand, and stared at the message in the yellow lamplight. Then she ripped it open, tearing the note inside, holding the ripped pieces together to read it. She read it several times.

Not sure about what any of it meant, she felt strangely calm, or maybe just too afraid to move too fast, as she went out into the cool night air. While walking along the moonlit beach, the note repeated itself in her mind as if beyond her control. Please meet me, it said, on the veranda of Casa Feliz. The message had not been signed, and she thought it must be another one of Jurgan's perverse tricks, another twist to his "investigation". But the ambiguity of the note lured her. Cregan? She recited it aloud as she walked, "You may not understand who I am, but we must meet again."

The moonlit surf surged onto shore rhythmically as it had done for eons and music floated in the night air. Susan could hear blaring brass horns, and her heart beat rapidly as she approached the veranda with its red and yellow light bulbs outlining a long patio curving onto the beach. She searched the tables, crowded around a glossy, wooden dance floor, colored lights reflecting from the shiny wood. Who sent the note? Where was he? She looked for him on the dance floor - a young woman wearing a full-length skirt, swimsuit strapped over small breasts, gyrated to the blasting horns. Was that woman having fun, truly, Susan thought, and watched her partner grinning like a monkey and swiveling his hips. A different kind of life, she thought, easy, like Elizabeth's, but she knew that anyone's life could change dramatically, whimsically, for no apparent reason. As hers had, several times.

*We make choices*, Susan thought, her heart pounding, *increasing, or decreasing, our chances at . . .* In the far corner, a man wearing white trousers and white shirt sat staring out at the gringos. As the band played and more people crowded onto the dance floor, Susan felt drawn to the man and moved slowly around the empty tables. *Chances at what*, she questioned, *finding the truth?* With each step she felt her insides tighten. She could turn away, run, decide to forget the note, bury all possibilities deep into her subconscious. Try never again to think about what might have happened. What good was the truth? But some things weren't easy to forget. The man stood and stepped away from his table. A few feet from him, she stopped. No way to turn back now, even if she wanted to. *I chose this*, she thought, *I'm in control. Just be reasonable*. She studied his face fully, as well as she could in the colored lights and distracting noise from the band. He appeared sunburned, or was it the red light? A graying beard was cropped close to his jaw, and a thin scar ran diagonally through the bridge of his nose and touching his forehead; his eyes were deep set and shadowy. But when the lights brightened, the man's eyes glared, reflecting red, like a serpent, and there was no doubt this snake was her long dead husband now returning to haunt her - alive - the clues falling into place like the slamming of a tomb's door.

Susan felt her knees buckle, but quickly recovered, bracing herself against the cold hard reality - her husband had left her, lived a lie, hidden from her. Questions flooded over her. Had he left her to die in the wilderness? When did he decide to run? Did *she* do something to cause this? No, she thought, she had grown far beyond feeling guilty about her husband's "death". But this was different. What was this? *How am I supposed to feel?* Then suddenly and forcefully her whole body filled with hatred.

"You bastard!" She lunged at him, flailing her fists against his chest. But his arms wrapped around her and held her. She pushed and clawed, and broke free, running, stumbling past a chair, flinging it aside as she made her escape into the dark. *Forget it*, she thought, *he's dead, should be dead. Should have left it alone, never met him again*. But she wasn't the one who was digging up the past, was she? Why was he back tormenting her with his betrayal?

She ran into the pounding surf, stopping only when the cold waves slapped hard at her legs, then pulled - her footsteps sinking heavily into the cool, soft sand. But she resisted. Turning, she emerged from the surf only to stare once again into his face, his shadowy eyes, black against moonlit skin. His eyes had been black on that other night when the moon cast shadows, and now the water was white again, the surf pounding on the beach. Yes, it was her husband, and *nothing* could justify him - despite the pull of his quiet, subdued voice.

"I understand. Run. I did."

She stood defiant, glaring at him. She could not move. He blocked the path. "Get away!" she screamed, refusing to back down, allow him to dictate what she would do.

He stood firm, but said nothing.

"Get away from me!"

"Is that what you want?"

She bent her fingers like claws. "I want to gouge your eyes out!"

He backed away, and she ran down the beach, splashing through the encroaching waves. "Susan," he yelled.

But she ran through the unstable sand, back to her hotel. She passed through the revolving door to the lobby, and headed up the stairs, but stopped. She looked for Jurgan. Telling him that she had seen her dead husband alive was the only sane, smart thing to do, but the bar was so crowded she couldn't see across it. She ran up the stairs, down the gaudily decorated hallway - gold wallpaper with tightly wound red serpents. She locked and bolted her door. How could she have been so stupid, she thought, ignoring the proof? David had broken into his own home, "stolen" a check, jacket - what else? Had he spied on her? Laughed? Screwed other women? She phoned Jurgan, no answer, again his voicemail, so she tried his hotel, but he wasn't there either. She left a message: "I found him", the clerk asking if that was all. She hung up, feeling ugly, even though she knew that she was innocent. She had done nothing wrong. She had worked hard, gained a new life for herself without him. Even so, she felt guilty now wanting to kill her husband, make him pay for his lies.

Susan lay on the bed, stared at the pink stucco ceiling. The Aztec woman, she thought, had to be smart to gain equality . . . to survive. She punched the pillow, then threw it across the room, knocking over a lamp. I must go on with my plans, she thought, the museum tomorrow, then on to the excavation . . . But then what? Must go on, like it never happened, couldn't let it interfere with her life. "Bastard," she screamed, pushing her books off the table, papers fluttering to the floor.

She paced to the front wall, threw open a curtain covering a small porthole of a window, and stared out at the moonlight - white water, the rapids hurling her through space, her life speeding out of control, changing her forever, then pitched into darkness - nothing left but her battered self, her soul abandoned in the wilderness. She survived then. And she would survive now.

# Chapter Forty-Four

David watched his wife disappear into the lights from the high-rise hotels. His legs felt rubbery. But he couldn't let her go that easily. Her angry shouts only made him more determined - he had to face up to her scrutiny. Bear the full brunt of her anger, accept the consequences of his foolish lies. He followed her path up the beach, stopping at a circular drive in front of her hotel. He pushed through the revolving entrance door, and scanned the lobby - a couple at the front desk, a bar, an elevator, stairs curving up to the second floor and Susan's room. A young woman staggered out of the bar, laughing, walking into David. He dodged her, turned, and faced Jurgan, who leaned forward, squinting in the bright lobby lights.

"Excuse me," David said, but Jurgan blocked his way.

The insurance agent reeked of alcohol. "Hey, don't I know you?"

David glanced at the exit. "No."

"Yeah I do." Jurgan stared. "Who are you?"

"None of your business," David said, and tried stepping past, but Jurgan grabbed his arm.

"I *do* know you," Jurgan insisted.

David blinked, turned his head. "Let go of me." He tried pulling his arm away but Jurgan tightened his grip.

"Dave Cregan?"

David thought, this isn't the way he wanted it. He needed Susan alone, not with this jerk hounding him.

"Yeah, has to be you." The insurance agent leaned close, brow furrowed, and he almost fell. "Yeah," he said, "green eyes, but . . ." He stared.

"I said, let go." David wrapped his hand around Jurgan's wrist and pulled himself free.

"So why'd you use a David Brooks prescription number?"

David shook his head, then turned away, walking out the revolving door, and ran onto the beach.

Jurgan stumbled outside, and shouted, "You *are* Brooks."

David circled the hotel, across the street, away from the high-rise hotels, and into downtown Puerto Vallarta. He walked past beggars asleep at doorsteps, cradling tequila bottles, and all-night joints where horns wailed, patriotic music blasting out into the night. A tequila bottle rolled into the street, and water spilled from a doorway, small rivulets. Like blood, he thought. The blood of Aztec warriors. He watched the moon slowly arc across the starlit sky and fall toward the ocean, and he returned to her hotel where he peeked in the windows. Jurgan was gone.

The desk clerk told him that Susan wasn't in. Maybe that was good, he thought. By the time she returned, the shock of seeing him alive might have worn off, and she would feel better. He sat in a large leather chair, drifting off to sleep, waking, thinking he saw a woman in a white dress floating across the lobby. He started to get up, then realized he was watching a maid rolling a rack of white sheets. The clerk stared at him, and a security guard arrived. David went back out into the night and found a recess in the building hidden by maguey plants. He hunched up and slept like a beggar. When he woke again, the sky had turned gray. He went back inside, the gray light filling the lobby. He shuffled over to a small table, drank black coffee, and felt his body tense, his hands sweat, and he thought, what if she had left Puerto Vallarta? The "not in" message at the front desk a trick?

Susan emerged from the elevator, walked across the lobby, and through the revolving door. David spilled coffee, burning on his arm as he saw her climbing into a taxi, and he followed her.

After only a few turns, a drive into downtown, he watched Susan get out in front of a building with smooth stone columns and wide steps rising to a big wooden door.

As the door shut behind her, David ran up the steps, grabbed the oversized handle and pulled. Inside the museum, a high-domed room soared over ornate pillars around the periphery forming a hallway. The circular hall was lined with glass cases full of artifacts. He spotted Susan far across the room, talking to a man in a business suit, the museum curator. She followed the man to a room with a red-lettered sign in Spanish. They shook hands, and Susan went behind the door. David approached the curator. "*Ah perdon, señor, que es la puerto*? What is this door?"

"You may speak in English if you wish."

"Sorry. That door . . . what does the sign say?" He felt anxious, wanting to know if Susan could go out another way. But he didn't ask, not wanting to arouse suspicion.

The curator turned. "It says 'museum personnel only'. Why do you ask, señor?"

David shook his head. "No reason . . . *no razon*." But the curator did not move, apparently waiting for an explanation. David pointed to a sign on one of the pillars. "And that one?"

"Cameras are forbidden . . ."

"It says 'no photographs'? *Fotografias?*"

The curator smiled politely and said, "*Bueno, senor, en este pais muchas personas hablan en español*." He walked away, his footsteps echoing in the large room.

David stood near the door and looked at a display. Inside the glass case, several small figurines squatted around a life-sized stone figure lying on its back with flexed legs, hands holding a receptacle on its chest. He tried reading the display's plaque. He recognized only one word - *corazon*, heart.

He looked up and saw Susan pulling the office door shut, gripping her notebook close to her chest as she faced him.

"Get away from me!"

"I can't . . ." David hesitated, knowing that he would have to choose his words carefully.

"I have work to do."

"I know the feeling," he said. That's what he had done, he thought, when they were together. He worked harder, and harder, unconsciously avoiding the more daunting challenge of their marriage.

She glared. "You're full of answers, aren't you? I don't need any answers from you. You're sick."

She tried to get past him, but he stepped in front of her. "Just look at me," he pleaded, "Maybe I've changed."

Susan stared at him, his face a pre-Columbian mask. "What do you want from me?"

He wanted to give her something, show her that he wanted peace. Didn't want to hurt her again. He felt the trinket necklace against his chest and carefully lifted the chain over his head, holding it in front of her, the small, silver-plated serpent with its two heads facing opposite directions. Maybe, he thought, she would accept the serpent. Proof that he had given up his duplicitous life.

Susan's eyes widened, face reddening, and she slapped the necklace out of his hand.

David watched the trinket slide in pieces across the floor, then looked at her. It's okay, he thought, he deserved it and he would accept it.

"What's wrong," she said. "Didn't your girlfriend like blue eyes?"

David touched the corner of his eye. The contact lenses had become part of him. He no longer felt them. He carefully pinched the rim of the lens, peeling it away, one eye blue, the other green. With the lens in his palm, he held it out to her, his vision momentarily blurry and skewed. He needed to unravel all of his lies, fully.

"You hid behind those? You left me to wonder what happened, never knowing if you suffered! You're pathetic." She pushed him, and he grabbed her. "Let go!" She jerked her arm away, and started to walk, but he blocked her way, trapping her against the display. She turned and stared at the artifacts.

David stood next to her, his heart pounding, not wanting her to leave but unable to say anything, unable to think of anything that would make her stay, make her understand. How could he, when he did not fully understand? He wanted forgiveness, but *how do I get it?* He looked at the plaque, then tapped the glass. "What does it say?" he asked.

"Read it yourself."

"I can't," he said.

"What makes you think *I* can?"

David closed his eyes and exhaled. What could he tell her? That he'd been stalking her through the streets of Puerto Vallarta? "Just talk to me . . ."

She leaned hard against the glass. "Chacmool," she said. "It's for sacrificing human hearts." She lifted her hands off the display. "The figurines are called laughing heads."

David felt her anger and looked closer at the ancient, molded clay with the pixie-like face and triangular head. "Somebody had a bizarre sense of humor."

"The Aztec believed that the dying man was responsible for his own death . . . in collusion with the Lord of the Dead. He must confess the collusion." She turned and faced him. "Heard enough?"

His mask-like face reflected in the glass. "I've changed," he insisted, thinking, she had to see that, didn't she?

She turned back to the display and read, "The living had to endure abstinence . . . further ritual . . . nightmares."

He grimaced, tense, his mind reeling off excuses - didn't mean to cause any harm, thought you'd be okay with the insurance money, didn't think you'd miss me. Then he shrugged, and tried to fend off the impact of his lies, calculate the math - other universes, just testing a theory. "You want me to confess?" he asked.

"I hate you," she said.

He knew she would feel that way. But, even with knowing, his heart now sank at her words. He stared out across the museum. *Okay,* he thought, *I'm ready to tell her everything, confess my cowardice in the Canadian wilderness, my perverse decision to "die".* But then he saw Jurgan walking across the smooth floor, toward them as they stood leaning against the glass case.

"That's good," Jurgan said. "Mind if I take a few pictures?" He aimed his camera and it flashed like lightning in the cavernous museum. "Hope your eyes don't show up red." Then he turned to Susan. "You were good. Especially that last message. Found who? Cregan or Brooks? Guess it depended on *what* I found out?"

"I'm responsible," David said. "Susan's done nothing wrong." He looked down and murmured, "Except maybe marrying me in the first place." He had been ready to confess. Could he now only admit he was worthless? He felt his resolve slipping away, and fought to keep it.

Jurgan looked at Susan. "Now it looks like you will owe us."

"Why?" she responded. "You haven't paid anything."

"You think this investigation was cheap?" He smiled, his face ashen and eyes watery, hung-over, hands trembling.

"There he is, alive, you won't have to pay the damn claim. You want to suck my blood now?"

"We'll just want to recoup expenses. Maybe sue for attempted fraud . . ."

"Leave her alone," David said.

Susan screamed at Jurgan, "You're a fool if you think we planned *this*?"

"No," Jurgan responded. "You're fucking innocent. But you never know what a court will decide." He aimed his camera again, the flash filling the museum.

Suddenly, the curator ran toward them, yelling. Susan responded in Spanish, as two *policia* arrived, one grabbing Jurgan's arm, the other taking his camera. "No photographs," the curator said.

Susan turned away, and David followed her out of the dark museum. He wouldn't give up, couldn't let her ditch him in the streets of Puerto Vallarta, not like this. Afternoon sun beating down on him. Her words rang true. The Aztec warrior must *confess his collusion with the dead*. Only then could he offer himself to the gods. And to Susan if she wanted his heart.

# Chapter Forty-Five

David followed his wife across the busy street, then lost her in a crowd. Bumping into several people, saying excuse me, *perdon,* he caught a glimpse of her turning down a street headed back toward the hotel, and he ran, gaining on her. He watched her hurry through the revolving door, into the lobby, up the stairs. In the hallway decorated with serpents, he saw a door closing, and stood waiting. Waiting. She emerged from her room with a pack over her shoulder, and she brushed by him. "Get out of my way," she said.

But he wouldn't give up. Not now. He watched her check out of the hotel, and followed her into the sunlight, where she finally stopped. "Leave me alone," she said.

"I can't."

"Should I get the police?"

"Don't."

"What do you want?"

David looked at her. He did not feel anything like an Aztec warrior, standing on the curb in front of a tourist hotel. A car pulled up and a young couple, apparent newlyweds, climbed out laughing, holding long-stemmed glasses full of champagne.

"Can we go somewhere," he asked, "to talk?"

But he wasn't sure what he needed to say. Of course, he should confess his years of living another life. But how? Was there an explanation or would mere confession free him? And what about the specifics - should he ask to be forgiven for sleeping with Janice? And for their marriage, his inability to talk to her then? Had he gotten any better at that?

"You can't hurt me," Susan said, her own authentic blue eyes upon him, "can you?"

"That's right, I won't. I never wanted to—"

"Stop it," she said.

David looked at her. Making excuses, he thought, no he couldn't do that. "Let me come with you," he pleaded.

"You can't hurt me," she said again, more forcefully. "I won't allow it."

David watched her staring blankly across the street, toward the downtown, traffic noise receding into the air but the smell of exhaust lingering.

She looked at him. "I'll wait here," she said, then shrugged and added, "You'll need to get your pack?"

David felt immediate relief, her tone less accusing, but then he thought, maybe she was just trying a different tactic - deception. While he went to get his backpack, she would disappear.

"You won't leave without me?" he asked.

"What's wrong, don't you trust me?"

David stared into her calm, perhaps calculating, blue eyes. He had no choice. If he was going to gain her confidence, he had to trust her. So he cautiously started walking toward his hotel, glancing over his shoulder, watching as she drifted behind him. He took one more look - Susan sitting on a bench far up the street - and he went inside the hotel. He ran to his room, stuffed everything haphazardly into his pack, and checked out, finally emerging to find his wife standing, moving away, but still there. He ran to catch up with her.

"Where are we going?" he asked, out of breath.

"I'm going to do my work." She squinted her eyes. "I'm not sure about you."

They hiked quickly through the city streets, finally stopping at the bus station. They bought tickets and sat without speaking, the station crowded with campesinos and smelling like raw meat, the smell itself constricting, David swallowing, making sure he could breathe. The air felt thick in his throat, and his heart worked hard, beating against his chest. What's wrong, he thought, he had taken his medicine. Maybe it was merely the smell of the meat that made it hard to breathe. More likely, he now realized, a side effect. He had become increasingly thirsty with taking the pills, and now his mouth felt pasty, the bitter taste of the medicine still lingering. He rummaged through his pack and found a water bottle, the water warm and stale, but he drank it anyway, swallowing hard. The bus station was cramped, crowded, and suffocating. But as he looked around, his wife sitting next to him, he felt on the verge of discovery. He sensed an adventure, and he thought, yes, of course, he could only gain redemption in the wilderness. Where else? He didn't need to know where they were going, only that they would be out of Puerto Vallarta, out of the crowded city.

The bus arrived, squealing, stopping, swerving into the pick-up lane, and everyone rose out of their seats, picking up bags, clothes, food, boarding, the driver taking their packs and strapping them on top.

David leaned against the window, and it fell open with a loud thwack. Gears grinding, the bus lurched on its way up a steep winding road then down along a river. Trinkets and tassels dangled from the windows and swayed with the vehicle's rocking motion. A plastic Mother of God statue was glued to the dashboard.

He looked at Susan sitting next to him, staring ahead, the muscles of her jaw tight. The bus jerked to a stop, and he watched a stooped old woman with a large sack of grain on her back climb aboard. The weight bowed the woman's legs out as she heaved the sack onto the seat across the aisle, then she pushed it onto the floor and sat with her small feet resting on the grain, her knees up. She pulled a black shawl over her head, thick wrinkles folded in around her glazed-over eyes and pursed lips. A man less burdened, carrying only a satchel, climbed over her and sat near the window. The bus hit a pothole and bounced heavily. David heard them laugh. Then the old woman looked across the aisle, directly at him, and smiled. *La hora*, he thought, *la hora de la muerte.*

David felt comfort in the wisdom of the campesinos. They had confidence, enjoyed a simple joke and small pleasures despite the heavy burden of their lives. *They* would enter paradise. The old woman on the bus was like the old woman in Tijuana - time was only for measuring insignificant events before death and ascension.

Soon darkness settled upon them, and David watched Susan, her eyes closed, head rocking with the motion of the bus. Up the aisle, he could see the driver pull the steering wheel first in one direction, then the other, following the headlights into the mountains. Dust and fumes drifted in the cracks and windows. Passengers appeared on the side of the road all night, the bus grinding to a halt, lurching back into motion, making it impossible for him to sleep. He looked at the space between him and his wife, the seat torn and frayed. For a moment, he allowed himself a false belief - his cowardly act had been for her own good. But he knew he had reacted like an animal and disguised it as an intellectual choice. He had wrapped his fears in theory. Sure, he had thought, no problem, he would leap into another universe, another life, as if it were an equation, easily calculated by Savgren, impossibly testing a theory that only worked on the chalkboard, or in Savgren's mind. But he felt like he was implicating his climbing friend and that wasn't right. David understood now more than ever how numbers and probability had helped Savgren - weeping while holding his baby boy dying eleven hours from the womb. No, David thought, he couldn't and he wouldn't blame Savgren for anything. David Brooks had run. No one else.

Eight in the morning, minutes after he had finally fallen asleep, the bus jerked to a stop, and he slid from his seat. He watched the old woman heave the grain onto her shoulder, everyone getting off, Susan near the front. Out the window he saw their packs fall past the window and hit the ground.

David got off the bus and watched Susan slip her pack onto

shoulders, then start hiking through town. Exhausted, he stretched the stiffness out of his arms and legs and followed her up a hill. The streets were nothing but ruts and gullies, smashed beer cans as pavement, with scrawny chickens pecking erratically at the dry ground. A pig ran by squealing chased by a man with a stick. Drunks leaning against the clapboard-shuttered windows of a saloon wearily lifted their hands in a friendly, hopeful wave. His pack loaded with gear, David nodded at them as he passed, feeling compassion for drunks and beggars. He knew it could get bad, and he wished he could help them.

About a half-hour walk out of town, a white house with peeling paint and narrow doors sat perched on the edge of a steep hillside. Susan knocked on the shutters. A slight brown man wearing a dirty serape opened the door. David watched as Susan smiled and shoved several pesos into the man's calloused hand. As they were walking away, David heard him say in English, "Good luck."

He followed his wife through thick shrubbery and forest, then on a footpath that rose precipitously into the forested mountains. As Susan hiked faster, David lagged behind. He had had little sleep, felt emotionally drained, his mouth more parched than ever. Each time he sucked in air, his throat felt sore, his chest tight, causing him to breathe heavily while hiking over a ridge then down a ravine. The medicine was useless, he thought. No, it was worse, side effects made his throat *worse*. Susan finally stopped, leaned against a tree, and picked a lime-orange. She tossed it to him, the juice feeling good in his gritty mouth. Each time they rested, David searched her eyes. Was she ready to forgive him, had some of her anger ebbed with their hiking, the tranquility that often came with such physical effort? But she avoided him. He looked out over the trees. Below them lay a heavily foliaged ravine with a river snaking through it and pouring over a ledge into a narrow canyon.

While zigzagging down switchbacks, he fell to one knee,

sweat pouring from his brow. He looked up and saw Susan sliding down a steep incline, then drop out of sight. David almost fell, catching himself at the top of a cliff. He slowly eased himself over the edge, searching for handholds. He opened and closed his hand, unable to put much pressure on his fingers. Seemed so long ago, he thought, when he injured them. Thinking about his past life, he felt lonely, lost, never to recover, as he gripped the sheer cliff over the wilderness. Was he a fool to think he could be forgiven? If he were Susan, could *he* forgive? He climbed down through the trees and into the bushes where the river rushed by on its way to the canyon, the roar of a waterfall filling the air, cool mist on his face and the smell of damp earth. He looked upriver, and saw no sign of her, only black boulders with water crashing around them. He started hiking through the brush, then heard a branch snap. "Susan?"

Upriver, Susan climbed onto a boulder slanting into the water. She waved, then leaped across. David pushed through the brush and followed her, jumping over the surging water, then hiking uphill through broad-leafed shrubbery and thick woods, mist evaporating in the dry air, and the smell sharp with maguey plants. At the top, Susan stood waiting for him in a small, level clearing, littered with shards of broken pottery.

David looked up at a mound looming behind her, and a narrow stairway, the stone steps old and crumbling, leading into the mound where the crest of a temple remained buried. Along the stairway, serpent heads jutted out from the dirt, with human-like grins, eyes with lines spiraling out from an empty center. Of course, he thought, the Aztec, the serpents, the temple where proud Aztec warriors went to be sacrificed. But also where victims, prisoners captured to provide blood for the war god, were slaughtered like animals, their entrails decorating the garb of the high priests. Would he be a victim, or would he be a warrior who willingly offered himself to the gods? His heart pounded in anticipation, and he felt dizzy, the stone serpents lifelike. For a second, he swore he saw one of them move. Would Susan be the Aztec priestess? He stared at her, and she turned away. But, he thought, she brought him to this place for a reason. And she now left him standing before the temple. He started off alone, ascending the mound along the crumbling steps, digging his hands into the slope to keep from falling, his face scraping against the carved stone of the serpent - a small cut, blood mixing with sweat and dirt. He climbed up, the steps disappearing into the mound, reaching the crest where he could see miles down the canyon, water snaking into the valley, merging into another river.

Falling to his knees, he begged for forgiveness. He deserved to have his heart ripped out and offered to the gods. Come on, he thought, where are the gods? Suddenly, he felt light-hearted, the thought of freedom making him giddy, and he laughed. Where were the bloody gods of the Aztec? Buried here? He dug his hands into the cool earth, letting dirt slide through his fingers, the smell like ashes. He saw a laughing head, its tiny, cupped hand held up to a toothy grin, cheeks pushed up and eyes narrowed. Down along the steps, the ancient stone was turning red in the setting sun, and he saw forked tongues slithering from the serpents. He thought he heard an echo, screaming, from the canyon. A huge black bird spiraled overhead, wings feathered out and silhouetted against the crimson sky, a snake in its claws. David raised his arms, then leaned backward, lying on the buried temple. He closed his eyes, tears streaking through blood and grime, mouth dry as the baked earth, and he reached out and clutched the soil, gripping small pebbles - the Aztec placed a jadestone in the mouth of the dead, transporting them to the afterlife. David shoved a small stone into his mouth. Nothing existed but the screeching of the bird and the pounding of his heart. *Here*, he thought, *take it, carve it out of my body, and give my soul to the gods, transport me from my hell, and deliver me to whatever paradise awaits.* In his twisted position, he felt his back tighten, while his mind frantically searched for an intellectual explanation (medicine side-effect), his muscles circling around his chest pulling tight and suffocating him - the hand of God wrapped around his heart.

David felt a surge of adrenaline, his emotions like a cresting wave, sudden order in the chaos. Gasping, he rolled onto his side, coughing, spitting out the stone, mouth gritty. But, he still lived. He felt sure he would die. But he had been spared. He felt exhausted, relaxed. And he felt optimistic that he could go on, finally gaining a new life. The world was full of random events, he thought, but his beliefs affected his decisions, and he could make decisions that (if he were lucky) might bring some order into his universe. He made an awful choice to run away, and now he was finally facing up to it.

On the way down, his legs felt rubbery, his skin tight, pulling at his eyes. And the doubts, the worry, returned. While he had been spared his life, he still had doubts about what sort of life it would be. Why hadn't Susan taken on her role as Aztec priestess? She wanted him to come to this temple. She must have wanted that. Was she ready to forgive him? Near the bottom, he fell, then sat and stared at scratches like claw marks on his hands. He got up, brushed at his pants, pushed back his hair. Across the clearing, Susan was setting up her tent, using a rock to pound in the last stake. David remembered when they first met, walking with his wife along a gentle stream - deer lazily drinking, then looking at them, and the fireflies lighting the woods, the cool starlit night. Before his death. The memory evaporating. He was ready to give Susan whatever she needed, but was she ready to accept? And who was she really? The person he married no longer existed. Who was this new Susan, this person who hiked so confidently into these Mexican highlands, who communicated so effectively with the local people, and who explored ancient Aztec worlds?

Susan stared at the tent, the memory of her husband flooding back upon her, tents pitched in darkness, wilderness, and that last night together when she had to tear it all down and climb into the canoe, and the fire. Almost drowning. Struggling out alone. Had David left her there? Did he know that she was alive? When exactly, and where, did he decide to leave her? She hated him. She wanted him dead as he pretended to be. But David wouldn't go away. When she checked out of her hotel, she considered complaining, telling the clerk to get the police. But when she faced her "dead" husband, she felt her heart pound out "why?" Why did he leave her? She did not doubt her anger, her desire to get away from him. But she needed an answer. Only he could give her that answer. Whatever it was, she was confident that her ability to reason would shield her from the gut-wrenching emotions, her feelings of betrayal and hatred.

Determined to go on with her plans despite him, she let him follow her to the temple. Many times, she wanted to scream, but she held in her emotions. She would not allow them to interfere. She would wait for the right moment, and very logically, she would question him, gather the information she needed. And she, Susan Moore, through the strength of her intellect, would discover why he'd left her in the wilderness.

Now she held the rock in her hand, and saw that she had been cleaning it, standing there, staring, unconsciously rubbing dirt from the rock, revealing a sharp obsidian stone. Obsidian, she thought, used to make weapons for the Aztec.

She could feel her husband nearing her, and turned around, holding the rock like a knife. The Aztec butchered thousands of prisoners to the war god, Huitzilopochtli, rivers of blood nourishing, flowing into the earth. Aztec warriors, she thought, willingly sacrificed themselves to the gods. From death sprang life. She stared at David. He was saying something, she thought, his words forming slowly, unintelligible at first.

"*Tu eres,*" he said, "*una mujer muy bonita.*"

The Spanish, coming from her husband, startled her, and she

quickly translated, *You are,* he had said, *a very pretty woman.* But, she reasoned, *mujer* could also mean "wife". And she felt compelled to defend herself, in English. "I'm not your pretty little wife."

"That's right," he agreed. "You're not my wife. You're not the same woman I married."

She stared. "I made it to that cabin. You knew—"

"Yes, I knew, I saw you fall near the bridge. I confess. I saw you go in the wrong direction."

Susan heard his words, but she struggled against them. He was a lie, she reasoned, so everything that he said must also be a lie.

"I tried to yell, but couldn't move, couldn't talk, my throat was raw, but I tried. You must believe that."

"Don't tell me what I should believe."

"I followed you—"

"You knew I was alive," she said. "And you ran. You left me." She watched the shadows knifing through him, thinking she should plunge the obsidian stone into his chest. "I didn't cash in on your body," she screamed, "your so-called *death.* I made it on my own. Earned my degree and I'm working on a Masters. I've learned a new language."

"I'm sorry. I didn't—"

"You left me to wonder what happened, never knowing if you suffered! I *felt* you alive! I . . ." She gripped the sharp stone as the ruins glowed in the descending sunlight. "David?" she asked. "Why?"

"I tried to save you," he said. "But . . . I fell . . . then you were gone . . . Forgive me. Rip my heart out if you want. I deserve it."

"Why?" she asked again, searching his eyes for an answer, his form dreamlike, fluid in the failing sunlight, arms reaching for her, the temple looming behind him, and the blood-red sky.

"I made mistakes," he said.

She glared. "How many *girlfriends* heard you say that?"

He grimaced, averted his eyes and, for a moment, Susan felt

content; she'd inflicted a wound. But, she thought, was she after revenge?

David leveled his stare at her and said evenly, almost a whisper, "You wanted me out of your life, didn't you?"

"I don't know what you're talking about."

"Forget it," he said. "*Nothing* excuses what I did . . . and now, I understand how you must have felt . . . with your father leaving—"

"*He* didn't leave me! You did!" She gripped the sharp stone. "You must think I'm stupid."

David reached for her. "Susan . . . I—"

"Stop!" She lunged, the sharp obsidian stone ripping his shirt, cutting his chest, but he stood firm, and her hands trembled. She felt the nightmares rushing back, Susan as priestess ripping out his still beating heart and staining her breasts with spurting blood. She threw the stone into the brush, trying to rid herself of the nightmare. How could *he* say *anything* about her father? She felt stiff, paralyzed with anger. He touched her cheek. "No," she screamed, staggering back, turning away and running into the shadows.

Sick, ironic joke, she thought, that she should feel anything. Her work was supposed to protect her from this. She hiked to the river, leaped across on the boulders. She started climbing - the cliff red from the sunset slashing the horizon. She heard him behind her, yelling, but she refused to listen. She wanted to run away. Nothing else, just get away from him and everything in the past, her emotions sweeping her away, out of control. Unable to stop as he called out her name.

"Susan!" He leaned against the base of the cliff, his wife's unearthly form above him in the dusk light. Wait, he thought, he hadn't fully explained, but immediately knew there was no simple explanation, only forgiveness. He climbed after her, rock crumbling in his hands, until there was nothing left to hold onto. Please take my heart, complete the sacrifice. While balancing on a ledge, he searched desperately for a way up, then jammed his injured fingers into a small seam, pivoted, and felt lightning quick pain. For a moment, he felt weightless, floating, then fell. He tried grabbing another ledge, missed, cut his hand. He landed feet-first and tumbled backwards, coming to a rest with his ankle bent beneath him. Throbbing, searing pulses flowed through him, followed immediately by numbness, and a wave of nausea and blackness.

Rolling over onto his side, he pulled on a tree, and struggled to stand. "Susan," he yelled, then fell, face in the dirt. He rolled onto his back and stared past the trees into the dark sky. Had he missed his chance? Would he remain unforgiven, doomed to die alone and unloved surrounded by artifacts - laughing heads bouncing up and down with their laughter, ridiculing his failed efforts, and serpents slithering away into the darkness, abandoning him. No, he thought, he would rise again. He had survived before; he would drag himself out. No matter what it took, he would find a way up over the steep ridge, and if he got back alive . . . he would try again. He loved Susan deeply. He broke his *own* heart long ago when he couldn't just hold her, ask what was wrong, and now again, losing her. "Susan," he called, his voice barely audible in the night, "I love you."

Susan heard the fall, rocks hitting at the bottom, the heavy thud. She jammed her hand into a large crack, balanced on a ledge and looked down, listening. She heard nothing but the white water. She climbed down and found him lying on his back, then she thrashed through the underbrush gathering sticks and formed a splint. She bent over him, a gash on his forehead. One eye was swollen shut, the other dark with a faint glint of blue, blood filling his scar, his face a pre-Columbian mask. He grimaced, back arching. My nightmare, she thought, my husband pushing his heart out to me, for me to carve out in a bloody sacrifice. And why not tear it from his chest? Why not, she reasoned, hadn't it been David who had failed to "save" her? He moaned but she stiffened, shoulder back. *He deserved it. He said so himself.*

"This time," Susan said, "I admit it. You're right, just like you said. I am *not* the same woman you married."

Susan stood over him, her face tilted to the red sky and the Aztec gods, mist rising from the river roaring into the canyon, and she felt besieged by the rituals she'd been studying. Rip out his heart?  She closed her eyes - *blood oozing between her fingers and streaming down her arms, holding the still beating heart while her victim howled in pain.* She turned away, and walked along the river, white water, mist spraying her as she absently headed toward the excavation. She had seen the body; she could justly collect on the 300,000. He owed her for his lies anyway, didn't he?  She felt a perverse sense of freedom, maybe happiness, and she almost laughed out loud. But the joy was momentary. Who was he?  The David who was not David? Or simply evil. Feel *nothing*. Logically, she thought, she should leave him there, leave him to die in the ruins of their discovery. But what had they discovered by digging up their past?

Susan stopped. She was standing on a boulder, white water crashing around her. Could she cross over to the excavation, pick up her gear, and leave him?  Could she leave anyone to die? Susan closed her eyes and felt the cool night air, mist on her face, the smell of moisture on the surrounding trees. She took a deep breath, leaped off the boulder and hiked back along the cliff, pushing through the brush and kneeling, touching his dry, cracked lips. She stared into his one open blue eye. He had been a coward, hiding from her. But she had also hidden, from him, from herself, from the beginning. She knew, and had known for a long time, but couldn't accept it until now. She married him, tried to be his wife, married like everyone else, maybe start a family. But she didn't love him. Not fully. She couldn't. Susan scanned the rugged terrain as night blanketed the excavation. Her father had died long ago in these Aztec mountains, but it wasn't her fault, or his. Now, she just wanted to live. And she wanted her husband to live. *I accept*, she thought, *I accept your heart and complete the sacrifice.* Then she stared down at him, his face shrouded in the dim light. "You are forgiven," she whispered.

She pulled David's arm around her, the two of them crossing the river, staggering back to her tent where she wrapped him in a sleeping bag, then crawled in next to him. They would survive the night together.

Lying on her back with her head resting outside, she watched stars fill the sky and listened to the rhythm of his breath while he slept. She could feel the quiet beating of her own heart, her body as if it were melting into the ground, and she smiled, closing her eyes, knowing that she would help him out of the wilderness.